The Fallout Of Deception

A Different Kind of Kidnapping

Lou Knight

ISBN: 978-1737823728

Dedication

I dedicate this book to my ETSU Kappa Delta sorority sisters, Debbie, Jane Ellen, Ann, Jane, Cindy, and Kathy, and our adopted sister, Sissy. Forty years of beach trips have forged a bond like no other and created beautiful memories of laughter and love but also loss. I specifically dedicate my book to Carolyn, whose trips with us ended way too soon. Years ago, I wrote a fictitious version of her funeral and read it at the beach as we eight toasted her with champagne and cried. Down the road, that scene became part of chapter five. I hope she likes it.

And to the friends I've made along the way: Whether we met as toddlers, schoolmates, neighbors, or coworkers, I couldn't have written a book that leans on the bond of friendship without your influence. So, I dedicate this book to those who accept me, warts and all.

Genetically, DNA connects us to others. Some people hit the jackpot as far as relatives go. Others do not. But everyone gets to select their friends. Our paths cross, and something clicks, but not just on the surface. It's deeper than that, and we consciously choose to keep each other in our lives. But not in a creepy way. That becomes stalking.

Acknowledgments

Without the Soleil Critters writing group, this book would still be rattling inside my head. We took this journey together, and your edits, suggestions, and sense of humor kept my points of view in order and dialogue in check. Thank you, Jack, Erika, Fred, Brad, and Brian. Special recognition goes to the club's leader, author, teacher, and mentor, Josh Langston. Your constructive criticism was never unkind, and your encouragement kept me moving. Thank you for filling my head with knowledge and crazy ideas.

Thanks to my first-draft readers: my sister, Anne, who kept me on the straight and narrow, made intelligent observations, and questioned the profanity but finally gave in; Jane, my first-grade friend, one of the funniest people on the planet, and someone who knows what a dangling participle is; and Sally who found things no one else caught. To my hometown friends and coworkers, who told me I should write a book, thank you for helping me believe in myself. And to F.F. Martha, you were the perfect choice for the launch. Thank you. To my husband, Mickey, who answered odd questions about men, tolerated being ignored while I wrote and said all the right things to lift my spirits; thank you. I love you. Finally, to our two Goldendoodles who constantly interrupted me with wet muzzles, watch out. My next book may be a double Doodle murder mystery.

Introduction

Present Day

CeeCee Montgomery drove up to the log cabin and studied the familiar structure that held so many secrets. For some, it would be easy to hate this place, but not her. And not today.

She hesitated for a moment, then gathered a few things from the front seat, and stepped out onto recently poured concrete. *Somebody's been busy. Hiding evidence?* She smiled.

Grateful for one less tripping hazard, she plopped her cane down onto the smooth surface and made her way to the side porch. Each slow step reminded CeeCee of her limitations, and it pissed her off, but if she wanted to play tennis anytime soon, the damn cane had to come along. The rooster comb injections had helped with the pain but not enough to get her back to her A-game. Because of the incident ten years ago, her left knee continued to give her problems and would never be something to crow about.

She let herself inside the house, slung her bag onto a dining room chair, and scanned the first floor, listening for signs of life. No bodies in sight. *Always a good thing*.

CeeCee wrapped a woven scarf around her neck and secured it in a casual knot. The colors brought out the highlights in her hair and the fire in her opal earrings, and the new Coral Blossom lipstick completed the look just as the young salesgirl promised. After a quick pit stop, she checked her make-up in the mirror and touched the small scar on her cheek, which was hardly noticeable now. Nevertheless, she considered it her badge of honor earned many years ago when she came close to death. She turned off the bathroom light and entered the great room, where she heard a shriek from the top of the stairs.

"Aunt CeeCee!"

Kathryn's Birkenstocks clomped down the steps, and her ponytail bobbed up and down as she squealed again and ran into the arms of her mother's best friend.

"Whoa, don't knock me down," said CeeCee. "I'm like one of those fainting goats these days."

"You used to do cartwheels with me."

"I know. Now I tip over when I put on my underwear. When did you get so tall, or am I shrinking?"

Kathryn giggled. "You haven't changed a bit. Pretty as ever."

"Thank you, dear," said CeeCee as she took a step back to examine the little girl who'd turned into a beautiful young woman. Wearing distressed jeans and a white tee-shirt, Kathryn stood 5'-7" tall with a thin frame that would be a photographer's dream. "And you... you look just like your mother. If she could only see you now."

"I like to believe she can."

"Me, too, kiddo. Me, too." CeeCee looked away before she teared up. "Where is everybody? I expected a big reception, at least a 21-gun salute."

Kathryn laughed. "They're at the dock, but as Uncle Bill would say, expectations only lead to disappointment, so it's best not to have any."

CeeCee frowned. "You can't believe everything a shrink says, but don't tell him I said so."

"Is there wine down there?"

"Is that a serious question?"

CeeCee laughed, then made her way to the door. "Aren't you coming?"

"In a sec," Kathyrn said. "See you in a few."

CeeCee wondered if 100 years from now, people would speak complete sentences or do away with them altogether. She stepped outside and headed towards the path that led to the lake. As she looked down at the large flagstones, memories flooded in, and she saw younger, prettier feet in designer sandals taking the same steps she took now. And no cane.

She stopped at the floating ramp that connected the shore with the oversized dock and watched her friends mingle and chat, often touching each other's arms or shoulders in relaxed familiarity. As CeeCee approached, shouts of her arrival led to hugs and kisses and a few tears. Mostly hers.

Lynn cut a path through the group and, with hands on hips, shook her head as she scanned CeeCee from head to toe. "Oh my *God!* You're using a *cane*? You look like you're a hundred."

"You're looking pretty worn down yourself," CeeCee replied. "You finally have to quit the pole dancing?"

"Why would I? Your husband is my best customer."

"He's nice to the elderly. What can I say?"

"What happened to you *this* time?" asked Lynn, eyeballing her friend's cane again.

"Oh, *now* you want to know." CeeCee pushed by her and held the cane up threateningly. "It's a weapon, too, if you remember."

"Are you going to tell me?" Lynn asked again.

"What do *you* think?"

Lynn shook her head. "Once a jackass, always a jackass."

"Why would I mess with perfection? Especially *this* ass."

No one said anything or moved while the two women glared at each other. Then after the perfect comedic pause, when they could hold it in no longer, CeeCee and Lynn cracked up and fell into each other's arms. The group clapped and cheered, and the two women curtsied.

Their routine of make-believe disgust started in college, but neither remembered when or why, and they never knew what they'd say until they said it, making it even more fun. Instead of hugging as ordinary people do after the summer break, they'd stop in their tracks, squint like two gunslingers ready to draw their revolvers, and throw verbal zingers at each other. It might happen in the dormitory hallway and on the lawn, where students lugged boxes from cars and said goodbye to parents. It was their schtick, and they loved it, almost as much as seeing people's alarmed expressions. So the tradition continued.

After a lot of back-patting, questions, and hugs, the group returned to catching up with each other while nibbling hors d'oeuvres and drinking wine. It was a wonderful reunion, and everybody was there, save one. As the sun lowered over the lake and conversations wound down, Kathryn flipped a switch that illuminated the dock with tiny white lights, creating the perfect setting for old friends with a long history. She sat down next to CeeCee. "Will you tell the story?"

"What story?"

Kathryn rolled her eyes.

"You've heard it a million times," said CeeCee.

"I know."

"It's getting late. Maybe tomorrow."

Lynn piped up. "She's an old woman now, Kat. Probably needs to go to bed. It's almost 7:30."

"I'm not too old to kick your scrawny ass," CeeCee said.

Everybody laughed.

Kathryn grabbed CeeCee's hand and kissed it repeatedly, making loud smooching sounds, then formed her lips into a child's pout. "Aunt CeeCee, please?"

CeeCee shook her head and looked up at the stars. "See what you created? She's relentless." She looked at her best friend's daughter, knowing she could never say no to this precious girl. "Okay, but if I tell it, it's got to be done right, so don't complain that it's taking too long."

Expressions of anticipation spread across each person's face as they maneuvered their seats into a large circle. CeeCee waited until everyone got settled, gathered the folds of her gauze skirt around her legs, and focused on the only empty chair. She took a deep breath and began.

Chapter One

Ten Years Earlier

It was a beautiful Sunday afternoon that soon became one of the worst days of Molly Baxter's life.

She and her husband Bill attended church, something they did on occasion but not faithfully, then went to lunch at Fat Boy's Pizza Parlor. With leftovers in hand, they strolled through the small downtown of Harelton and stopped in front of a shop where a giant ice cream cone hung from the pink and white striped awning. They briefly discussed the calories they'd just consumed, shrugged, and stepped inside to order their favorite sundaes, small ones this time. They sat on red vinyl swivel stools that overlooked the sidewalk, a great place to people-watch and make snarky remarks they hoped no one heard.

On the corner across the street, a young man with blue and green spiked hair climbed out of a rusty car and unloaded musical equipment. He set up shop by opening a black guitar case, placing it on the sidewalk, and sitting on an upside-down bucket. He plucked at the strings until they were in tune.

"I didn't expect lunch, dessert, *and* a show," Molly giggled. "Best date this week."

"You've had others?" Bill asked.

"Didn't mean to let that slip out."

They laughed, cozied up to each other, and held hands while the music drifted into the shop through the vintage screened door.

Bill looked at his watch. "Maybe it's time we gave up these front-row seats. My butt's numb, and I've got things to do before work tomorrow." Molly spun around on her stool twice, like she always did, and licked her spoon one last time before tossing it into the trash bin.

"I'll be right back," Bill said.

She watched her husband lope over to the musician and put some bills into the guitar case. The young man nodded and continued to strum and sing.

****

The couple took their leftovers to the kitchen, climbed the second-floor stairs, and headed for the new walk-in closet. They still weren't used to the size of the space, and more than once, the 4' x 8' mirror at the other end scared the bejesus out of them when they turned on the light. As they changed from their dress clothes into jeans, sweatshirts, and sneakers, Bill pranced around in his underwear, flexing muscles and posing like a bodybuilder. He smacked his bicep. "Go ahead. You can touch it."

Molly rolled her eyes and grinned. "Don't you have work to do?"

Bill finished dressing, turned to walk out, and slapped Molly's rear end. "Nice ass."

"That's what all the guys say."

Molly closed the closet door and walked through the bathroom, where she caught her reflection in the mirror. She barely recognized herself these days and spent too much time thinking about her aging body. It depressed her and dragged her down. *If I feel this way now, what will it be like when I'm 70?* She sighed, turned off the lights, and went to find the novel she'd started last night.

She looked around their recently-redone bedroom, now her favorite place in the house. She called it her happy place because it lifted her spirits. The custom upholstery, bedding, and window treatments gave the room a designer feel, but they weren't so formal that she wouldn't jump on the bed and plunge her face into the pillows. It was perfect.

When Molly bent to grab her book off the ottoman, she spotted something under the bed. *Could that be the mysterious missing sock?* She'd been looking for the damn thing since Valentine's Day, so she got down on her hands and knees and peered into the dark abyss. There it lay, one red sock with white hearts.

She was shoulder-deep under the bed when her cell phone rang, startling her and triggering a headbang on the side rail.

"Shit!" She quickly lunged at the sock, groaning as she got up to follow the lilting sound of her ringtone. The caller ID, however, made her heart sink with dread. Her legs, too, reacted and weakened but somehow got her to the window seat before she collapsed.

"Hello?"

In a shaky voice, Josh said, "Molly? She's gone. About an hour ago."

Molly gripped the device tightly but wanted to throw it out the window along with the words she'd just heard. She felt like she'd been gut-punched and quickly grabbed a wastebasket sitting next to her desk. Covering the phone with the Valentine sock, she retched, hoping Josh couldn't hear it. Her mouth remained open in anguish, but no sound escaped as tears streamed down her face. She finally gasped for air and tried to slow and deepen her breathing. She zoned in and out of the discussion until she heard, "At least she went peacefully."

Molly's eyes flew open at the words meant to comfort people, but she wasn't like most people. Her take was very different. Does *going peacefully* imply your loved one died *better* than others? She guessed so. *You're no less dead, though.* They were talking about her best friend, and she didn't want to be comforted. She wanted to feel pain, to suffer for still being alive when someone better than her was not.

She didn't want a kind phrase. She wanted one more beach stroll with her friend, talking about nothing and everything, one more happy-hour toast to sisterhood, and laughing until she cried. Happy tears. Not sad ones. She wanted to see Carolyn's beautiful green eyes dance as she smiled, to hear her bracelets tinkle against each other as perfectly manicured hands gestured, and to feel one more hug. More than anything, Molly wanted time to rewind before cancer invaded her friend's body. Before she was gone. Peacefully or not.

Of course, Molly's wants were insignificant, so she sat up straight, put on her imaginary armor, and said what Josh needed to hear.

"She's in a better place now. No more pain. No more suffering."

Then she used an old trick and forced herself to smile so the inflection in her voice would sound light and cheerful. "And you *know* she's walking on a beach somewhere in a beautiful swimsuit, her hair and cover-up blowing in the wind, and she's basking in the glory of the sun and God."

Josh sort of chuckled. Not much, but a little, which indicated she said the right thing.

"I'll let Lynn and CeeCee know," said Molly. "We'll get there as soon as possible to help you and the kids. Don't worry about anything."

Molly put down the phone and barely made it to the bed, where she folded herself into a ball and sobbed. A part of her brain interrupted several times, nagging her with a to-do list, but she surrendered to her emotions instead, crying and moaning until sleep overcame her. Her body needed rest for the days ahead.

When Molly awoke, Carolyn's beautiful face floated across the back of her swollen eyelids, and for a second, she didn't recall the bad news. But reality broke her heart all over again. Her friend was gone.

Chapter Two

Wednesday

CeeCee leaned her head on the passenger side window, ignoring the blur of telephone poles, cornfields, and boiled-peanut signs whizzing by. Her mind was numb. The two-hour journey so far had been silent except for the wipers moving across the windshield, creating a soothing rhythm, but a pothole suddenly jolted her back to the present. The skies had turned dark, like her mood. She thought she'd prepared herself for the inevitable, but Molly's phone call three days ago proved her wrong. She watched the water drops zigzag across the passenger window and disappear, reminding her of the people who enter and exit one's life.

Cory reached for her hand and squeezed it. "I wish I could help."

She kissed the back of her husband's hand, which smelled like Old Spice body wash, the same fragrance her dad used once upon a time. She took another quick whiff, then burrowed into the warm leather seat. "I'll come out of my funk in a little while. And thank you."

"For what?"

"Being here. Your support. Everything that's going to happen in the next few days."

CeeCee knew Cory was giving her space to gather thoughts and deal with emotions. He'd always been good at reading others' needs, but few knew it. At first glance, people saw bulging muscles on a large man with a shaved head and a chip on his shoulder, but inside, he was marshmallow cream. Cory was her hero, too, and their community seemed to agree. Cards and letters of appreciation filled a drawer of their dresser, and he was so touched by the sentiments he refused to throw any away. Sometimes he'd point at the drawer and say, "This is why I became a fireman." Not for the cards but knowing he helped save someone or their home.

Hopefully, no one would need Cory's firefighter skills on this trip, but his social skills would be tested. Typically the buffer, CeeCee kept things flowing, staying close to help him feel comfortable and included; this week, though, he'd be on his own. She blew her nose for the eightieth time, tossed the tissue onto the floorboard, then stared at the accumulating pile. *My mother would be mortified.*

Instantly her mind traveled back to childhood trips in the family station wagon. The radio knob held a small plastic bag, promoting a national movement to prevent highway trash.

"Remember when we were kids, and there was all that stuff about litterbugs?" she asked. "Businesses gave out bags with a big hole in the top? Wonder what happened with all that." She could use one now.

Cory looked at her quizzically. "Ours was green with yellow letters: 'Don't be a Litterbug!' And if I remember right, we thought it was pretty cool. Like being the first one on the block to have a hover car or something."

CeeCee laughed. "I hardly think it was *that* cool. It seems absurd now, but at some point, someone said, 'I have an idea! We shouldn't throw all this crap out of our cars. Why not put it in a little bag and empty it when we get home?' Such a simple concept, but humans had to be told. Kind of sad."

"Couldn't have those now. All we have are push buttons and touch screens." He glanced at his wife. "I know your mind flies all over the place, but what in the world brought this up?"

CeeCee pointed at the pile of tissues.

"That's gross. Don't be looking at me to clean that up."

Before she could answer, a billboard with gigantic red letters caught her attention. It said, *aRe yoU iN Pain? For answers, call 1-800-R-U-N-PAIN.*

"Look at that. Like anybody will call someone who puts up a dilapidated billboard in the middle of nowhere."

"You never know. Maybe it's a sign from God."

She snorted. On a typical day, she'd grab her phone and punch in the numbers, just for fun, and make up some bizarre story to see what they would say. But today was anything but ordinary. She *was* in pain, and Molly and Lynn were the only people who could help.

They'd met as college freshmen when they all joined the same sorority. Molly had bent down to get a closer look at her nametag, then grimaced. "Cynthia Corrine? Your parents have a weird sense of humor."

"You have no idea. My brothers' names are Jerald Jermaine and Peter Patterson, plus our last name, of course."

"Which is?"

"Fitzgerald."

"You're shitting me," said Molly. "I don't have time for that many syllables. You got a nickname?"

"Sometimes I use the initials CC, but I spell it CeeCee."

"Much better. Glad to meet you, CeeCee."

As pledges, the group of four, Molly, Lynn, CeeCee, and Carolyn, became instant friends and eventually housemates. They were inseparable until graduation, when they hugged, cried, and vowed never to lose touch. Five years, four marriages, and three kids happened before someone suggested a beach trip, which quickly became an annual tradition. No one ever missed. Until this year. They tried to carry on as usual, but it wasn't the same. They'd even discussed canceling the trip and visiting Carolyn instead, but she would hear nothing of the sort. "Please do this for me," she pleaded. "I don't want to be the reason you don't go."

So, the three honored her wishes but insisted on calling her every day during happy hour to entertain her with ridiculous stories, made up and authentic. It was fantastic to hear her laugh, which turned out to be the last time they heard it.

****

Lynn Ferguson stood at her second-story bedroom window, watching Adam methodically pack his brand new SUV. It glistened like a black diamond in the sunshine. She knew the suitcases, coolers, tote bins, and hang-up clothes would be in perfect order, every item in its place and a place for every item, as he said often. Too often. He didn't need her help nor want it. God forbid she should throw something in sideways or lackadaisically. Or worse. Scratch the paint.

Her husband's attention to the minutia in all matters closely mimicked an addiction. She didn't know how much more she could tolerate, but today, no amount of bullshit thrown her way would keep her from her friends.

As Adam closed the hatch, Lynn looked around the room one last time, checking for anything amiss, then turned off the lights and went downstairs, where she found her husband standing in the foyer with a scowl on his face. "I thought you were ready. What have you been doing all this time?"

"I didn't want to get in your way while you put things in the car," she answered meekly, then smiled. "I know you have a system."

He squinted at her. "Whatever. Let's roll."

Lynn thought about using the restroom one last time but didn't. Adam's tolerance of her stomach issues caused problems, especially if he was on a schedule. Missing a deadline, real or imagined, was not an option. She walked out the door, locked it, and saw their neighbor walking his dog along the hedge they'd worked hard to perfect. Adam threw up a hand. "Morning, George. Is this a gorgeous day, or what? Gonna tee 'em up later?"

The man jerked Daisy away from the shrubs. "I am. What about you?"

"Not today. We're headed up north, staying a few days."

"Ah. Safe trip."

"What an asshole. Once again, he was letting that scroungy mutt piss on our azaleas."

"I don't know what's wrong with people," Lynn agreed. "It's pretty obvious we care about our yard."

"I know, right? I'll remind him when we get back."

Lynn hoped the interaction with George wasn't enough to set Adam off. On a good day, he was an aggressive but safe driver. In a foul mood, the monster showed its ugly head, and Angry Adam cussed, yelled, gestured, blew his horn, and tailgated any poor schmuck unlucky enough to be in front of him. He acted like he was king of the road, and other drivers should bow down to let him pass. *Or kiss his ass.* She smiled at the unintended rhyme.

The radio played a familiar song, an oldie from years ago, and Lynn hummed along. It brought back memories of fraternity parties, beer kegs, and dancing—t*he good ole days.*

"You want music or news?" asked Adam.

"Music, please."

"Okay, but at 9:00, my guy comes on."

"That's fine."

It wasn't fine, but Lynn knew better than to debate it. She hated talk news shows where biased journalists belabored their points for hours and then speculated on things that hadn't happened. What-ifs drove her crazy. *Don't let the facts get in the way of a good story.* She tried not to let it bother her, but her body automatically reacted, thanks to her former job, where she had dealt with the media frequently. No matter the situation, reporters probed and poked, hoping she would screw up and reveal a hidden nugget they could exploit. Hypocrites, all of them.

They used her company's products daily. Everyone did. Eventually, Lynn moved to another position, but the anxiety and stomach problems remained her constant companion.

The sudden sound of a horn blasted Lynn off her seat. Kids scattered in different directions, then scampered onto the curb, where they screamed as the SUV nearly flattened their ball.

"Adam!"

"What?"

"You scared those kids to death. And me!"

"Oh, don't be so dramatic. I wasn't even close, but *somebody* needs to teach them a lesson. Obviously, it's not the parents. How about you relax and let me do the driving?"

Lynn reached into the back seat and grabbed a sage green sweater she kept in the car in case it got chilly, which was a given. She wasn't allowed to touch the temperature control knob because Adam didn't want to perspire and mess up his perfectly ironed, heavily-starched clothes. He had a *thing* about wrinkles and didn't trust anyone with his clothes except the dry cleaner he'd interviewed extensively. That was fine with Lynn. Adam could not blame their mistakes on her for a change.

Lynn grabbed her phone from her green leather purse and checked for messages. The three couples planned to meet in the hotel lobby for drinks, and the last thing she wanted to see was a text with lousy news about late arrivals. She couldn't wait to see Molly and CeeCee. Only they knew the sadness she felt.

"I thought we could have lunch at that little inn we like so much," she said. "What do you think?"

"The one in Middleton? I don't know. Last time it smelled funky, like beer and stale cigarettes. You know how it gets into your clothes and hair."

"Restaurants don't let people smoke anymore. Are you sure you're thinking about the right place? Maybe you're confusing it with something else."

"I don't get confused."

Lynn said nothing to his remark and continued staring ahead at the road. She saw an upcoming power pole and envisioned jerking the steering wheel hard to the right, causing a head-on collision with Adam's side of the car, leaving her unharmed. *My Lord, what is wrong with me?*

"If you're going to be a big baby about it, we'll stop, but don't say I didn't warn you. And if you get the shits, don't come crying to me."

"Thank you."

Around 12:30, they turned off the highway onto the half-grass, half-gravel driveway and approached a covered bridge. It sat elegantly across a small rocky stream and purple morning glories draped themselves across its handmade railings.

"Doesn't this make you feel like you're entering a magical land of some kind?" asked Lynn. "I could stare at it for hours. Would you stop for a sec?

I'd like to snap a quick pic." Already opening the door as the SUV slowed to a stop, she quickly stepped onto the running board, aimed, clicked, and climbed back in.

"That was fast," said Adam, nodding. "Impressive."

"Wanna see?"

"Later."

Large hardwood trees towered over the property of the Old Lakeside Inn, creating a canopy of arched branches adorned with Spanish moss. A red wooden sign boasted its establishment in 1902 and welcomed visitors. Adam grabbed Lynn's hand and walked in front of her as if towing a toddler. He opened the door to the gift shop, allowing his wife to enter first, which Lynn knew was just a show. She stepped inside and looked around to see if anything caught her eye. Over the years, she'd bought several gifts here and wondered if there might be something for Molly and CeeCee. Her husband seemed to have other thoughts and guided her towards the hostess stand, where a pretty little brunette bounced towards them. "How many are in your party today?"

"Two, please," said Adam.

"I have the perfect table overlooking the lake," she answered, looking at Adam, then down at her hands. "Unless you want privacy, of course."

Lynn noticed the girl was blushing. Women flirted with Adam frequently, so she was used to it, as was he. He carried himself confidently, a handsome man with a perfect olive complexion, deep brown eyes, and salt and pepper hair. His custom-made clothes were impeccable and expensive, just like his million-dollar smile.

"The lake view will be fine… Daphne."

"How did you…." The girl slapped her hand over her nametag. "Oh." Her face turned redder.

Lynn rolled her eyes and followed the hostess to a table with tall armchairs upholstered in white and gray damask fabric. A linen tablecloth held place settings of Lenox china and crystal water glasses, and sterling silverware flanked each dinner plate. She handed them both a leather-bound menu and disappeared.

Adam studied the splendor of the lush gardens outside and pointed at a ginkgo tree in the distance. "Look at the sun shining through those magnificent gold leaves. They're practically glowing."

Lynn agreed. "Looks like a painting."

"What do you think about planting one in the backyard?" Adam asked. "I know just the right place to put it."

I know where you can put it, too. "I think that's a great idea."

Their waiter appeared with drinks, hot sourdough bread, and the Inn's famous herb butter. Lynn raised the basket to her nose and squealed with delight. "It smells delicious!"

She placed a slice on her plate and piled butter on it. As they chewed, both raised their eyebrows and grinned with approval. Despite his earlier resistance, Adam looked like he was enjoying the restaurant, so Lynn relaxed some, grabbed more bread, and leaned against the seatback.

"I hope the entrée is as good as this bread, but I'm not sure how it could be."

"Better pace yourself. You don't want those love handles to get any bigger than they are." His eyes were serious, but he grinned as if he'd just said something loving instead of insulting.

Impersonating his shitty grin, she retorted, "Then I guess you'd better lay off, too, fat boy."

They were still glaring at each other when the waiter placed the food on the table and asked if they needed anything. Getting no response, he backed away.

Lynn stabbed at her grilled chicken and vegetables, barely noticing the flavors bursting from each bite. Once again, Adam managed to destroy a nice outing. She had her napkin poised to place on the table, signifying she was finished with her meal when she noticed a dollop of sauce clinging to the plate's rim. Placing her napkin back onto her lap, Lynn selected another slice of bread from the basket, waved it around in front of Adam's face, sopped up the sauce, and stuffed the whole thing into her mouth while looking straight at him.

"Real mature."

"Why do you have to ruin everything?" she hissed. "Can't you, just one time, be nice to me for a whole day?"

"I don't know what you're talking about."

"You never do."

"You're overreacting, as usual," he said dismissively. "You used to be able to take a joke. And I *am* nice to you. When you deserve it."

"I *deserve* a little compassion this week *and* your understanding. You know how much Carolyn meant to me." Her voice cracked. "Can't you see my heart is broken?" Tears rolled down her cheeks. "I can't handle that and your disapproval, too."

Adam tilted his head, looking baffled as if he were considering this for the first time. He leaned towards his wife and took her hand.

"I'm sorry, honey. I am. I liked Carolyn, too. She was one of the nicest women I've ever met." He spun Lynn's wedding band around with his thumb and middle finger. "I'll do anything you need. You know I love you."

"Thank you for saying that," said Lynn. "I'm trying to hold it together, and it would be easier if I knew you were on my side."

Adam frowned. "Of course, I'm on your side. Why wouldn't I be? I'm your husband, remember?"

His tone was becoming confrontational again, so Lynn quickly added, "That didn't come out right.

You know what I mean. I'm just thankful I have you to lean on."

Staring directly at his wife, Adam whispered, "I hope so. You know it makes me crazy when you question my feelings or disrespect me. And if I get upset, it's your fault. Not mine. You know I can't help it."

Lynn had heard this same old song for years and knew his apologies meant nothing. The blame was hers, just like all the other times.

"So, are we good?" he asked.

She smiled at him and lied. "Yep."

"Great! How about we look at the desserts?"

"I don't have room for one more bite," Lynn said, patting her stomach. "I'd rather get back on the road if you don't mind."

"Nobody forced all that bread down your throat, but as usual, it's all about you." Adam shook his head and pursed his lips. "See what I mean? Why are you like that?"

"Like what?"

"You said everything was good, but now you're being disagreeable. Nothing's ever suitable for you."

Even for Angry Adam, this was a fast repeat attack. It surprised her.

"I'm just in a hurry to get to the hotel, I guess."

"Don't worry. You'll see your little friends soon enough," Adam scoffed, waving at the waiter. "I'd like to order a piece of apple pie and a scoop of vanilla ice cream, please."

"Right away, sir."

"No hurry. We have plenty of time." He looked at Lynn. "Don't we, sweetie?"

Chapter Three

CeeCee and Cory arrived at the hotel earlier than expected, so they had plenty of time to tour the massive facility, which featured a conference center, indoor/outdoor pools, tennis courts, a golf course, three restaurants, shops, and a luxury spa.

"This place is magnificent," said CeeCee. "If we were here for any other reason, I'd want to stay for a week."

"It's something all right," Cory agreed. "I checked out the restaurants online, and boy, do their selections look good. Their prices, on the other hand, are *not* so good."

They laughed and continued their stroll, eventually circling back to the lobby a few minutes before five o'clock. The modern furniture, Sputnik-like chandeliers, and blown glass sconces gave the room a futuristic look. The designer had chosen muted tones, but pillows, textured drapes, and artwork provided a pop of color that could change with each season. CeeCee gave her secret nod of approval and found a strategic spot next to the fireplace, where she could watch the entrance. Of course, there was never a problem finding Molly. At 5'-9", she and her red hair were easy to spot in any crowd. On the other hand, CeeCee herself stood only 5'-1" and could get lost among the racks in a dress shop. Together they made quite the comical couple when walking down a street together.

A tall figure wearing an emerald green dress walked into the room, followed by a slightly taller, bespectacled man. CeeCee jumped up and waved both arms, making the bell-shaped sleeves flap like flags in the wind.

"Molly! Over here!"

"Ceeeeeeeeeee!" They flew into each other's arms. "Oh my God, I'm so glad to see you. I'm sad. Really sad. But it's great to see you."

CeeCee smiled at her friend and hugged her again. "I couldn't do this without you."

"I know. I feel the same."

Bill wrapped an arm around each woman, then looked at his wife's longtime friend. "How are you holding up?"

"Okay, I guess," said CeeCee. "Just doesn't seem real, ya know?"

He nodded. "Have you seen Lynn?"

As if on cue, CeeCee heard her name and turned to see Lynn running in their direction. The three women enveloped each other, kissed cheeks, talked over one another, and finally let the tears fall. They remained in their small huddle for a few minutes, then sat down on a massive sectional sofa and dabbed at their eyes and noses.

"I just can't believe it," said Molly. "I thought we'd have more time."

The other two nodded and looked down at their laps.

"Oh God," CeeCee said. "We forgot the guys."

The husbands stood nearby, hands in their pockets, silently watching their wives' sad reunion. The men had met at a wedding years ago but didn't know each other, so the girls made introductions and tried to include them as they discussed the details of Carolyn's funeral service. When the conversation started waning, CeeCee nudged Cory with her elbow.

"Hey, anybody thirsty?" he asked. "I say we migrate to the bar and order some drinks."

"You're talking my kind of language," said Adam as he took Lynn's hand and stood up.

While the women slid two tables together, the guys went to the bar, ordered drinks, and busied themselves with the contents of their wallets.

"Look at them up there, avoiding each other like the plague," CeeCee whispered. "I kind of wish the guys had stayed in the room. Remember Sharon's wedding? They sat like posts, and we spent the entire evening making sure they didn't feel left out. We worked our asses off."

"When we should've been dancing them off," said Lynn. "It was exhausting! I think Adam and I had a little quarrel afterward, come to think of it."

"And the wedding lasted just a few hours," Molly added. "What will three days in the same house be like?"

Instead of heading home after the funeral on Friday, the women jumped at the chance to extend their trip through the weekend when Josh offered his lake cabin. It was the perfect place to decompress, spend more time together, and give their husbands an opportunity to get to know each other.

"It's so beautiful there," said Molly. " I just hope it doesn't backfire on us."

"What's backfiring?" asked Bill as he handed the light pink martini to his wife.

CeeCee jumped in. "We were talking about our part in the service and hope we don't say anything inappropriate."

Bill chuckled. "I think that's probably a given, but I know it will come from your heart, so don't waste time worrying about it."

"Worrying about what?" asked Cory as he plopped beside CeeCee. The three women and Bill laughed, then Adam walked over. "What's so funny?"

For two hours, the group ate appetizers and talked about light-weight topics or told stories about Carolyn. When the couples gathered outside the bar, Adam kissed Lynn on the cheek and whispered something into her ear before he headed for the bank of elevators. On the outside, it appeared to be a loving gesture, but Lynn's expression told CeeCee something completely different.

****

Molly waved to Bill and turned to walk down the wide corridor with CeeCee and Lynn toward the hotel café, a much quieter place that suited their need for privacy. The room featured round tables with white tablecloths and napkins; small vases held pink and lavender flowers. The lights in the crystal chandeliers caused the sliced lemons to glisten on the rims of the glassware. It was a gorgeous place for discussing the unimaginable.

"How do you think dinner went?" Molly asked. "Did Adam or Cory give you any hints?"

Lynn and CeeCee shrugged.

"Bill thought it went okay."

"Well, of course, he would," said CeeCee. "He's a psychologist. He probably had a good ol' time, studying everybody's oddities."

"Yours in particular," Molly shot back.

A waiter approached wearing a black suit, white shirt, and plain black tie. His gloved hands caressed a sterling silver coffee pot. "Ladies, may I pour coffee? Decaf, of course." They nodded; he poured and then disappeared.

Molly lifted the delicate china cup to her lips, blew the steam away, and took a sip. "Dammit." She plopped her cup on the saucer and plunged her burned tongue into the water glass. She let out an audible sigh. "Jesus, can this be happening? Are we really about to bury our friend?" She patted her eyes with her napkin.

CeeCee touched her shoulder. "She's counting on us, Mol. We can't fall apart. Not yet."

Molly shifted her weight in the chair, sat a little straighter, and then grabbed a pen and pad from her purse.

"Okay, ladies, let's plan the send-off our girl deserves."

The three friends raised and clinked their coffee cups together. "To Carolyn."

Two hours later, Molly climbed into bed, the pad and pen still in hand. "I drew the short straw, which means I'll be speaking."

"You'll be fine," said Bill. "Better than fine."

"I think the story is okay, but you know how this kind of thing terrifies me. I wish I had your public speaking ability."

Bill pulled her to him and draped his arms around her. "I'm transferring my skills from my body to yours. Are you receiving it? Do you feel it?"

Molly giggled. "I feel *something*."

"Be serious. You have to feel the energy. Concentrate and repeat after me. I am a great storyteller. I am a great storyteller."

Molly rolled back to her side of the bed. "You know I don't believe in that psychobabble."

"Excuse me, these techniques have been proven by the greatest thinkers of all time and even published."

"In comic books, maybe."

They both laughed and said good night. Molly lay in the dark, overthinking the funeral service and the things that could go wrong. She couldn't shake the angst and finally got up, took her notes into the bathroom, and worked on the eulogy until it was perfect. All she had to do now was read it.

"I am a great storyteller. I am a great storyteller."

****

Thursday

The following day Molly climbed into the car and clicked her seatbelt. "I'm smacking my lips already. The hotel staff couldn't stop talking about this bakery. Must be something."

CeeCee adjusted the rearview mirror and started the engine. "Just don't get us lost. The roads on the map look like a pile of spaghetti."

"Well, they did admit it's off the beaten path."

Path turned out to be an understatement. After driving miles through open farmland with no signs of life, the asphalt ended abruptly in front of a yellow sign nailed to a barbed-wire fence post. *Anna's Goods* was hand-written in red paint, and a large blue arrow pointed at a dirt road that disappeared into an archway of large oak trees.

CeeCee stopped the car. "Is this some kind of joke?"

Lynn leaned in from the back seat. "Should we turn around?"

Molly rolled her eyes. "What's up with you two? I don't believe the hotel staff would send us to an unsafe place. They seemed very sincere when I spoke to them."

"Oh, did they? Sound very sincere?" asked CeeCee. "Well, that changes everything. Why didn't you say so?"

"Bite me."

CeeCee checked the door locks and veered the vehicle to the right. The density of the branches created a tunnel-like effect, making the headlamps come on and the dashboard lights brighten. She looked at her co-pilot. You have 9-1-1 on speed dial?"

"Of course I do." Molly grabbed her phone and glanced at it. "But there's no service."

"Are you shitting me? Cellphone towers sprout like weeds all over the planet, and we're in the one place it doesn't reach?"

Molly shrugged. "Probably the trees, but you rely way too much on that phone. Unless it's a stun gun, too, all it can do is make a call. It doesn't protect you. It's a false sense of security."

"Who *are* you?"

"Well, it's true. You've seen TV shows where some chick is in danger, and all she does is back away, stumble, scream, and punch at her phone. She doesn't even try to defend herself. It's stupid when you think about it. And let's assume the soon-to-be-Jane Doe reaches someone. She's still dead. It's not like a genie pops out and kills the bad guy."

CeeCee shook her head and looked at Lynn in the rearview mirror. "I don't know what's down this road, but it can't be worse than being lectured to death."

The three friends cracked up and were stunned when the trees opened, revealing a white picket fence and pink roses surrounding a Victorian house. A large welcome sign hung from the gingerbread trim on the front porch, which held four rocking chairs with floral cushions.

"You can thank me later," said Molly.

CeeCee parked the car alongside a few others, and they all slid out. Lynn took a few pictures of the house and the tunnel of trees. "Just in case we need evidence."

"Now *that's* a good use of the phone," Molly snapped. "If something happens, the investigators can do a digital dive and track our last movements."

CeeCee shook her head and walked away.

The aromas of freshly-baked pastries encircled the women as they entered the house. It was heavenly. Molly inhaled deeply, wanting to take it all in, and moved to the enormous pie case holding scads of delicate treats. She felt like a kid in a candy shop and placed her face close to the glass, tapping on it when she saw a favorite. After several moans and oh-my-gods, they placed an order, then strolled to a table tucked away in the corner. The girls had a schedule to plan and needed some isolation, but their chairs scraping on the hardwood floor caused more than one customer to turn in their direction.

CeeCee rolled her eyes. "So much for privacy."

Molly pulled her trusty pad and pen out of her purse and laid them on the yellow and white checkered cloth.

"Do you take that thing everywhere you go?" asked CeeCee.

"Maybe. Yes. What's it to ya?"

They laughed, more like cackled, again causing people to stare.

"Listen, you two," Lynn whispered. "We don't have all day to screw around."

"How about part of the day?" asked CeeCee.

Lynn ceremoniously thumped her fork twice on the table. "I hereby declare this meeting to order, and today's agenda is to plan a weekend where fun is had by all."

Before they started, their pastries arrived, and CeeCee studied the mouth-watering dessert in front of her. She took a bite, licked her fingers, and moaned.

"Oh my God, this is better than sex."

Lynn giggled. "You must be doing it wrong."

"Cory would be thrilled to know he's been replaced by an apple fritter," said Molly.

"Oh, he knows."

"Can we please get back to the weekend?" asked Lynn. "Adam has asked about it several times, and I had no answers. He doesn't like that."

"Bill doesn't either," said Molly. "Here's what I know. Josh stocked the cabin and told me not to worry about anything. But what does that mean to a guy? Beef jerky and cheese puffs? I wanted to ask him, but in my mind, it sounded ungrateful. Ya know?"

Lynn nodded. "Yeah. It's like checking to see if he chose things up to our standards, so I say we don't take any chances and take whatever we want."

They all agreed, then turned to the real issue at hand, keeping the guys pacified. After some brainstorming, Molly put down her pen. "Well, that settles it. The only thing they have in common is us."

"Ya know what I wish more than anything?" asked CeeCee. "That they would become friends. Real friends. Like us."

"Wouldn't that be something?" asked Molly as she thought back to Bill's initial reaction to the cabin-in-the-woods idea. Even though he loved hiking and the outdoors, he just wanted to support her through the funeral and not be saddled with strangers for days. And she'd bet big money he had no plan to make new buddies.

CeeCee pointed at Lynn's untouched blueberry muffin. "Don't you like it?"

"Hmm? Oh no, it's delicious. I'm just trying to watch my weight."

"*What?* You're in better shape than anyone I know."

"Adam mentioned my love handles, so I'm—"

"Stop. Don't even finish that sentence. We've had this conversation before. You can't let him—"

"I know."

"What's changed?"

"Nothing. That's..."

Suddenly a short, stocky lady stood at their table, drying her hands with a striped towel, which she promptly threw over her left shoulder. She looked at Lynn's plate. "Would you like something different, dear? Or a to-go box?"

"No, 'mam. It's perfect. I'm just taking it slow."

"You sure? I'm happy to get you anything. Just say the word, and please, call me Anna."

When the women realized she was the owner, they barraged her with questions about the food and the odd location of the bakery. Anna called a man over to the table. "I'll let Frank tell you. It's his doing."

Thirty minutes went by before the owner's husband stopped talking.

"Interesting people, especially him," said CeeCee.

Lynn jabbed at a crumb with her fork. "I bet *she* doesn't have to choreograph every move when they're out somewhere. We have to write a script for our guys."

"Listen, I like to bitch as much as the next girl, but we've beaten this dead horse," said CeeCee. "We don't have all day, as you said, and Frankie boy just ate up a big chunk of time. Let's get back to a plan."

"Why do *we* always need a plan?" Lynn continued in a whiny voice. "Why can't they say, 'How about we play poker or a dice game?' How hard can that be? Then they couldn't complain if it all goes to shit."

Molly and CeeCee exchanged glances, indicating a suspicion that something deeper was happening, but Molly kept things light. "Why, Lynn Michelle, are you suggesting the menfolk *communicate*? With each *other*?" She gasped and put one hand over her mouth.

Lynn smiled. "I blame it on their mothers, coddled to the very end. And it's just like that wedding dinner all over again. I'm sick and tired of negotiating deals with Adam."

"What kind of deals?" Molly asked.

"It's not important."

"I know what you mean," said CeeCee. "I feel like Cory's personal tugboat, not making any waves and pulling him along while he just floats and looks at the scenery."

"My friend calls that driving the bus," said Molly. "Always in charge. As long as you keep driving, people keep riding, happy to let you do the work. All they have to do is show up and have fun. But sometimes you just have to kick 'em off or stop the bus and get off yourself.

CeeCee raised her finger. "Just once, wouldn't it be nice if the guys drove the bus, planned it all, and then invited us to come along?"

"It'll never happen," said Molly and picked up her pen. "At least not today. So, what do our men like?"

"Hookers?" asked Lynn playfully.

"I thought you gave up that career," Molly said. "Seriously, do Cory and Adam like to fish, hike or canoe?"

"Any sports on TV keeps my Cory happy for hours," said CeeCee. "And the food channel."

"Anything outdoors?" asked Molly.

"Like shooting things?" CeeCee asked.

"Well, sure. Who doesn't like to do that?"

"Me," said Lynn. "Guns scare me to death. Adam likes to watch TV, too, and it's football season, so some games should be on. Hope the reception is good."

"So, while they are not fishing, not hiking, and not canoeing, they'll stay indoors and watch TV," said Molly. "They could do that anywhere."

"Well, hell, let's just leave them at the hotel then," CeeCee said.

"It's funny you mentioned that," Molly said. "When I talked to Josh, I told him we were apprehensive about how things would go this weekend. He said if the guys were that big a problem, leave them at the hotel. He was joking, of course."

"Was he?" asked CeeCee. "Either way, Cory would be in Heaven, vegging out in his underwear on top of the unmade bed, propped up on six pillows, watching ESPN, and getting room service from those fancy restaurants."

Lynn snorted. "Don't forget the scratching of different crevices."

"Bill would be analyzing me, looking for clues for my uncharacteristic behavior," Molly added.

"And Adam would be drawing up divorce papers," said Lynn. "Hey, he could do it for the other guys, too, thus forming a new kinship."

"So what you're saying is, they'd be friends, we'd be friends, and we'd all be divorced," said Molly, giggling. "Quite the conundrum."

"I can see Adam's expression when I tell him," Lynn continued. "Like, 'Hey, Babe, we've decided to go to the cabin by ourselves, so you're off the hook. I'll be back in a couple of days. Love you!'"

"That's where you're messing up," CeeCee said. "Too much time for confrontation. It would have to be a surprise."

"You mean, just leave, no explanation, no nothing?" asked Lynn.

"Oh, we'd leave a note or something. We wouldn't want them to think someone abducted us."

"V-e-r-y interesting," said Molly as she theatrically drummed her fingers on her chin. "First, they'd be in disbelief. Then pissed. Then they'd start plotting our murders. I want them to be friends, but not that bad."

"Wait a minute. This won't work," said CeeCee. "Being in a hotel doesn't force them together. They could leave town and never look back."

"You're right. They need to be in one place, without a car, and unable to leave," said Molly. Her eyes lit up. "The cabin!"

A server with purple and blonde hair popped into view and whispered. "You gals look like you're planning—or maybe plotting—something fun. Can I join you?"

"Sure," said CeeCee. "You know anything about abandoning men in the woods?"

"Honey, I've been married four times. What do you think?" She winked. "Just don't forget the blindfolds, gags, and zip ties."

Molly frowned, wondering if she was in the presence of a sociopath who was still talking. "Not to bother you, but we have some fresh bread right out of the oven if you want to try it. On the house. Plus, we have a great wine that pairs perfectly with it."

"Sounds delish," said Molly. The other two nodded.

"That was weird," Lynn said.

CeeCee giggled. "Maybe, but she's not wrong about the supply list. Something to think about." She tapped Molly's pad. "Write that down."

The waitress soon returned with hot rolls, various kinds of butter, and wine glasses filled to the rim. Even though they'd just consumed large pastries and iced tea a short time earlier, the girls dug in. They continued to knock around ideas for the weekend and soon were laughing at things that weren't funny.

"It might be the iced tea talking..." said Molly.

"You mean wine," said CeeCee.

"What. Ever. But I'm telling you, the more we talk about this idea, the more it grows on me."

"Speaking of growing," Lynn said. "If I eat one more bite, I won't fit into my dress tomorrow."

"Which idea are you talking about, Molly?" CeeCee asked.

"Leaving the guys at the lake and skedaddling."

"You're not serious," CeeCee said.

Molly burped. "Yep. I mean, it's the craziest thing we've ever cooked up, with no time to think it through, which makes it terrifying but exhilarating at the same time. So we have to decide. Right now. What d'ya say? Can we do it?"

CeeCee scrunched up her nose. "Nah. We could never pull that off."

"Never say never, my friend. That just encourages me," said Molly.

CeeCee nodded. "That is true."

The long-time friends looked down at their empty bread plates for a few seconds, locked eyes, and clinked their empty wine glasses.

"Could we?" asked Molly.

"Should we?" CeeCee responded.

One hand, palm down, was placed in the center of the table, then another, and one more capped it off. It was official. The Kappa Delts were going to kidnap their own husbands. For better or worse.

Chapter Four

Friday, the day of the funeral

Last night CeeCee and Cory were too wound up to sleep, so they watched an old movie they'd seen several times and munched on popcorn from the vending machine. When 8:00 a.m. rolled around, they were still groggy and unprepared for the sound of a foghorn emitted by the alarm clock. CeeCee moaned and slapped at the clock, aiming for the snooze button that escaped her grasp. Finally, she traced the wire down the wall and jerked the cord out of the receptacle.

"Dammit. I hate getting pissed off before I even wake up. It ruins my whole day."

Cory pulled her to him and kissed her. "I think I know how to fix that."

"You do?"

"I do."

An hour later, CeeCee watched her husband's reflection in the bathroom mirror as he put his arms around her waist. He nuzzled the back of her neck and kissed it.

"Thank you for taking my mind off things," she said.

Cory sighed. "It was tough, but duty called."

She rolled her eyes and leaned forward to check her waterproof eyeliner and mascara. Both would be tested today.

Cory looked at his watch. "Time to go."

"I don't want to."

"I know."

****

Molly woke and snuggled up to Bill while he continued to doze. She'd hoped to sleep in, but too many things weighed on her mind: sorrow for her friend, fear of screwing up at the funeral, and abandoning her husband this evening.

Her emotions and nerves were raw, and her stomach felt like it had an ice pick in it. She had a severe phobia of public speaking, and no amount of positive self-talk alleviated the racing heart, sweaty hands, or squeaky high-pitched voice. Most of the time, she could avoid it, but she'd drawn the short straw the other night, and there was no way to back out of this eulogy.

In addition, the plan to leave Bill at the lake terrified her, and she wasn't confident she could do it. Lynn and CeeCee agreed to think about it during the drive to the cabin, where they'd give each other the nod if the plan was still a go. Delaying the final decision for several hours did not stay her anxiety, however, which seemed to grow by the minute.

Bill made coffee while Molly showered, and afterward, they shared four stale powdered donuts.

"We know how to live, don't we?" asked Molly. The word *live* made her tear up, and she dabbed at her eyes with her robe. "Dammit. I can't start this now. I'll never stop."

Bill brushed white sugar from her nose, then held her tightly. She could hear his heartbeat and feel his chest rising as he breathed. She loved this man. *Can I do this to him? Will he ever forgive me?*

Molly slumped onto the vanity stool in the bathroom and slid closer to the counter. A magnified make-up mirror awaited to enhance her wrinkles and flaws. She didn't want to look at it, so she busied herself by opening a case filled with little bottles and jars of beauty supplies, products that promised to make her look ten years younger. *And I lapped it up, just like all the other suckers.* Just the other day, she passed a storefront window, and the reflection of a slightly-overweight woman accompanied her. For a nano-second, her brain registered the image as a stranger. Then it hit her. She was looking at *herself*, a revelation that hit hard and stayed with her all day. This aging shit sucks.

She tilted the mirror toward her face and smeared on tinted foundation, shadows and liners on her eyes, and blush on her cheeks. Once she styled her unruly red hair, she didn't look half bad.

"You look beautiful," Bill said, kissing the top of her head. "I'm jumping in the shower."

"I'm going downstairs to get some real coffee. Then I need to review my notes."

Molly returned shortly with two steaming cups of coffee and two bran muffins and sat in the chair next to the room's sole window. Like many people, she carried her stress in her shoulders and neck, and the sun's rays on her back and warm coffee helped to ease the tension. As Molly stretched, she looked outside, happy to see clear skies and a sunny day. A florist hurried across the grounds to the hotel entrance, where he handed an arrangement of yellow mums to a bellboy. The mums immediately took Molly back to college many years ago.

It was a crisp fall day, and golden hues of leaves swirled in the air and landed on the green fescue grass. The college campus buzzed with Homecoming excitement, and blue and gold decorations were draped everywhere, urging students to show their school spirit. In a strategic location near the stadium, a football player hung in effigy, although it looked more like a giant red and white pinata. It served as a stern warning to State's rivals and would be the first thing they'd see when stepping off the bus. It was there every year. Only the uniform colors changed.

Everyone went to the game. Fraternity and Sorority Rush ended a month earlier, and all pledges in the Greek nation proudly wore their shiny lapel pins symbolizing their lifelong commitment to an organization they loved. It was a feeling similar to falling in love.

Molly addressed the new pledges using her most authoritative tone, giving advice and guidance about the weekend. They mustn't do anything to smudge their reputation or the sorority. If they did, there would be severe consequences.

"I know you want to have fun. We all do," said Molly. "But don't get caught up in bad decisions other people make, especially drunk boys. They're immature and don't have any sense. If you need help, call anyone in this room. We're sisters now, and we look out for each other."

As a tradition, the girls dressed in their best fall outfits, and their dates bought corsages made of yellow mums and blue ribbons. Molly disliked the smell of mums, even to this day, and warned Bill years later it could be a deal-breaker if he ever bought any. He'd never forgotten it and loved to tell the story of her flower restrictions.

During the football game, the guys secretly sipped whiskey out of hidden flasks, and occasionally the pungent aroma of marijuana wafted through the crowd. The girls thought about more important things, like the Homecoming dance.

Halftime featured a parade of floats that only 15 hours earlier were empty shells of chicken wire.

Students sometimes pulled all-nighters stuffing each hole in the wire with a colorful square of tissue paper, finally revealing the theme designed by the sponsor. The finished floats lined up on one end of the field, waiting to circle it during halftime. The last float carried the Homecoming Court, elected by the student body, and the 300-piece marching band paved the way while playing the school song. Those were the good old days, except for the mums.

Molly felt a hand on her shoulder.

"Are you ready?" Bill asked.

"As ready as I'll ever be."

****

Adam lay on his right side facing the window when he woke up. The sun peeked through a gap where the curtains didn't quite meet, and dust particles floated along the beam cutting through the room. He closed his eyes, rolled onto his back, and yawned. He thought about last night and felt pretty good about it. He'd gotten through that awkward dinner with Lynn's friends and used his charm to show interest in their trivial lives. It was one of his favorite games—to engage, smile, ask questions, make good eye contact, and nod his head in response. It worked every time and made him look good in Lynn's eyes. He liked that.

As he chose the shrimp scampi from the menu, Adam had looked unwaveringly at his wife, who hated the strong garlic breath caused by the dish. She should feel lucky he came on this stupid trip, and she needed to know he was still in control. He stretched his arms up towards the ceiling, smiling. *Now it's time for my reward.*

He reached across the king-sized bed to pull Lynn towards him but came up empty-handed. He opened his eyes and saw her tiptoeing to the bathroom.

"Hey. Come 'ere, baby."

"Gotta go!"

The bathroom door closed, and he listened for the sound of the lock, knowing it wouldn't come. He grinned. He'd taught her well, maybe too well. *It's almost no fun anymore.*

****

Lynn leaned against the bathroom door and took a deep breath. She'd been awake for quite some time, listening to her husband's rumbling snore. With each exhale, she got a whiff of garlic from last night's dinner, and her nostrils flared at the pungent odor.

She'd gently moved her left leg towards the side of the mattress, trying not to rustle the covers or vibrate the bed, but Adam's snoring halted. Before he could paw at her, she threw herself out of bed and scurried to the safety of the bathroom.

The thoughts of today's upcoming events and the potential consequences of her escape from Adam swirled in her mind, making her anxious. She looked at the knob, wanting badly to lock it, but knowing she wouldn't. Instead, she sat down on the commode, placed her elbows on her knees and head in her hands, and let her long hair flop forward, creating an auburn cocoon. With her field of vision narrowed, Lynn stared at the gray and white floor tiles, studied the intricate mosaic design, and admired her shiny red toenail polish. She lingered, listening for sounds outside the door, and, hearing none, took the silence as a good sign.

Lynn stepped into the shower and welcomed the warm water pulsing on her back and head. The tightness in her chest faded, and her body relaxed as she breathed in moist air and the soap's fragrance. Before she turned into a prune, she reluctantly turned off the water and reached for a towel. Suddenly Adam grabbed her wrist and jerked the shower curtain violently to the side.

Lynn screamed, jumped back, and reflexively covered herself with the towel. Adam stood there, naked, with a scowl on his face.

"What are you doing?" she shrieked, still trying to catch her breath. "Are you trying to scare me to death?"

"The question is, what are *you* doing? You knew I'd want sex this morning."

Trying to ignore him, she blotted her face and hair with the towel. She was getting cold and wanted to get dressed. "I was awake and needed to pee and didn't want to disturb you. So I decided to get a headstart on the day."

"Didn't you hear me say, 'come 'ere, baby'?"

"Wasn't sure what you said. Didn't think it meant anything."

"The problem is you *don't* think. Period."

"Well, I admit my mind is distracted," she said. "I barely slept and kept thinking about Josh and the family. It's just so sad. Today is going to be horrible."

"Well, my little friend here can perk you right up." He moved towards her wiggling his penis to get her attention.

You mean perk you *up*. Lynn stepped out of the tub, gave him her best smile, and gently put one hand on his chest. "I know he can, big guy, but not today. Why don't you get back in bed while I get ready? Then you can have the bathroom."

Adam grabbed her face with one hand, squeezing her cheeks, and forced her to look in the mirror. Black streaks from her eyeliner dripped down her face, and her hair was matted to her head.

"Look at yourself. You look like a drowned sewer rat. Do you know how lucky you are to have someone like me? Someone willing to make love to *this*?"

Lynn said nothing, but her eyes stayed on his until she finally looked away as if feeling shame. It was something she'd learned that sometimes slowed the building rage of the monster before her.

"I'm sorry. I just can't," Lynn said softly, trying not to cry. "I'll make it up to you later. I promise."

"Same old story with you," he jeered.

"What do you mean, same old story?"

"There's always some excuse."

"You mean like burying one of my best friends today?" She wanted to say a lot more but dared not. Instead, she looked down at the heavy make-up mirror on the counter and, for a split second, imagined swinging it like a bat and watching his bloody head roll on the pretty tile she'd admired earlier.

"I need your support today, Adam, not a fight."

"I came, didn't I?" acting as though he was doing her a favor, but his cold, dark eyes showed nothing but anger.

Lynn braced herself. "I just don't know what you want from me."

"You know precisely what I want, and I'll expect it tonight." He turned to leave. "No excuses."

Lynn watched with relief as he walked out and slammed the door. *I won't need an excuse tonight, asshole.*

Chapter Five

The couples arrived at the church at 10:45, and a man with an orange traffic wand directed them into parking spaces. Molly's nerves were getting the best of her, so she focused on the architecture of the gray stone church. "This is magnificent. It's like a mini version of a cathedral, flying buttresses and all."

"Now you're just showing off," said Bill. He shut the engine down and turned to his wife. "I know you have a thousand things running through that pretty little head of yours, especially the eulogy, but try not to let that dominate Carolyn's Life Celebration. I don't want you to miss the experience or ignore the emotions you need to feel because you're wondering about tripping over your tongue. Others will share things about her you'll want to hear, so don't question what you've written. Don't question your ability to speak clearly and from the heart. You've done your best, and it will be spectacular. But if you can't go through with it for some reason, there is no shame in letting someone else take the reins. Your story of friendship will still get told."

Molly smiled. "Now *you're* just showing off." She took his hand and kissed it. "Thank you."

When she stepped out of the car, the others were waiting. The girls all wore black hats with short fishnet veils and looked like they had just stepped out of Vogue Magazine instead of an SUV. They'd decided weeks ago to dress up for the service and hold nothing back. The men also looked dapper in black suits, white shirts, and tasteful silk ties. On a typical day, Molly would suggest taking a group photo, but this day was anything but typical.

She and Bill led the way to the red, arched doors that stood at least ten feet tall. They proved to be as heavy as they looked when Molly pulled on the forged-iron handle. "I'm not sure they want people to get in here."

A pregnant lady in a purple dress rushed over to them when they stepped into the entrance hall. "I'm sorry about the door. Some gismo that makes it swing easily broke, and the young man stationed to greet people had to take a potty break." She pointed to the guest book. "The family would like you to sign the register if you don't mind."

As Molly signed her name and drew a few hearts, she heard an old hymn coming from the adjacent room. It seemed familiar and comforting, but she still shuddered.

"Are you cold?" Bill asked. "Do you want my jacket?"

"No. I'm just... I'll be okay." *I hope.*

An usher handed a folded bulletin to each person as they entered the sanctuary and, in a hushed voice, told them about the reserved pew in the front. They filed in quietly, then busied themselves reading about the service as the organist played a different song, one a little more uplifting. Molly turned the bulletin over, and Carolyn's face met her gaze. Below the picture was the date of birth and death. *Date of death.* She stared at it, then flipped it over, still not wanting to believe why she was there.

Bill placed his hand on hers, and she leaned into him, putting her head on his shoulder. The angle brought the tall ceilings to her attention, as well as the hand-hewn beams and massive chandeliers. Paneled walls and flickering candles on the window sills gave the church an old-world feel. It was beautiful and sadly filled with sad people waiting to say goodbye.

The music stopped, and the priest motioned for everyone to stand as the pallbearers pushed the casket to the front of the church. Carolyn's family followed and filled the seats in front of Molly. She reached over and placed her hand on Josh's shoulder, causing him to turn. When his eyes met hers, they teared up, then he shut them, nodded, and squeezed her hand. She looked at Lynn and CeeCee and almost lost it, but Bill put his arm around her, which again helped Molly pull herself together.

Twenty minutes into the service, the priest said, "I'd like to ask some of Carolyn's friends to come forward. They are called the Beach Buds, I believe, or Babes, but I'm not sure I'm supposed to say Babes in church." He smiled and sat down.

The women rose, held hands, and took the steps to the pulpit. CeeCee and Lynn flanked Molly, appearing as a unified force, and had promised if she passed out or did anything equally stupid, they would take up where she left off and revive her later. Their presence comforted her, but Molly's hands shook as she placed the notes on the podium. She noticed a small glass of water, probably meant for the Father, but she sipped some anyway.

"We crossed paths as 18-year-olds, hailing from different states, who happened to choose the same university and the same sorority. We had no idea how those choices would impact our lives at the time, but since we're standing here today, you know it was significant. We were excited to be independent, make our own decisions—good and bad—and meet new people, especially boy people."

Everyone chuckled as Molly had hoped.

"We took up terrible habits we hid from our parents, like smoking in the dorm, eating pizza and Twinkies, staying up all night to study, and drinking cheap beer at fraternity keg parties. These were the days of miniskirts, bell-bottoms, and halter tops." Molly made air quotes with her fingers. "And rebelling against The Man.

"This is when we met and fell in love with Carolyn. Like a moth drawn to a flame, she had a way of pulling you in, figuratively and literally. As you know, she liked hugs, not just regular hugs. Bear hugs. So when she pulled, she did not let go. I can still hear the jingling of her 14K gold bracelets as she reached up to embrace me and kiss my face. And that smile of hers? You couldn't find one more genuine, bright, or infectious, and her green eyes reflected her happiness as well. Carolyn was probably the nicest person I've ever known."

Molly saw people nodding their heads and smiling at each other.

"Even now, she's making us smile. Soon after graduation, we served as bridesmaids in Carolyn's wedding. She was *so* happy, even though our southern belle married a Northerner. A Yankee, for God's sake."

Molly picked up a lace fan from the podium, fanned her face dramatically, and she, CeeCee, and Lynn said, "Oh my," in a heavy southern drawl. "Turns out Josh is a great man, and their marriage flourished. I don't know if Carolyn doing laundry in the nude had anything to do with that or not."

Molly picked up the fan again, and the girls repeated, "Oh my." The audience laughed while Josh shook his head and blushed. She looked at him. "You knew it was going to be in here somewhere.

"The next five years, we concentrated on careers and learning to be adults—they call that *adulting* now. Once we earned vacation days and could afford to travel, we planned a beach trip that became an annual tradition. That meant we met at the beach every May, come hell or high water, starting up where we left off the year before. We'd cram in as much talking, laughing, and love as we could handle, and instead of eating pizza and Twinkies, we drank wine and ate chocolate. We'd become quite sophisticated, you see. It was and still is magical. We shared hopes, dreams, man troubles, job changes, and talked about people who drove us bat-crap crazy like... well, I'll just say we left no stones unturned."

Molly turned and looked at the priest. "Sorry about the bat-crap phrase, Father. It slipped out. And while I'm confessing, I drank some of your water." He grinned, waved her off, and the people laughed.

"Every morning, while we sat in our pajamas drinking coffee, we'd hear Carolyn's flip-flops slapping on the stairs before she'd appear in the kitchen, dressed for the beach and sun, towel in one hand, tote bag in the other. Then out the door, she'd go, promising to save us *slackers* a chair at the pool. She walked miles on the beach before we ever got there and stayed after we gave it up. She loved it so much.

"Carolyn has been in our lives a long time but not nearly enough. If only we had one more beach trip, one more hug. This year she didn't come. She was busy preparing for her son's wedding and didn't have the energy to do both. We understood, of course, but we were also thinking...can't they change the wedding date?"

The congregation laughed again.

"A few years ago, Carolyn and I were walking

on the beach. I can't remember why, but I said, 'you must be *the* sweetest person on earth.' With a devilish smile, she cracked up and said, 'If you only knew.' Please keep that last statement in mind because this next part may be somewhat inappropriate. But since Carolyn and someone else who shall remain nameless—CeeCee—mooned us from the back of an SUV, we believe our sometimes-devilish friend would approve. Now, getting approval from the church? A whole other matter. Turns out the priest has a good sense of humor, and I'm pretty sure he's expecting a sizable donation before we leave town."

Molly stepped away from the podium. A chair behind her held four fluted glasses and a bottle of Dom Perignon, uncorked. CeeCee took one flute to a small table near the casket, poured champagne, and returned to fill the other three. They raised their glasses and sang.

Let's drink a toast – to the Kappa Delts!

The greatest girls we know.

The fact is notorious. They're simply glorious!

That's why we love them so.

And when I die, if I get the chance,

To choose 'tween heaven and hell.

I'll say Lord pardon me, but I'd rather be,

Down with the Kappa d–d-d-d–d-Delts!

The room filled with applause as Molly stepped back to the mike.

"Some volunteers, our husbands, will bring out small cups of champagne, so we can make another toast."

A low buzz came over the crowd as they waited, and more than a few children tried to grab a cup of their own, only to be met with a parent's scowl.

"Will everyone please stand and raise your glasses? To Carolyn!" Molly shouted.

"To Carolyn!" they replied.

The three women sang in harmony, and others in the congregation joined them.

We love you, Carolyn, oh yes, we do-oo.

We love you, Carolyn, and we'll be true.

When you're not with us, we're blue.

Oh, Carolyn, we love you.

As the women made their way to their seats, they inserted a white rose, the sorority's symbol, into the floral spray on top of the casket.

The priest nodded at the women. "All I can say is, I'm glad I spoke first. I can't compete with that."

After the service, the three couples left the church through the beautiful arched doors, bookmarking a permanent change in their lives, one they'd hoped would never come. They climbed into their cars and got in line for the drive to the cemetery, where they'd say a final goodbye. Unthinkable until today.

The family held a reception at an old inn

restored to its original 1859 décor and listed on the historical register. Wood banisters gleamed from recent polishing, and crystal chandeliers shone brightly above mahogany tables holding mounds of food on silver platters. People milled around and nibbled on hors d'oeuvres and drank champagne punch.

Due to the sad occasion, conversations were whispered, but as time passed, much-needed giggles and laughter filled the room. Several women approached Molly, praising the toast to Carolyn's life and asked if she'd speak at their funerals someday. She thanked them for the offer but assured them this was a one-time gig. She didn't want to think about attending another funeral anytime soon.

Molly scanned the room for Josh and walked over to hug him again. "We'll be leaving soon. You know we love you, and we're here for you. Anytime. Anywhere."

"I know, Mol. I feel the same way. And thank you again for your tribute to Carolyn. She wouldn't have expected anything less from you bat-crap crazy girls." They both laughed, then locked eyes.

"Is everything ready?" she asked.

Josh nodded. "As we discussed. Good luck."

We're going to need it.

Before starting the drive to the mountains, the couples changed clothes, and the girls said goodbye to a few people on their way out, promising to keep in touch but knowing they wouldn't. As the convoy of dark SUVs pulled onto the road, it reminded Molly of a motorcade for political officials. The only thing missing were the little flags on the hoods.

"I sure hope I can remember how to get to this place," she said. "I've only been there once, and it's literally in the middle of nowhere. That's why we can't use GPS."

"I hope you're kidding," said Bill. "You talked to Josh and got directions, didn't you?"

"Well, I meant to, but things got sort of busy. One thing led to another, and I didn't get the chance. Take a right at the next light."

Bill snorted in disbelief. "Are you messing with me, Molly Elizabeth?"

She looked at him, shrugged her shoulders, and smiled. "Maybe. Maybe not."

****

Bill checked the rearview mirror for the tenth time to ensure the rest of the convoy was behind him. His was the lead car, but he had no idea where to go, and his co-pilot was incommunicado. The breathtaking scenery and smooth jazz on the radio helped melt the day's tensions, but he still needed to talk to Molly. Bill reached for his wife's hand, but her arms were under a blanket, eyes closed. He put his hand back on the steering wheel.

Usually, on car trips, Molly chatted nonstop, asking Bill what he thought about this and that. Today, he got the silent treatment while wondering about the weekend and how things would go. A trip with a bunch of strangers didn't fall on his list of fun, but Molly promised to discuss it on the drive up to give him some clarity. They were getting closer to the cabin, or at least he thought so, and he'd received no additional information. It bugged him.

He looked over at his wife again and thought about nudging her. She hadn't been herself since Carolyn's death, and the funeral was another stressor, so he knew she was tired. She'd spent a lot of time on the phone with the girls, often leaving the room to talk privately. *Making all the plans, I guess. Plans that didn't include my input.* But since Thursday, she'd been especially quiet. W*hat's the big secret?* Bill felt shut out, and he didn't like it. If they weren't in this post-funeral haze, he'd call Molly on it.

Up ahead were several little signs on the side of the road. LAST CHANCE TO GET SUPPLIES! GET 'EM AT BIG JON'S. ONE MILE ON THE RIGHT. Bill knew they had all the stuff they needed for the weekend but thought, what the hell. *I'm stopping.* He put his blinker on well ahead of time and saw the others do the same.

The crunch of the gravel parking lot got Molly's attention. "We're stopping? Are we there?"

"Seeing as I know nothing about the place or where it is, the answer is no." His tone was a little chippy.

"Uh oh, you're mad at me. You have on your pissed-off face."

"Nope. Just want to stretch my legs a little and get a soda. The others stopped, too."

"Okay, can you grab some water for me? And maybe some cookies?"

"Sure."

The store's front porch featured splintered wooden posts holding up a rusted tin roof with barbed wire draped around the edges for decoration. Windows with metal bars flanked each side of the front door, which featured an old horseshoe as the handle. Bill stepped onto the weathered floorboards, each one creaking, and walked into the past.

The interior floors hadn't been exposed to the outside elements, but they weren't in much better condition than those on the porch. Dusty racks and shelves holding various goods took up most of the space, and rusty lanterns and old tools hung from the ceiling. Metal signs from days gone by and expired license tags were nailed haphazardly to the dingy walls. Bill loved it. When the other two guys entered the store, he saw they were taking it in as he had.

A man behind the counter asked, "Help ya?"

"Howdy," said Bill, getting caught up in the rusticness. "We'd like to get something to wet our whistles and maybe a snack."

The man looked at him quizzically. "You from Texas?"

"No. Maryland."

"Ah, crab country. Ever wet your whistle at the Burley Oak Brewing Company?"

"Yes, lots of times! You been there?"

"One time with the Missus on a weekend getaway. Well, help yourself but check the expiration date on the snacks. I don't get many visitors up this way, and most come for bait and beer, not the nutritious food in cellophane wrappers."

"Good fishing up here?" asked Bill.

"Oh, you bet. Especially striped bass. You thinkin' 'bout dipping a line, now's the time to get what you need." He pointed his thumb at the shelf behind him that held several Styrofoam cups. Handwritten labels identified the contents as live crickets, worms, and minnows.

Bill nodded as if considering the idea, but he was actually acknowledging the fishy smell he'd noticed earlier. "Maybe next time." He placed four items on the counter. "What do I owe you?"

Before the man could answer, a wall phone rang loudly. It had the original old-fashioned ringtone that cell phones replicate these days. *I haven't seen one of those in a long time, curly cord and all.* Bill remembered the avocado green phone they had in the kitchen where he grew up. The cord got so stretched out from people—his sister mostly—trying to talk privately that it never returned to its original spiral shape, something his mother did not like one bit. He remembered feeling terrified when calling a girl to ask her out, sweating as he tightly gripped the handset and praying he didn't get shot down. *Boy, were those days different.*

The man turned toward Bill, pointed at the phone, and rolled his eyes. "Yep. Yep. I know all about the weather this weekend, Joe. I got a TV, too, ya know. Yeah, saw it might hit Friday night. I'll be outta here by then. Gotta go. Got a customer." He hung up the phone. "That'll be $4.27."

Bill laid a $5 bill on the counter. "Haven't seen a wall phone like that in a long time."

"Yeah, I know. I get razzed about it all the time, but I'm grateful for it. Cell phones are no good here."

Bill climbed into the car and handed Molly the water and chocolate chip cookies. "Interesting place."

She jammed a cookie in her mouth, chewed for a second, and said, "Is that a fact?" Then she opened her mouth and stuck out a tongue covered with half-chewed food.

Bill rolled his eyes and smiled. "Gross."

They both did this on occasion to make each other laugh, and it usually worked, especially during awkward or stressful times. He leaned over and gave her a quick kiss. "You're weird, you know."

She smiled. Bill started the engine and waited for everyone else to get in their cars. As they eased onto the highway, he squeezed Molly's hand.

She swallowed her cookie and took a sip of her water. "I guess you're going to interrogate me now."

"If you're asking would I like to have a conversation, then the answer is yes. Do you think you're up to it?"

"You promise not to analyze?"

He almost analyzed the analysis question but stopped himself. His training as a psychologist sometimes got him into trouble with Molly, and he needed to be a husband right now, not a shrink. "I'll try my best."

"Okay, fire away."

"How do you think this weekend will go?" Bill asked. "Is there anything specific planned, or are we just winging it?"

"Depends on your definition of a plan, but I'd say it will be a combination. We brought some games if there's any interest, but I'm hoping the weather will be nice enough to be outdoors hiking, enjoying nature, and lazing on the dock. I know one thing for sure. Lots of adult beverages will be consumed."

"The guy at the store mentioned some sort of storm coming in."

"Did he? Well, crap." She scratched the palm of her hand, a familiar habit when she got a little uneasy.

"He also said the fishing is great. Think there's any gear at the cabin?"

"Knowing Josh, that cabin has anything and everything, so my bet would be yes." Molly looked at Bill. "I've never heard you talk about fishing. You know how?"

"Do I know *how*? Do I know *how*?"

"So, the answer's no." They laughed. "Listen, I know you're nervous about being around a bunch of people you don't know. I get it."

You're the one who seems anxious. "I'm not nervous. I'm *curious* about what I signed up for. I think you know that." Bill tried to keep from sounding impatient, but dammit, they were almost there, and he still didn't know a friggin' thing.

"You're right. I do know that, and I'm sorry for being inattentive the past few days. Dealing with Carolyn's funeral and speaking in front of all those people had me freaked out, and then making plans for the weekend sucked up the energy I had left. I guess it dominated my thoughts."

You got that right.

"I hope you know I love you very much. I don't know what you'd do without me."

"Very funny."

She grinned. "Seriously, thank you for being so patient with me. How about this? How about we look at this weekend as an adventure? You love to study different personalities, and you happen to be very good at it. We could compare notes afterward. Might be the makings of a good book. What do you think?"

You're avoiding questions. That's what I think.

Chapter Six

The vehicles turned off the main highway and maneuvered over rough terrain, making their progress slow and tense. Molly took pride in getting them there and only steering them down one wrong road, but she didn't mention it to Bill. Getting three large SUVs turned around on that one-lane path had been challenging, and she'd noticed more than one glare in her direction from the drivers, including her husband.

Road trips brought out a different side of Bill, who was usually laid back. That wrong turn cost them thirty minutes, and his body language showed his frustration. Molly didn't understand the importance men put on the time it took to get somewhere. *Aren't we supposed to enjoy the journeys we take, as well as the destination?*

Everyone piled out of their cars, some grunting as they stretched and twisted to get the kinks out. Adam walked around his vehicle, inspecting it for scratches, and he didn't look happy. Molly didn't blame him. His car was brand new, as was hers. She didn't remember the road being so bad, or she would've warned Lynn about it, but that kind of detail hadn't entered her mind.

"This place is amazing," yelled CeeCee, making a 360, looking all around and up. "I'm glad you knew how to get us here, Molly. I *never* would've found it."

Molly grinned and looked at Bill, who frowned and rolled his eyes.

The log cabin stood two stories tall and had a deep wrap-around porch supported by logs at least ten inches in diameter, but they looked small compared to the ones used to construct the walls of the house. Natural stone adorned the 40-foot tall chimney, which oddly had a television antenna attached to it. But the real star of the show was the expansive lake at the edge of the property. The leaves were just beginning to turn, and a few twirled in the breeze before landing on the flagstone path leading to the water. Even though the days were still warm, it wouldn't be long until chilling temperatures would force them all to the ground. But today, it was perfect. Molly envisioned herself on the dock, book in hand and soaking up the sun, but she snapped herself out of it before she changed her mind about the plan.

"Okay, you guys, let's get this stuff into the house," said CeeCee. "We'll figure out who's sleeping where later. It won't be daylight much longer, and I'm pretty sure those chairs on the dock are calling our names." She winked at Molly.

Each couple busied themselves, pulling things out of the cargo holds and setting them on the side porch. Bill caught Molly looking at him, smiling.

"What? Something on my face?" He swiped at his chin.

"Nope. Just love you. That's all. In case I haven't said it already, thank you for coming on this trip."

"You don't have to thank me. I'd do anything for you—within reason."

I hope that's true. She squeezed his arm and turned away, pointing at one of the coolers.

"Hey, guys. How about taking that blue cooler down to the lake, and we'll grab some snacks. Josh said he stocked the place with all kinds of goodies, so we'll check it out. We'll be down in a jiff." She paused. "And save us some beer!"

The men seemed relieved they didn't have to do any more work, so they did what Molly asked. Cory and Bill grabbed the cooler, and Adam ambled along behind them with his hands in his pockets. Once the men were beyond earshot, the girls looked at each other. Molly took a deep breath. "It's not too late to change our minds."

"No!" Lynn exclaimed, then lowered her voice. "No. We've been through this, and we all agreed."

Then she clenched her teeth together. "We even did the secret handshake."

The friends joined hands and, one at a time, nodded. Time to execute.

****

The men made their way down the flagstone path in single file. Cory led the way with his arm behind him, holding one handle, which caused his muscular tricep to perk up. This didn't go unnoticed by Bill, who was hanging onto the other end, trying not to trip. The cooler blocked the view of the path, making his footing uncertain, so he walked slower than Cory, which caused a mini tug of war. No effort was made to communicate this problem until Bill got smacked in the head again by a branch Cory pushed out of his way.

"Hey, man. Hold up for a second. I need to switch hands."

They set the cooler down.

"You want in front?" asked Cory. "I noticed you were pulling back."

"You noticed that, huh? Besides getting pummeled by boomerang branches, I couldn't see where my feet were going. I'm running a marathon with some of my former Eagle Scouts next month, and the last thing I need is a twisted ankle."

"Oh. Sorry, Scout. Sometimes I'm like a bull in a china shop. At least that's what CeeCee says."

He didn't sound sorry, but Bill half-grunted and half-chuckled anyway. The two changed positions and continued their descent to the lake. The pathway's design escaped Bill's attention before, but now he noticed small colorful stones, artfully placed in the ground between the larger ones, creating a striking pattern. Framing the rockwork were large-leafed, variegated hostas, jumbo azaleas, and mushroom-shaped, low-voltage lights.

"Even the path to the lake is beautiful," said Bill. "Someone put a lot of thought into every detail. I would've dumped a load of gravel, spread it out, and called it a day." Neither guy responded, so he stopped talking.

They got to the water's edge and stepped onto a floating ramp that led to the enormous dock. Cory and Bill plunked the cooler down next to eight Adirondack chairs arranged in a semi-circle. Four were grayish-blue, the others tan. A lumbar pillow with the same color scheme lay in each chair.

The three men looked around, admiring the beauty and breathing in the crisp, clean air.

"My God, this is something else," said Adam. "Look at that water. It's like a sheet of glass."

"Can you imagine skiing on that?" Bill asked.

"I can. Talk about a smooth ride. Lynn told me no motorized crafts are allowed, though, at least not that kind. Electric only. Keeps it quiet so you can sneak up on the fish."

"You fish?" asked Bill, hoping for something to talk about or do later this weekend.

Adam grinned. "No. Lynn urged me to find a hobby years ago, but I didn't have the time for it. Or patience."

"Yeah, I know what you mean. Some say it's not about the fish so much but more about man connecting to nature. Looks like the perfect spot to do it." Bill looked around again. "Get a load of this dock."

The massive structure, 30 feet long and 20 feet wide, was built with composite decking, a product of reclaimed wood and plastic. Bill nodded his head in appreciation. "This stuff is meant to last forever. No splintering, no rot, no fading."

"And *no* issue with funding," added Adam.

Bill smiled. "Yep, that, too." He put his hands in his pockets and walked around. Two metal ladders gave swimmers easy access to the lake, and next to each stood a short post holding a red and white life preserver. The back corner of the dock had a screened enclosure with a picnic table that seated 12 people, and over it stood another tier of decking that provided more space for hanging out. Bill climbed up two or three rungs of the captain's ladder and saw several lounge chairs scattered about and built-in benches attached to the railings. In one corner, a tall bamboo pole held a faded windsock that waved slightly with the breeze, and a few feet away, a blue fiberglass diving board hovered over the lake. Bill eyed the board, estimating it to be about 15 feet above the water, and pictured himself doing a cannonball. He smiled and shouted to the others. "The lake must be deep here."

"I hope you're not thinking what I think you are," said Cory. "Way too dangerous. You never know what's floating under the surface."

"That's true," said Bill. *But I'm going to do it anyway.*

Adam nodded at Cory's statement. "I've seen too many cases where people broke their necks diving into a hidden log or something, paralyzing them for the rest of their lives. Not worth it, man."

"Speaking of money, wonder how much cash Josh laid out for this little piece of paradise," said Cory. "I couldn't afford this dock, let alone the cabin." No one ventured an answer. "So, I've made a decision. I call dibs on Josh becoming my new best friend."

Adam laughed, "Dibs, huh? As official as that sounds, you may have to fight me for that position. How good are you at arm wrestling?"

Cory held up both his arms and flexed his biceps. "I don't know, but you can ask gun number one and gun number two."

Bill walked over to the blue and white cooler, opened the lid, and grabbed a beer. The familiar pop-hiss echoed across the lake. "Anybody wanna beer?"

Cory and Adam wandered over, sifted through the ice, chose a beer, and sat down. The guys left a chair in between them, probably for the girls to fill the void, physically and socially.

Bill heard a buzzing overhead, which turned out to be the sputtering engine of a small yellow bi-plane circling in the sky. Occasionally it caught the sun's reflection, making it glow like a fireball. Other than the plane and a distant quack somewhere on the lake, things were eerily quiet and still. *I hope Molly gets down here soon.*

As if reading his mind, a giant bullfrog sitting on the muddy bank behind them croaked loudly. "I guess we have another friend," said Bill.

"Let's hope he's the only reptile around here," Cory said.

"Amphibian," said Adam.

"Huh?"

"Frogs are amphibians, not reptiles."

Cory smirked, then shrugged.

"But, I know what you mean," Adam continued. "Not a big fan of snakes myself, but I hear most of them are harmless."

"I know a guy who used to hunt rattlesnakes," Cory said. "He used this long stick with a little lasso at the end."

"No kidding. Why would somebody do that?" Adam asked.

"He ate them, believe it or not, and he sold the skins," he said. "It's not bad. Ever eaten rattlesnake?"

"Nope. Let me guess. It tastes like chicken?" Adam chortled.

Cory grinned. "Yeah, kind of like Mr. Bullfrog's fat legs over there. Excuse me, the *amphibian's* legs. In fact, he may be in danger if those girls don't get down here pretty soon. My stomach is talking to me."

Ten more minutes went by, and no wives were in sight. Between sips of beer and not-so-muffled burps, the men discussed the weather, the drive to the cabin, the stock market, the lake water temperature, and whether or not it was considered uncouth to pee off the dock. All safe topics. And still no women. No food. No nothing. Just the sounds of nature and their friend, the frog.

Ordinarily a very patient man, Bill's aggravation grew. "Where the heck are those girls?"

"Probably got to gabbin' and can't stop," said Cory. "Sometimes CeeCee doesn't get her priorities straight, even though I've tried to teach her a million times. Y'all got that problem?"

Bill cocked one eyebrow at that statement.

"Sure! I tell Lynn all the time that I'm going to teach her something," Adam said and laughed at his secret joke. "And then I pick myself and my teeth up off the floor. Who's got a phone? I left mine with Lynn."

He took a swig of beer, crushed the can, and got up to get another one. He looked around. "Well, for the dock that has everything, it's missing a trashcan."

Cory dug around in the pocket of his beige cargo shorts and produced a phone. "I'll call Cee and tell her to bring some garbage bags, along with the food. She *has* to know I'm getting hungry." He looked down at the phone. "Shit!" He looked like he wanted to slam the phone onto the dock, like spiking a football.

"What is it?" Bill asked. "Something wrong?"

"There's no fucking service here, that's what."

"Dang, man. I thought it was something serious," said Bill. "You scared me. Maybe having no phone service is a good thing. Just us and the elements." He raised his beer at the trees as the leaves rustled. He liked the sound, but Cory's sarcasm cut through the air.

"Now, *how* would that be a good thing, Bill?" He heaved his large frame out of the chair. "I'm going up there, and I better get a good reason for this bullshit."

His motion, however, was interrupted by a sound not typically heard in nature. A single staccato bleep echoed across the lake and bounced back, making it sound like six or more. Cory cocked his head, listening, then turned to Bill. "Hey, Scout. Is that some weird bird?"

"Only if it has a horn. Sounded more like a car when it's locked."

"Did the girls mention going somewhere?"

"Not that I know of. Maybe someone sat on the remote. Who knows? Besides, where would they go? Big Jon's?"

They all laughed.

"Yeah. Maybe he promised some special candy that expired three years ago," said Adam.

"I bet they're playing a joke on us," said Bill. He pushed up the nosepiece of his glasses, a habit more than a need for adjustment, and got up for another beer.

"By locking the car? What's the joke?" asked Cory.

"No clue, but we're jumping to conclusions here," Bill said, trying to gain control of this runaway train. "We hear one little sound and automatically leap to the worst-case scenario." *Typical distortion thinking.*

"Yeah, that's what little girls do," said Adam with a smirk.

"Let's give it some time and let it play out *if* there is anything to play out," suggested Bill.

A few more minutes went by. Adam and Cory stood near the cooler, with one hand in a pocket and the other holding a beer. They appeared to be studying their shoes.

"I'll tell you one thing. If this is a joke, it's not funny," huffed Cory. "If it's not a joke, I know a curly blonde who will catch hell. She *knows* better than to do something like this to me."

"Hey, man, calm down," said Adam. "I'm sure we'll have a big laugh about this later. Have another beer."

Cory looked over at him. "I'm not laughing now, and I for damn sure won't be laughing later. This little get-together is over as soon as I see her stupid face."

"Whoa, don't you think you're overreacting? Thought you agreed that was for little girls," Bill teased.

"No. I think *you're* under-reacting, Scout."

"Sounds like you don't want to be here," said Bill.

"Hell no, I didn't want to come!" His voice carried across the lake, causing him to lower his tone a bit. "Did you?"

"Well, I admit I put up resistance," said Bill. "But it seemed very important to Molly. What about you, Adam?"

"I got the same speech, important, blah blah blah. She knows how I feel about being around strangers—no offense—and having to chit-chat about nothing. So, we did some negotiating. Lynn promised to skydive with me on our anniversary if I came on the trip."

"That's quite a negotiation, dude," Cory said, obviously impressed. "What are you, a lawyer or something?"

"Afraid so."

"Should've known," said Cory, his admiration vanishing as suddenly as it appeared.

Adam locked his eyes onto Cory's. "Yeah? Why's that?" He paused. "Cory."

"Look at you, man. Tassled loafers, no socks, expensive cologne, starched and pressed designer shirt, tailor-made slacks. You think you were going to the Country Club or something?"

Adam tilted his head. "So, is this what you do when something doesn't go your way? Lash out at people who have done nothing to you? What the hell is your problem, Bubba?"

"Well, I'll be damned. I figured you for a fella who wouldn't say shit if you had a mouth full of it."

Adam took a deep breath, exhaled, then turned towards Bill. "I don't know about you, but I'm going to the house and see what's up. This guy's going to make my head explode."

Bill stayed seated and waited for Adam to put some distance between them. *What is going on with this Cory guy? He goes from zero to one hundred in two seconds.* He stood up and looked at him.

"Hey, man. I know you're frustrated, but taking it out on us is not the solution. We aren't your enemies, not yet, at least. I don't think this trip is what's bothering you, and I suggest you figure it out before you do something you'll regret."

"Oh, and what are you, my shrink now?" Cory asked.

Not in a million years. Bill turned and walked away, ignoring Cory's following remark.

"Jeez, you *are* a shrink, aren't you?"

Bill caught up with Adam, who seemed to have slowed his pace towards the cabin.

"Everything okay down there?" asked Adam.

"Who knows with that guy?"

Adam suddenly stopped. "Hey, what the hell is going on?"

"What is it?"

Adam pointed to the side of the cabin. "Your car is gone."

They looked at each other and hurried their pace, finally bursting through the cabin's front door.

What they found, they never imagined.

Chapter Seven

No one spoke as the car made its escape from the cabin. The sun hadn't set, so there was no need for headlights, which helped keep their departure unnoticed. Years ago, the road was part of an old logging operation, but once the large equipment left the area, lack of use gave way to erosion, exposing rocks and old tree stumps. The same ride the women endured just 45 minutes earlier was again uncomfortable, bumpy, and slow-going.

Lynn sat forward on the front passenger seat to keep the jarring to a minimum. Anxiety already had her stomach in a knot, and the constant jolts could cause unexpected mishaps. *Nobody wants that.* She felt like she'd been holding her breath since they crept away, or to be honest, since she left home on Wednesday. She knew shallow breathing caused anxiety, so she inhaled through her nose and breathed out through her mouth. While repeating the process, she became aware of a pleasant aroma of perfume, lotions, and hair products circulating inside the vehicle. The scent instantly brought up a childhood memory she hadn't thought about in a long time. A girl lived on Lynn's street with her mother and aunt, who both worked in the cosmetic business. They'd set up one bedroom like a small shop with floor-to-ceiling glass shelves displaying sample products of all kinds and colors. A manicurist table sat in the middle with stools on either side. Miniature perfumes, lipsticks, nail polish, and powders lined the walls and fit perfectly in a little girl's hand. The whole house smelled nice. Girly. Lynn had never been in a place like it, a far cry from the baseball field where she spent most of her time competing with the boys.

In a barrel-sounding radio voice, CeeCee said, "Earth to Lynn. Earth to Lynn."

"Shush, I'm in an alternate dimension, and you can't see me," joked Lynn, although she felt anything but joyful. She looked down at her shirt and brushed off lint that wasn't there, a nervous habit. Needing to do something with her hands, she finger-twisted her hair—another giveaway of her state of mind. "God, I could use a cigarette. What were we thinking?"

"First of all, you don't smoke anymore," Molly said. "Second, I know what we were thinking. We were hoping—against all odds—*hoping* that our husbands get to know each other and form friendships. Of their own. Without us. They don't know it yet, but they need each other. Who knows what can happen to any of us?"

Lynn sighed, turned to the window, and watched black tree trunks slowly pass. *Even the trees are warning us to turn back*. The car suddenly rocked sideways, and she banged her head on the window. "Shit. Can't we turn the god-dang lights on now?"

Molly said nothing but flipped the lever for the running lights. "I'm doing the best I can. It gets a little smoother at the fork. I just can't remember if we go left or right."

"Molly!" CeeCee yelled from the back seat.

"I'm kidding. I'm kidding. You all need to lighten up."

At the fork, crushed gravel helped smooth the ride and Lynn's jumbled nerves. She scooted back in her seat and tried not to worry about Adam blowing a gasket that would somehow end up around her neck like a noose. She also wondered about the rising lump on her head and if she had a concussion.

Molly asked, "Where've you been, kid?"

She never misses a thing. "Inside my head."

"See anything in there?"

"I'm a little worried," Lynn said. "That's all. Adam's not exactly crazy about surprises, and this one will shock his socks off."

"I don't think he's wearing socks," said Molly.

Lynn gave her a go-to-hell look.

CeeCee snorted. "You wouldn't believe what I had to promise Cory to get him to agree to this trip."

"Yeah? Like what?" asked Molly.

"None of your bee's wax. That's what. Stick to the subject."

Molly shrugged. "That was the subject."

"Well, I bet it's not jumping out of a perfectly good airplane," Lynn said.

Molly's head jerked to the right. "You didn't."

She nodded. "Afraid so. On our anniversary. 'Course, if we don't survive the weekend, I won't need to worry about it."

"Why wouldn't we survive?" asked CeeCee.

"I mean the fallout. You know, from the deception. They'll never trust us again."

"Look, Lynn, we're all nervous," said Molly. "But I thought you felt good about it. What changed?"

Nothing's changed. That's the problem.

Suddenly the car jolted, and Lynn screamed. Molly struggled to control the steering wheel as it jerked hard to the right, but it was too late to prevent the crunch of metal on the bottom of the vehicle.

****

Molly pushed on the accelerator, and the car churned, swayed, and rocked before easing forward.

"Oh, my God, what just happened?" Lynn asked. "Are we stuck? This is a sign. I knew it. We'll have to walk back, look them in the eye, and explain everything. Adam's going to kill me! Oh my God!"

"Okay, we're not stuck, so let's all calm down," Molly said. "I think we should get out and see what I hit and if there is any damage."

"By *we,* you mean... who, exactly?" Lynn looked around. "We don't know what's out there."

Molly looked in the rearview mirror and saw CeeCee rolling her eyes.

"Oh, for Pete's sake," said CeeCee. "You stay here and guard the wine. We'll check it out."

Molly grabbed a flashlight out of the glove compartment, made her way to the back of the car, and waited for CeeCee to join her. She pressed the button on the side of the flashlight, but nothing happened. She did it again. Nothing. "Are you freaking kidding me? Dammit."

"What now," CeeCee whispered as if someone were in the woods listening to them.

"Why are you whispering?"

"I don't know. It's kind of creepy out here. Remember all those horror movies we used to watch?"

"Yes, I do, and thanks for bringing them up." Molly continued beating on the flashlight. "Listen, Lynn's already freaked out. I don't need you to join her. There might be a penlight in the console. Could you check?"

CeeCee went to the driver's door, reached inside, and quickly jumped back. "Jesus, Molly! There's a gun in there."

"I know. Did you find a light or not?"

"Well, is it loaded? What if it went off? And no, I do not see a penlight."

"Of course, it's loaded," said Molly. "It's not much good if you have to stop and put bullets in it. Since when are you afraid of guns?"

"I'm not afraid of them," CeeCee said as she joined her friend behind the vehicle. "I just like to know where they are."

Molly marched to the other side of the car, where Lynn sat, and tapped on the window with the flashlight. Lynn practically jumped out of her skin. "You scared the shit out of me!" she yelled through the window.

"Why is everyone so jumpy?" asked Molly. "Will you get in the driver's seat and put the car in reverse? But don't back up unless I tell you." *The last thing I need is to get run over.*

The backup lights lit up the road and the wooded area to the left and right, where tall trees and thick underbrush grew. Molly checked around for anything moving or crawling, then crouched near the large rock and knobby tree roots that caused the car to jolt. CeeCee squatted beside her. "All I see are some scrapes on this rock and gouges out of that pointed stump. No fluid anywhere and no parts lying about, but I think we should look under the car. It would make me feel better."

"What are we going to use for light? A match?" asked Molly. "Maybe a lightning bug?"

"See? If we were still smoking, I'd have a lighter," said CeeCee. "And you don't have to get snippy with me, or you just might find one of those bugs stuffed up your nose."

"Even if you *did* have a lighter, I'm not lying down on that ground with God knows what slithering around," said Molly. "I say we take our chances and get the hell outta here. And one more thing. I'm sorry."

Lynn switched seats with CeeCee and climbed into the back. "What did you guys see?"

"Nothing. I think we're okay," said Molly. "We're going to mosey on. Carefully."

She put the car into drive and looked at the gauges. The Check-Engine light was not blinking, nor were any other symbols. *So far, so good.*

Chapter Eight

Cory regretted making an ass of himself and paced the dock, trying to control his anger. He needed to apologize and headed for shore.

Someone yelled. "Hey, ham hock! Get up here!"

Very funny. Not wanting to appear too interested, Cory slowed his gait as he walked up the path to the house. He approached the steps, took two at a time, and strode across the massive front porch. Although the firefighter worked out regularly, he was out of breath from the incline, so pride kept him outside while his heart rate slowed. He peered through the door's glass at Bill and Adam, who both held something in their hands. *That's odd.* He grabbed the door handle and pushed his way into a vast space with a soaring, two-story fireplace. Two leather couches sat perpendicular to the hearth, and three club chairs completed the u-shaped grouping. Adam had claimed a seat on a sofa.

"What's up, ladies? Need me to open a jar for you?" No one laughed, but why would they? He'd just behaved like a total jackass. Sometimes Cory's mouth spoke before his brain could think it through, causing him trouble more often than not.

Bill walked over and tried to hand him a piece of white paper folded in half. "Here."

"What's this? Another stupid joke? Or are you Nancys reading poetry to each other?" Again, instant regret.

"Good God, is there anyone that's hands-off?" asked Adam. "Or do you hate everybody equally?"

"What is it?" Cory asked again.

Bill dropped the paper and walked away. "Look at it, or not. Up to you."

Cory picked it up, his creaking knees complaining, and immediately recognized CeeCee's handwriting. "Where the hell is CeeCee?"

"I guess you didn't notice a vehicle is missing," answered Bill in a slow, calm tone. "I think these letters explain it, but we waited for you before reading them."

"Why don't we just call them and demand answers?" asked Cory.

"Remember your tirade down at the dock about having no service?"

"Oh, yeah. About that," said Cory. "I apologize for getting out of hand."

"Appreciate that," Bill said as he plopped down on the leather couch opposite Adam. Cory remained standing while the men read the notes from their wives. A few minutes went by before Bill spoke. "Well, the bottom line is, we're on our own until Sunday at six p.m. At least that's what mine says."

Adam lept up and walked over to his bag. "The hell we are. I'm getting my keys, and I'm out of here." He ripped open the zipper, searched inside, and upended clothes and toiletries. No keys. He then headed towards the kitchen area, an expansion of the great room.

"You're wasting your time," yelled Bill. "The keys aren't here."

Adam returned from the kitchen, patting down his pockets, and glared. "How do you know they're not here? Did you know about this? You did, didn't you?"

"Had no idea. But I know Molly and her attention to detail, plus she told me in her letter."

"What else did she say that you're not telling us?" asked Cory. "You look pretty calm. Too calm. You sure you're not in on it?"

Bill closed his eyes and sighed. "No, Cory. I am *not* in on it. I'm not any happier about this than you are. In fact, I'm seriously *pissed*." He stood up and put his hands in his pockets. "But it is what it is."

Cory snorted. "Hear that? It is what it is. I hate that saying. Like that's supposed to settle everything. Thanks for the psychological interpretation, Doctor."

"What do you propose, Cory?" asked Bill, frowning. "Wanna ransack the place, throw bottles at the wall, break out windows, and run around the house with our hands up in the air, screaming—what were Adam's words—like little girls? Hell, why stop there? Let's burn the whole fucking house down!"

Cory dismissed Bill's overreaction with a wave of his hand.

"Yes, Cory. I'm calm because I choose to be that way, which doesn't mean I'm not upset. I don't get hysterical, and I don't throw fits. Unless my legs are on fire, I tend to internalize things, mull them over, and try to come up with a solution. That's just the way I'm wired. If you can't deal with that, well, it is what it is."

"Wish you'd stop saying that," Cory said.

"Yeah yeah, we're all grown men, blah blah blah," said Adam. "And I know all about solving problems. I make a living doing it, but it's just a little hard to believe this is happening, and since you mentioned it, I might take you up on burning the place down."

Bill stared at him.

"Don't worry, I'm not going to damage any of Josh's precious belongings," Adam said. "I bet *he* knew about this."

"You could be right about that," Bill said as he walked towards the kitchen. "We'll find out in due time, I suppose."

Cory heard him open the fridge and pop open a beer.

"Hey, there's all kinds of food in here if you're interested," Bill shouted. "At least the girls weren't lying about that."

Cory and Adam walked into the kitchen and surveyed the stash accumulating on the kitchen island. "I'm starving," said Cory.

Bill continued to pull plastic containers with red, yellow, and blue lids out of the refrigerator and then searched for plates, utensils, and napkins. "I don't know about you, but I can't think on an empty stomach."

"Do I smell bar-b-que?" Cory grabbed a chicken wing and gnawed on it. "Any hard liquor around here?"

"Do you mind?" asked Adam, stepping away.

"What?"

"Talking while your mouth's full and chewing with your mouth open."

Cory smacked his lips loudly and grabbed another wing.

"Jeez." Then Adam muttered, "Once a hayseed, always a hayseed."

"You say something?"

"Nothing you'd understand."

They locked eyes, and Cory smiled. *Oh, I understand dip-wad.*

"Come on, you two," Bill interjected as he grabbed some grocery bags from the counter. "Somebody look for the bar." His hand rattled inside the bags, and he announced the inventory. "Carbs! Oh boy. Corn chips, crackers, sandwich bread, blueberry muffins, raisin bran cereal, and uhm, hamburger buns with sesame seeds on top."

Cory spied a mahogany cabinet next to the long dining table that accommodated ten chairs. He opened the doors, revealing every kind of alcohol a guy could want. "Bingo!"

He grabbed a cut-crystal, highball glass and looked at the array of bottles. Glenlivet's XXV label jumped out at him. He'd never had that quality of scotch, but there it sat. Free, and he deserved it. He found a mini ice maker in the bottom of the cabinet, dropped three cubes into the glass, and slowly poured the amber liquid. He put his nose to the rim. The whiskey smelled spicy and nutty with tones of sherry, making Cory's mouth water. He took a sip and rolled the alcohol around inside his mouth before swallowing. "Ah, man, that's good stuff."

Adam walked up. "Is that Glenlivet XXV? Come to papa!"

"Might be, but how would I know, being a hayseed and all? Never learned those X and V numbers."

"Hey, that was a joke," said Adam.

Cory moved away from the bar. "We both know that's not true, but once an asshole, always an asshole. And *that* wasn't a joke."

The men shuffled around for the next few minutes, avoiding each other, fixing drinks, and piling food onto their plates. They sat in the same places they'd chosen before and ate silently. A grandfather clock proudly announced the seventh hour with loud bongs that echoed off the wooden beams and floors. Cory turned and stared at the intrusion, as did the others.

"Mind if I turn on the tube?" he asked, grabbing the remote. "I can't stand all this crunching or that ticking time bomb over there."

"Says the guy who chews with his mouth open," Adam added.

Cory flipped him a bird but kept his eyes on the television. "Let's see what this antique TV has to offer." He pointed the remote, and the TV sprang to life, revealing a fuzzy panorama of someplace out west and a roaming bison herd.

"Wonder where that is," asked Bill.

"Who knows?" Cory responded. "It could be the prettiest place on earth, but we can't see it."

"You like areas like that, just you and nature?" Bill asked.

"Sure, who doesn't?"

Bill stroked his chin and grinned. "If only we could be in a place like that."

Cory looked at Bill, studied him a bit, and rolled his eyes, but he appreciated the sarcasm. "Point taken."

After helping themselves with more food and alcohol, the guys were on their way to inebriation. Cory found a football game on a station that was halfway clear and, hearing no objections, left it on. The men made a few remarks about players' skills and referees' bad calls, but other than that, they stayed quiet. The mood in the room seemed to relax, but there was no telling how long it would last. A TV commercial promoting national zoos appeared on the screen, and a cute baby elephant rolled around in a muddy swimming hole.

"Speaking of elephants in the room," Bill said, wiggling his eyebrows up and down. "Should we talk about the notes our wives wrote? Maybe we can piece some things together."

No one volunteered.

"Why don't I go first, then?"

Bill pulled Molly's letter out of his pocket and pushed his wire-rimmed glasses up on the bridge of his nose. He looked through the top of them at Cory. "Could you turn the TV off, please?"

Cory muted it instead, not willing to concede to anything.

"I'm not sharing all of Molly's comments because some are personal, but it seems they want us to get to know each other. Carolyn's death reemphasized the importance of friendship, and as you know, they feel very strongly about it. I found this part particularly interesting. She says, 'These friends are very important to me. *You* are important to me. And these men are important because *they love* the women *I love*. We're bonded together in this life for a reason, and we have a choice. We can ignore it or we can explore it. I'm hoping you'll choose the latter and find out who these guys are.'"

"CeeCee wrote something similar," said Cory.

Bill looked over at Adam. "How about you? Same kind of note?"

Adam jumped out of his chair and headed towards the bar. "This is bullshit. Pure manipulation by these women. Lynn would never do this to me without being forced." He looked at Bill. "Who do you think is the instigator?"

"Why are you looking at me?"

"We know Molly is the ring leader of that group," Adam said. "I'd bet a hundred dollars she came up with this idea."

Bill stood up. "I'll take that bet. And what difference does it make? They each committed to it. All we know at this point is our wives left us here for a reason, and I'm guessing it was no small undertaking. The question is, what are we going to do?"

"I still wanna know why you're not upset," said Cory.

"I thought we already plowed that ground," Bill replied.

"Aren't you the least bit jacked out of shape?" Cory asked. "I mean, our wives deceived us, man. They went behind our backs and planned this whole scheme—who knows how long ago—and kept this big secret, all under the guise of us supporting them through Carolyn's funeral. Shame on them for using their friend's death to hijack us." Cory slammed his glass down on the coffee table. "And did you notice this is something *they* want? It's all about them. *They* want to feel good. *They* want to know we will be okay should bad things happen. They're trying to force us to do something we don't want to do, so *they'll* feel good. It makes me madder every second I think about it. *Nobody* controls me like that."

"It's a little surprising I admit," Bill said.

"Well, I guess being surprised is better than having no emotion at all, " Cory said. "Try not to lose control."

"If I do, you'll be the first to know."

"Uh oh. Sounds like he's about to blow," said Adam. He walked like a robot towards Bill, speaking in a monotone. "Hello. My name is Bill. I remain. Calm. At all times. I do not. Get upset."

Cory cracked up, only encouraging Adam to continue walking stiffly around the room, ending his routine of jerky movements at the bar.

"I don't know about you guys," Adam said, his voice slurred, "but I plan to *explore* this bar and get drunk on somebody else's expensive booze." He lifted his glass towards the ceiling and took a sip. "Then tomorrow, I'm going to find Lynn and make her sorry she ever laid eyes on me."

Chapter Nine

CeeCee tried to help Molly navigate the obstacles that might pop up, but she grew impatient as the car bobbed and weaved through the woods. "I could walk faster than this. It's driving me crazy."

"Feel free to get out if you want," said Molly.

CeeCee smirked but was soon rewarded when the paved highway came into sight. "Thank God."

Molly wiggled her fingers and clinched and unclinched her fists. The movement made the diamonds on her wedding ring wink in the light from the instruments. "Guess I didn't realize I've been gripping the wheel like a squirrel on a bird feeder. Remind me to get a hand massage at the hotel."

CeeCee laughed. "I've been wondering if those white knuckles would burst into flame. Good job, by the way." They slapped a high-five. "Smooth sailing from here on out."

Molly looked in both directions, eased the car onto the road, and headed south. The tension inside the cabin seemed to lift a little as the women leaned back in their seats and settled in for the ride. CeeCee slipped off her shoes and put her bare feet on the front console. "Civilization, here we come."

"Hey, girls," Molly said. "What do you say we pull over at that little store and break out the wine. We missed happy hour tonight, and I think we need to toast the completion of phase one."

"Great idea," said CeeCee. "I could use a drink after that catastrophic event in the forest."

"First, you might be exaggerating just a tad," Molly replied. "Second, get your stinkin' feet off my dashboard."

"We have crackers and Manchego cheese, too," said Lynn. "I'm starving."

Forty-five minutes went by filled with idle chitchat, but no Big Jon's in sight.

"Where is this place?" asked Lynn. "It seems like we've been driving forever."

"Well, we haven't passed it, so it should be showing up pretty soon," Molly said as she steered the car up a steep rise and around a hairpin curve. And there it stood. Big Jon's, their oasis. "Looks like our wish has been granted, ladies."

Lynn and CeeCee cheered when Molly pulled into the same spot Bill had parked in a few hours ago. The store itself was dark, but an old, rusty tin light hung from the porch ceiling, the only beacon of light for miles.

"Look," said CeeCee. "Big Jon left the light on for us."

The women got out of the car and grabbed the wine, corkscrew, cups, and snacks.

"Let's sit on the porch in those rockers," said Lynn. "I'm tired of being cramped up in the car."

"Yeah, I can see why you'd rather sit on a splintered, half-rotted piece of wood instead of the pristine leather seats of my SUV," said Molly. She smiled and plopped down in one of them. "Owww!" She picked something out of her pant leg. "Can't get to that spa fast enough."

"To Carolyn. Our husbands. And a successful mission," CeeCee said. The women clacked the plastic cups together and raised them towards the sky.

"Look at all those stars," said Molly.

"I heard a saying once," said Lynn, "that stars are the front porch lights of people in Heaven waiting for us to arrive. Isn't that lovely? I'd like to think that's true."

"I like that," said Molly. "Which one do you think is Carolyn's?"

"The brightest one, of course," said CeeCee. "She loved her bling."

"I wonder what the guys are doing," said Lynn in a downtrodden tone. She looked at her lap and fiddled with her paper napkin. "I'm sure they've found our letters by now and that Adam is going bonkers."

CeeCee frowned. "Wow, Lynn, way to be a Debbie Downer."

"I can't help it. I've got a knot in my stomach the size of a New Hampshire. Aren't you worried?"

"Yes, but dwelling on it doesn't help," said CeeCee. "It just gets me all worked up, so I think about other things."

"You know that doesn't work," said Molly, "pretending something isn't happening. Your body knows everything that's going on and will react accordingly."

CeeCee finished the wine in her cup and poured more. "I told you not to analyze me."

An engine off in the distance cut through the chirps of crickets and caught their attention. The noise seemed to be getting closer to them. Quickly.

"Looks like we're not the only ones roaming around in the middle of the night." Molly looked at her watch and laughed. "I don't know why I said that. It's not even 8:00."

"Feels later to me, too," said Lynn. "Probably because we're mentally exhausted."

Suddenly the source of the engine noise roared by, a black truck sitting high off the ground with four yellow fog lights bolted to a rail on top of the cab. Two men stood in the truck bed, holding onto the rail, singing with the music blaring from the cabin. That, and the dual tailpipes, rudely disturbed the peacefulness of Mother Nature and the girls' happy-hour pit stop. As quickly as the truck appeared, it disappeared around the bend, noise dissipating until nothing.

Lynn's eyes widened from fear. "Do you think they noticed us? I don't know why we stopped in the middle of nowhere. We're sitting ducks." She stood up to look out into the woods, scanning the surroundings.

Molly shrugged. "Doubt they had time to see us, but I'm sure they have more important things to do than worry about three old women."

"Who you calling old?" asked CeeCee. "Funny how things change as you age. Twenty years ago, that would've been us in the back of that truck. Now I just shake my head and think, idiots. With one bad bump or swerve, your brains are splattered all over the highway."

"And *my* first reaction is to run like a little kid," Lynn said. "Getting old sucks." She took another gulp of wine, nibbled on a cracker, then grabbed another piece of cheese. "Do we have anything else to eat?"

"You're not going to get whiny again, are you?" asked CeeCee.

"I'm not getting whiny. I didn't eat much at the reception, and this cheese isn't cutting it for some reason."

"I may have some walnuts in my bag," said CeeCee. "I'll check."

She stood up and stretched her arms towards the night sky, again appreciating its beauty. Then she pretended to run in slow motion towards the car. She heard giggles behind her, which made her smile. She loved making people laugh and hoped it reduced Lynn's apprehension.

CeeCee opened the front passenger door, grabbed the overlarge hobo purse from the floorboard, and unzipped it. She found everything in it except nuts. She shuffled all the stuff around one more time, then looked under the seat just in case they had escaped.

"Hey, I can't find them. Aren't there some grapes in the back?"

No one answered.

"Hellooooo, did you hear me?" She felt a tap on her shoulder, causing her to jerk and hit the back of her head on the top of the door opening.

Next to her ear, a deep voice said, "Can I help you find something, beautiful?"

CeeCee screamed, recoiled, and fell backward into the front seat, her heart rate escalating. Standing two feet away was a bearded man with a red bandana tied around his head, looking her up and down. He looked dirty, smelled like BO, and his eyes were bloodshot. Over his shoulder, CeeCee saw three other men standing around her friends who still sat in the rockers. Silent. Lynn was shaking with fear, which made CeeCee's heart sink. She didn't know what to do, but her instinct made her lean away from the man as far as she could.

"Get away from me!" screamed CeeCee.

Instead, he jumped at her playfully and yelled, "Boo!" She screamed again, adrenaline racing through her body. She raised her feet, ready to kick if he came closer.

"Look here, guys, we got us a feisty one," he said. They all got a good laugh out of it, and the guffaw of one man threw him into a frenzy of deep rattling coughs that indicated the lungs of a heavy smoker. Something dislodged, and he spat it out on the ground beside him.

CeeCee gagged.

Now, come on out of there," the guy said. "We just want to talk and maybe get some of that wine you girls are drinking." He turned and winked at his buddies. "Besides, we thought you might need some help, seeing that you're out in the middle of nowhere. All alone."

Molly stood up. "Is that why you slithered in here, like a rat snake? So you could *help* us? Where's your big bad truck?"

"It choked out about a half-mile up the road," the man said as he walked away from CeeCee and towards Molly. "And I don't appreciate being called a snake."

Molly held up her hands in peace. “Look, guys, we appreciate your offer to help, but we’re fine. There is nothing wrong here. Just stopped to stretch our legs and meet some other friends. I just talked to them, and they’ll be pulling in any second.”

“From where I’m standing, I’d say you’re fine all right, but you’re not a very good liar,” the leader said. “Unless you got some special apparatus I don’t know about, your cell phone’s got no service, just like everybody else’s.”

Molly tilted her head, squinted her eyes just a bit, and stared at the guy. “So, what is it you want exactly? We’re old enough to be your mothers, for God’s sake.” She pretended to look at her watch. “Isn’t it past your curfew?”

“You’re funny. Ain’t she funny, boys?” He looked at her with a sneer on his face.

“I try,” said Molly, not releasing her stare. “Tell you what. We were just getting ready to head out, so we’ll leave the wine for you. And once we have cell service, I’m happy to call someone. Do you have AAA?”

He snorted. “Now ‘mam, do I look like a AAA-kind of guy? Besides, we both know there’s nothing wrong with my truck, and you’re not going anywhere until we say so.”

Molly shifted her gaze to CeeCee, who had retained her position in the car. Her hands were behind her, perched on the middle console, and her feet were in striking position should the guy return.

At least that's what she told herself. CeeCee studied Molly's expression. She knew that look and nodded. They frequently joked about having the same thoughts at the same time.

Not wanting to make any sudden moves or attract attention, CeeCee slowly moved her left hand, found the latch, and quietly lifted the storage compartment lid. Keeping her eyes on Molly and the man, she felt around, trying not to rattle anything, and grasped the cold metal. CeeCee nodded at her friend.

"All right," Molly said. "Let's all calm down. No one wants to do anything we'll regret."

"Oh, I ain't going to regret anything," he said. "What about you boys, you gonna regret anything?" They snickered and acted tough, one guy grabbing his crotch.

"You might want to rethink that," said Molly.

The leader took a step forward. "Yeah, why's that?"

"I'd hate to see you get hurt."

The men laughed. "Who's going to do that?"

Molly raised her eyebrows and tilted her head to the left. "Her."

The men followed Molly's gaze, and shock registered on their faces. CeeCee stood next to the car with the Glock in her hands. She methodically racked it, putting a round in the chamber, and took a tactical stance with both hands on the gun. She raised it, aimed in the men's direction, and looked through the sights.

The leader held up his hands. "Whoa, lady. We were just having a little fun here. We didn't mean anything by it."

Scared out of her wits, CeeCee tried to appear composed. *What in God's name am I doing?* She felt like her heart had leaped to her throat, and her ears rang like alarm bells. She tried to take slow deep breaths, but they remained erratic, which caused her to feel more anxious. She tried to grin at his attempt to lighten the situation, but she wasn't sure her mouth even moved.

She was sure of one thing. She had to protect her friends, frozen with fear, still sitting on the rickety porch. An image of Sharon Stone's movie, "The Quick and the Dead," jumped into her head. Stone played a gunslinger and ended up outdrawing her male competitors, ultimately killing all the men in town. CeeCee almost laughed at the bizarre thought.

She looked at the leader, and with all the calm she could muster, asked, "Ever played Simon Says?"

No one answered. Just stared at her. CeeCee knew the tiny wheels in their heads were spinning, trying to figure out how to overtake her, the gun, or one of her friends. She'd seen it on TV a million times. So, she nodded at Molly, cocked her head and her eyes to the right, signaling for them to come her way. The two scampered to the back of the car, where Molly immediately opened the hatch.

Feeling a bit relieved, CeeCee addressed the men again. "Now come on. Speak up. All kids play Simon Says."

The leader sneered. "So what?"

CeeCee spoke slowly as if they were children. "Well, we're going to play, that's what. It's pretty simple, but I'll explain it anyway. When I give an order after saying, Simon Says, you have to do it. If I give an order and you do it, but I *don't* say Simon Says, then I'm afraid there will be consequences."

"We ain't doing shit, and nobody's playing a stupid game." He spat on the ground, wiped his mouth on his dirty sleeve, and looked around at his buddies. One of them chuckled and started to take a step toward her.

"I wouldn't do that if I were you," yelled Molly from the back of the SUV. "Especially when a gun is aimed at you by an excellent marksman."

"Here's the way I see it." He took off his baseball cap, scratched his oily hair, and pointed in CeeCee's direction. "The little lady here is waving a gun around with an unsteady hand and threatening four strong men." He put his hat back on. "I don't see a cavalry coming to save your pretty little asses, so I figure there's only one way this can go. And that's our way."

Molly stepped away from the back hatch, raised the thirty-ought-six hunting rifle, and snuggled the stock against her right shoulder. "What about now? You see things differently?"

She took three steps to her right, putting distance between herself, Lynn, and CeeCee, who remained positioned at the front passenger door.

"Jesus H. Christ. What's up with you fucking lunatics?" He looked at his friends. "Let's get the hell outta here."

A loud, shrill whistle cut the air like fingernails scraping a chalkboard, stopping the men in their tracks and startling Lynn and Molly as well. CeeCee took her thumb and index finger out of her mouth and put her hand back on the Glock. "Excuse me, gentlemen. I don't believe I dismissed you." She smiled. "Now, Simon says, take off your right shoe."

They stood there. "Oh, for God's sake. Just do it," one of the guys said. Each man bent down to the ground. Instead of shoes, they wore boots, so it took a little time to untie the laces and squirm out of them.

"Simon says, back up two steps."

The leader nodded.

"Isn't this fun?" She glanced at Molly.

"Yep." Molly smiled, but her eyes told CeeCee something else. She looked terrified.

CeeCee looked at the men. "It's time for you boys to leave, so get your sorry butts out of here." The men turned to walk away. "Hold it! I didn't say Simon says," she said in a sing-song voice. They glared at her.

"Simon says, take your other boot off and one sock." The men repeated the boot removal process and stood up, waiting, hate written all over their faces. She'd feel the same way if the tables were turned.

Molly clenched her teeth like a ventriloquist and muttered, "Wrap it up. You're pushing your luck."

"Simon says, walk to your truck," CeeCee commanded and watched with relief as they walked, or occasionally hopped, towards the highway. When the men got to the road, they took a right, headed north, and disappeared.

Molly joined CeeCee and touched her shoulder. "You okay?"

CeeCee's gaze was still focused on the road where the men had left her sight. "No, you?"

"No, but if we can get our legs to work, we need to get out of here."

Molly and Lynn quickly grabbed their belongings off the porch and threw everything in the back of the SUV while CeeCee remained in her tactical stance, eyes on the highway in case the morons returned. The muscles in her arms and shoulders cramped, so she finally lowered the gun and racked it, causing the round to eject from the chamber. She stepped to her right to pick it up when suddenly her foot slid out from under her, slamming her left knee into the ground. Hard. The gun flew out of her hand and skidded underneath the car. "Shit, shit, shit!" She plopped down on her rear, grabbed her leg, and tears welled. "Dammit!"

Molly rushed over to her. "What happened?"

"I don't know," CeeCee said, looking around her. "I slipped on something and jammed my knee cap." She clasped both hands around it and rocked back and forth. "Crap! The gun's under the car, so keep an eye out."

Molly grabbed the rifle that was propped on the side of the vehicle and stepped in front of her friend as she tried to get back on her feet. But when CeeCee placed her hand on the ground, it slipped, too, and she dropped onto her left shoulder. "What the hell is going on?"

"What is it now?" asked Molly, not taking her eyes off the road.

CeeCee winced as she slid her phone out of her back pocket, turned on the flashlight, and looked at the oily liquid covering her hand. "What is this stuff?" She smelled it. *Fishy.* She rolled to her right to look under the car, holding her head up to keep her hair out of the goop.

"The car may be leaking something."

"Could it be from another car and not mine?" asked Molly

"Nope. It's coming from yours."

"I cannot fucking believe this!" Molly shouted. "Lynn, don't just stand there with your teeth in your mouth. Help her up."

Lynn did as she was told but muttered something under her breath.

Molly looked at CeeCee. "You stable? I'm going

to start the car, see what lights up, if anything." She went to the driver's side, slid into the seat, and pressed the ignition button. "Hallelujah! It's all good, I think. Jump in. Before those clowns come back."

"The gun's still under the car somewhere," said CeeCee. "Can you pull up a little?"

Molly shifted the car into drive, and it rolled forward. CeeCee quickly found the weapon and signaled, but the SUV kept moving. She tried again, whistling, but the vehicle went another twenty feet before it finally stopped.

Thanks for making me hop an extra 50 feet, Molly.

She gingerly put her injured leg on the ground to see if she could put weight on it and quickly got the answer. It hurt like hell, but she somehow got herself to the car anyway, more than a little pissed off. She rapped on the passenger window with the tip of her gun, making Molly screech and jerk in her seat. "Are you trying to kill me? Get in!"

CeeCee placed the Glock on the floormat and used the handle attached to the ceiling to raise herself into the passenger seat. "Thanks for the lift, by the way. What's your deal, Red?"

"You can get snarky later. We've got a problem."

Lynn leaned in from the back seat. "You mean besides you and CeeCee acting like total maniacs from the wild west? I cannot believe what just happened. You could've gotten us killed. What if they'd been armed? Were you just going to shoot it out?"

CeeCee shrugged her shoulders. "Maybe. What's the problem, Molly?"

"No, CeeCee!" Lynn shouted. "You and Molly will not ignore me like you always do. I'm sick of it. I'm sick of both of you taking charge, never caring what anyone else says, ordering me around like I don't have a brain cell in my head."

"What do you mean?" asked Molly.

"I mean, you two have done this since college, ramrodding things down everyone's throat, doing whatever the hell you thought should be done. Don't act like you don't know. It's one thing being lorded over by a husband, but I don't need it from you, too."

CeeCee turned in her seat and looked at Lynn. "What do you mean lorded over?"

"No. You do not get to change the subject, and Molly, you will not analyze me," said Lynn. "All you care about is yourselves. So continue like you always do." She leaned back and crossed her arms. "What's the big problem we have now?"

Molly exchanged looks with CeeCee, then explained. "I'm no mechanic, but I think something is wrong with the brakes." She pointed at her dashboard gauge, which displayed a small orange symbol and the words 'check brakes.' "That's why I couldn't stop sooner, CeeCee. Similar to braking on ice."

CeeCee closed her eyes. "I knew that odor triggered something, but it didn't register. Cory told me once that brake fluid smells like fish oil."

"Oh my God! What are we going to do?" Lynn's voice got higher, towards the hysterical level. "What if those rednecks come back? What am I saying? Of course, they'll come back after the way you humiliated them. Hell, I'd come back, too. And I'd be loaded for bear. What are we going to do?"

"I don't know," CeeCee replied. "Any ideas?"

"I knew we shouldn't have done this to our husbands," said Lynn. "We're being punished. We're going to die, and for what? So they'd have friends to play with?"

"Lynn, I know you're upset," said Molly. "We're all upset, but we've got to keep our heads screwed on straight and figure out what to do."

Lynn looked up from the tissue she'd reclaimed from her purse. "I have a problem, too, that can't wait, and when I say it can't wait..." A gas bubble rolled through her abdomen, making an audible gurgling sound. "I *have* to get to a bathroom. Now."

"Can't you go in the woods?" CeeCee asked.

"No. I can't go in the woods. *CeeCee*." Lynn smacked the back of the seat. "It's not number one."

"Ewwwwwww." CeeCee mockingly fanned her face. "I thought I smelled something."

"You think this is funny?"

Molly turned towards Lynn. "I'm sure she didn't mean to be insensitive, did you, CeeCee?"

CeeCee knew that scolding tone. "I'm sorry, Lynn. Seriously. You know how I run off at the mouth sometimes. No pun intended."

"CeeCee!" said Molly.

Jeez, can't anyone take a joke anymore?

"Listen, Lynn," said Molly. "I'm going to see if, by some miracle, the store is unlocked. I'm sure there is a restroom inside. Big Jon has to go somewhere."

CeeCee laughed. "Which begs the question, does big Jon go in the woods?"

"For God's sake, cut it out. Please." Molly hopped out of the driver's seat. "Lock the doors."

The car's passenger side faced the store, so CeeCee rolled the window halfway down in case her fellow ram-rodder needed something. Molly approached the wooden porch where just a short while ago, they'd been minding their own business and thinking their biggest worries were back at the lake cabin. CeeCee didn't want to admit it, but her courage was crumbling. *Simon Says? What an idiotic idea.* She clasped her hands together to keep them from shaking and tried again to calm herself.

Molly reached for the horseshoe knob and turned it. Nothing. She jiggled it, put her shoulder on the door, and leaned in using her weight. She looked at her friends and shook her head.

"It was a long shot," CeeCee shouted. "What about the windows?"

"You mean inside those bars where *anything* could be growing or living?" She pulled out her phone, turned on the flashlight, and studied the situation. Then she stuck her hands through the metal bars and pulled on the window sash. No luck. She walked across the porch and tried the other window with the same result. Molly put her hands on her hips and looked around, then peeked around the right side of the building and disappeared. She reappeared shortly, clapping dirt off her hands just as a lightning bolt crossed the sky.

Thunder rumbled, followed quickly by another sound in the distance. The roar of an engine.

Storm's a'comin'.

Chapter Ten

The urgency to get into Big Jon's just ramped up, and Molly ran to the passenger side window. "Unless two trucks sound exactly alike, you know what's coming *and* a storm. Bill mentioned bad weather earlier, but I'd forgotten. We've got to get inside this building ASAP. The last thing we need is another confrontation out in the open."

CeeCee stepped out of the car, but when her left foot hit the ground, she groaned and clung to the door to take the weight off her leg. She hopped toward Molly, used her friend's shoulder as a crutch, and turned to Lynn. "Will you be okay in the car while Molly and I look around the back of the store?"

Lynn scowled. "Why do I have to stay here? Why can't we all go? And what good are you? You can't even walk."

"There's not much room back there," said Molly. "We'd be like fish in a barrel if we all go. It's better if we split up—just in case."

"Oh, is that the final decision, commander Molly?" asked Lynn. "Once again, without getting input from others?"

Molly sighed. "Okay, what do *you* think we should do?"

"I'm going with you, and CeeCee stays here. She can barely walk, which makes her a liability."

"Don't be silly, Lynn," said CeeCee. She reached into the floorboard and grabbed the Glock. "Do you know how to use a gun?"

"Get that thing away from me!" Lynn shouted.

"Listen, get in the front seat and lock everything up," continued CeeCee. "I'll put the gun on the console. You probably won't even have to touch it, but if you do, be careful. It's loaded and ready. Put both hands on the butt, aim, and gently squeeze. Expect a kick. You can do it."

"What in the world are you talking about?" asked Lynn. "You expect me to shoot somebody? Are you nuts?"

While CeeCee explained Guns 101, Molly opened the back hatch and grabbed her rifle. When she slammed it shut, Lynn stood beside her, then walked towards the side of the building. "You coming, Molly?"

"Lynn. Just get in the car, please," CeeCee said.

"No. You're the gun-toting fool. You stay and be our first line of defense. Or not. I don't care. I'm going to help Molly get inside somehow."

Molly rolled her eyes. "We're wasting time." She looked at CeeCee. "Listen, if worse comes to worst, you can always ram somebody. The car still goes. It just doesn't stop."

CeeCee hobbled around the car to climb behind the wheel. "Did you just give me permission to crash your creampuff car?"

"I can't believe I said it myself," Molly said.

"*That* I can do. And I have a driving record to prove it." For the first time in a while, CeeCee smiled.

The back of Big Jon's store butted up to a rock cliff with rogue shrubs and leafy vines that somehow found a way to grow. The side of the mountain had simply been carved to house the small structure and nothing else, leaving only three feet of space between the building and the living wall. Molly turned on the phone's flashlight and peered into the gap, looking for critters or unexpected threats. Lynn did the same. A worn path gave Molly hope, so she walked sideways into the gap with her back towards the rocky terrain, her phone in one hand and rifle in the other. A strong stench of urine permeated her nostrils. "Jeez."

"Pee-ew," said Lynn as she held her nose. "What the hell? I hope this doesn't indicate no bathroom inside."

"Probably just indicates some lazy dumb-ass who likes to pee on rocks. Hey, I see a door." She approached it. "It's got a padlock on it, up pretty high. I'm trying to see if the latch has screws on the outside, which would be pretty stupid if you think about it."

"Let's hope the dumbass you mentioned is also the handyman," said Lynn.

Molly got closer, leaned her rifle against the rocks, and stood on her tiptoes. "Ha! It is!

"Think it goes inside Big Jon's or is this just a storage place?"

"Only one way to find out. I have a Phillips head screwdriver in my toolbox. Will you get it? Hurry. It's creepy back here, and I don't know how long I can hold my breath."

Lynn made the trip quickly and returned with the screwdriver. While Lynn held the phone to light up the lock, Molly placed the tip of the screwdriver into the metal screw and tried to turn it. No movement. "This thing is so rusted it may never turn."

"Maybe it got peed on, too."

Molly wondered briefly about the possibility, wiped her hands on her pants, and gripped the orange plastic handle. She grunted and tried again. This time the screw rotated a little. It took a lot of effort, but finally, the screw came out and fell quietly to the ground. "Okay, we have lift off. One down, three more to go."

"You want me to try one?" asked Lynn.

"Nah. You're too short. No offense. Just light her up for me."

It felt like an hour before the last screw fell out, followed by the thud of the latch and padlock.

"Let's see what we have in here," said Molly as she cautiously opened the door and stepped in. "Oh, great."

"What is it?"

"Another door."

"What? Let me see."

Molly stood in a small wooden closet of some kind, barely bigger than she. It smelled musty and old, like her aunt's attic, where she and her cousins used to play like they were pirates in an old wooden ship. Suddenly something brushed across her cheek, making her shriek, lurch backward, and knock Lynn into the rocky bank. Her phone crashed to the ground with a cracking sound, and the flashlight disappeared. "Something just touched me. Oh Lord! It's probably a spider. Is it on me? Is it on me?"

"Don't worry about me and my two cracked vertebrae," said Lynn.

"Hurry up. Tell me! It's a spider, isn't it?"

Lynn checked her over and in her hair. "Nope. You're good."

"You better be telling me the truth, Lynn Ellen. You looked good, right? You know those things freak me out."

"Believe me, I know," said Lynn as she shone the flashlight into the closet. "Look. It's just a string attached to a light bulb socket." She reached out and pulled at the knot. No light. "Dammit. Can nothing go right in this godforsaken place?"

Molly looked at Lynn, who never used foul language. It amused her.

"Let me try again." Lynn twisted the bulb. "Let there be light." She reached for the knob on the second door and pushed. It creaked but didn't go far before it stopped. The light from the bare bulb flowed through the small opening into the dark store, creating shadows of various shapes.

"I think something's blocking the door," whispered Lynn. She started to peer around the edge. "If something jumps out at me, I'll die right here standing up."

"Nothing's going to jump out at you," said Molly authoritatively.

"Says the girl who freaked over a string," Lynn retorted. She wedged her head and shoulder into the opening and used the flashlight to peek on the other side. "Okay, found the culprit."

"Is it a dead body?"

"Shut up. It's a bunch of boxes. Help me push."

Molly put her hands on the door and leaned in. "It could still be a dead body, just deposited in several boxes."

With teeth tightly clenched, Lynn jabbed her elbow into Molly's side and repeated, "Shut. Up."

Once inside the store, Lynn rushed to find the bathroom. A small sign, hanging from the ceiling by two strings, pointed the way. She walked in that direction, unbuttoning and unzipping her pants. "Thank you, Lord!"

Molly hurried to the front door and unlocked it, but before she could turn the knob, the door burst open. She screamed as CeeCee stalked in. "What took so long?"

"Dammit, CeeCee, you can't do stuff like that. You could've been one of those men for all I knew."

"Sorry. I guess I got a little nervous out there by myself."

Molly quickly closed and bolted the door. "Did you get what we needed out of the car? And lock it?"

"Yes, commander." She gave Molly a little salute.

"Any more noise from the truck?"

"No, but that doesn't mean anything. Why's it so dark in here?"

Lynn suddenly appeared behind Molly, her phone light shining upward, making her face look ghoulish. "Because there may be dead people in here. Bwah ah ah."

"Somebody's feeling better," said CeeCee.

"We have mixed feelings about the lights," said Molly trying to steer the conversation to something helpful. "If they're on and some local sees them, they may call the owner, if they know him, or the police. That's a good thing."

"On the other hand," Lynn added. "If our *friends* come back, they'll know we're in here, and that's a bad thing."

CeeCee looked at them like they were morons. "Uhm, hello-o-o? The car is outside. It doesn't take a genius to figure out we're here. I don't want to deal with those assholes again, but staying doesn't seem smart."

"Maybe. Maybe not if we keep low until they leave," said Lynn. "Maybe they'll think someone rescued us. Who knows? But what choice do we have?"

"Or maybe they don't want any more of *this,*" CeeCee said as she held up the Glock and blew on the tip of the barrel.

"Yeah, you're a real badass," said Lynn. "We need a plan, so let's find a place to sit before my legs collapse. I don't know about you, but my body's had all the excitement it can handle."

Because of the light shining from the back entrance and front porch, the women's eyes quickly adjusted to the dark store. As they familiarized themselves with the layout, Molly found batteries at the cash register counter and inserted them into her flashlight. She spotted some smaller lights hanging on metal hooks along with a sign. *SALE: two for $6*. She grabbed a couple and got more batteries. "Remind me to leave Big Jon an IOU."

Lynn went to the other side of the store behind some racks of potato chips, cheese crackers, peanuts, and tiny cookies. "Hey! Found us a place to sit. And snacks."

CeeCee and Molly wandered over to Lynn and found her wadded up in an old armchair with half the stuffing falling out. A matching brown sofa and chair in the same condition sat nearby, along with an old steamer trunk, serving as a coffee table. The furniture smelled like men's shaving cream, pipe tobacco, and coffee beans. Not unpleasant. The women settled into the comfort of the well-used leather and tried to collect themselves.

Lynn tossed out snack bags to her friends, stuffed four Cheetos into her mouth, and crunched.

"More dry, salty stuff," CeeCee said, starting to get up. "I need something to wash it down."

"Oh, good grief," Molly said. "Sit. Rest your leg. I'll get them."

She walked to the check-out counter where an old red Coca-Cola cooler sat. She slid the door open and saw various aluminum cans lying side by side like little soldiers. She grabbed three and returned to the girls. "One of these cans I shook pretty hard, so be prepared."

"You're kidding, right?" asked CeeCee.

"Maybe."

The soda can hissed as she popped the top.

****

CeeCee slouched into the lumpy couch cushions and watched Molly disappear among the store racks and shelves. She thought she heard her say, "Back in a jiff," and assumed she headed towards the restroom. Her eyes wandered, studying the stuff inside Big Jon's. It reminded her of a little boy's treehouse, trimmed with flea market finds or junk from an abandoned lot. Deflated bicycle tires, hubcaps, an old gas can, and weathered windows with no panes hung from large hooks screwed into the ceiling. Barely secured to the wall hung a crooked shelf holding an old boat propeller and rusted cans with blobs of paint dripping down the sides. No shelf or surface seemed unclaimed. Over CeeCee's head swayed a red and blue toy bi-plane with one wheel and a wing missing as if it had been to war. She pictured a miniature Lynn doll falling out of it, her frilly skirt billowing like a parachute.

"Lynn? Are you really going to jump out of a plane?"

"What made you think of that?"

CeeCee pointed upward. "I couldn't do that for all the money in the world. When did you get interested in that kind of thing?"

"I didn't," said Lynn.

"Then why on earth did you agree?"

"You know why. I had to make a deal."

"Of all the things he could barter, why that? Seems like his favor is a lot bigger than yours. He spends a measly little weekend with people he doesn't know, and you jump out of a plane thousands of feet above the earth? You could get killed, and what's the worst that could happen to him? A sunburn?" CeeCee stroked her chin at an imaginary beard. "A bit lopsided, methinks."

"Well, that's a district attorney for you. Always ready to pounce on the vulnerable. The old kick 'em-while-they're-down tactic."

Detecting something in Lynn's voice, CeeCee cocked her head and raised her imaginary antennae.

"Well, you have plenty of time to back out. What can he do? Sue his own wife?" She giggled.

Lynn sat quietly, neck bent. "I'm terrified. And he knows it." She dabbed her eyes with the hem of her shirt. "Being an ADA has taught him a lot of ways to manipulate people."

CeeCee quickly sat up. "Hey, what's going on?"

Lynn waved her hand as if dismissing a silly problem. "Nothing. I don't know what's gotten into me. Guess I'm wound up because of everything that's happened today. The funeral. The car breaking down. This place. Those men. Guns waving around. Adam. Especially Adam. I think I'm coming unhinged."

"You're right," said CeeCee. "Today has been insane. It's a wonder we're functioning at all. We need to talk about our next step when Molly gets back, but I think I know what we need first."

CeeCee got up and limped towards the cash register area. When she returned, she wore a pair of black plastic glasses with a big nose, bushy eyebrows, and a mustache attached. She threw a pair at Lynn, who managed to laugh through her tears. "Great disguise. I'm sure those guys will never recognize us."

"No. These were just a *bonus*." CeeCee held up a neon yellow Bic lighter and a pack of Virginia Slims. "*This* is what we need."

"We haven't smoked in years!"

CeeCee ripped open the package, tapped out a cigarette, and flicked the lighter. "I don't give a rat's ass. You in or not?"

Lynn sighed. "Oh hell, throw 'em over here. Might as well add puking to my list of issues."

Molly reappeared and saw two big-nosed, mustached, bespectacled women taking draws off cigarettes and blowing smoke towards the ceiling. She glanced from one to the other with a deadpan expression. "I left you for five minutes."

"Just easing the tension a little," CeeCee said with a grin. "Here. Put your glasses on."

Molly plopped down. "Are you happy now?"

"One more thing."

"I'm not smoking if that's what you're thinking."

"Nope." She held up her phone. "We need a selfie. Lynn, jump over here."

With cigarettes hanging out the side of their mouths, Lynn and CeeCee scrunched Molly between them.

CeeCee held out her phone as far as she could. "Okay, one, two...."

The phone flashed. A door creaked. The women froze.

Chapter Eleven

Lynn sat motionless, barely breathing as CeeCee lowered the phone and put an index finger to her lips. She shaped her hand into a gun, then pointed at her purse on the floor about six feet away. Molly's rifle leaned on the wall nearby, neither within reach.

Lynn nodded but still held a half-smoked cigarette between her fingers, causing a logistical problem, so she handed it to CeeCee, whose expression indicated her displeasure with that decision. Lynn shrugged and slowly stood, wondering if a heart could beat out of a person's body.

<Creak!>

She sprang toward the rifle and tossed it to Molly, then plunged her hand into the purse, pulled out the handgun, and whirled around, searching for any movement in the store. She saw nothing except her hand shaking as hard as her heart pounded. Molly motioned for Lynn to go to the right as she set off in the other direction.

Lynn managed to put one foot in front of the other until she got to the front door, where she checked the bolt and found it secure. She glanced out both windows. Seeing nothing out of the norm, she headed for the back of the store where the creaking sound seemed to originate. A tall, misshaped shadow appeared on the far wall. *Molly?* Her breathing became more rapid and shallow, and the Glock felt like a fifty-pound weight in her hand. She tried to remember what CeeCee told her about racking or the safety, if it even had one. She broke into a cold sweat but managed to place her finger near the trigger, unsure if the gun would go off or not. Lynn aimed it toward the shadow.

Molly's eyes grew wide when she rounded a rack of fishing supplies and saw the Glock pointed straight at her. When Lynn made no move to lower the weapon, Molly took a step closer and pushed the barrel of the Glock downward, then crept towards the back door and pushed it closed.

Lynn stood like a statue, but a thousand scenarios raced through her mind, the worst of them being the death of her friend. *What the hell are we doing?* Her legs suddenly felt unstable, and the nerve endings in her hands and feet were on fire. *Panic attack.* She guided herself to the floor and concentrated on deep breathing to raise the oxygen level in her blood. It would work eventually, but the medicine in her purse worked faster. In therapy, she'd learned to envision herself in a happy place, easier said than done when real—not imagined—danger lurked around the corner. Suddenly a loud crash and things shattering jolted her nerves into overdrive. And CeeCee screamed.

****

Molly moved towards the sound, feeling her way among the racks, and tried not to stumble. She needed the flashlight but didn't dare turn it on. She stubbed her toe on something and barely avoided a fall by grabbing onto a black bear carved out of a log. Several splinters clawed their way into her hand. *Shit.* She raised her rifle as she approached the sitting area, then turned on her light.

"Don't move, you hairy son of a bitch!" Molly shouted.

What she saw was hairy but not human.

CeeCee stood in the leather chair, clutching a purse to her chest like an old lady on an unfamiliar city street. "Shoot it! What are you waiting for, my leg to be gnawed off?"

Molly's heart thumped as she took in the scene. She was expecting the worst, encountering one of the men, but she wasn't ready to shoot an innocent animal. She'd much rather shoot a picture of CeeCee being cornered by a raccoon. *My phone is still outside.*

"Lynn?" Molly shouted, keeping her eyes trained on the raccoon. "I need some help, but move slowly. We don't want to spook him."

Then she remembered her friend had wilted to the floor before CeeCee screamed. "Lynn?"

"What's wrong?" CeeCee whispered.

"Don't know."

Before Molly could think of what to do, Lynn appeared on hands and knees, as pale as a ghost.

"Lynn, think you can open the front door? Maybe he just wants out."

"Who?" she asked, her voice oddly indifferent and weak.

"Him," said Molly, pointing at the big raccoon with the barrel of her rifle.

Lynn stared but made no move toward the door.

Holding her teeth together, CeeCee murmured, "Get it off me; get it off me!"

Molly got to Lynn just as she collapsed. "What's going on? What can I do?"

"Purse. Medicine," whispered Lynn.

The critter continued to stare CeeCee down. "Umm... Molly, a little help? This thing could be rabid."

Molly didn't know who to tend to first. "I'm doing my best." She looked around, grabbed a bag of chips, and tore it open. "Look, Rocky. Chips. Yum."

The noise caught the animal's attention as she shook chips onto the floor, creating a narrow trail to the door, but he soon turned back to CeeCee. Then the raccoon climbed into the chair with her, stood up, and put its front paws on CeeCee's legs.

"Oh my god, he's coming for me. Get it off."

"Stay still. How can I shoot him and not you?" asked Molly. "Lynn, what's in your purse? Is it heavy enough to knock out a raccoon?"

"Wallet, cosmetic bag, medicine, keys, tissues. Oh, and an apple."

"Apple?" asked CeeCee. "Don't raccoons eat fruit?"

She rummaged around in the purse and threw it to Molly, who showed it to the animal. "Come on, buddy. Let's go outside."

The raccoon unceremoniously hopped off the chair, waddled over to the door, and followed the apple as it rolled onto the porch.

"Close the door; close the door!" shouted CeeCee, "before it gets back in. Jeez, I could've been killed."

Molly rolled her eyes at the exaggeration. "Get Lynn's medicine out of her bag. Hurry!" She put her hand on the door to close it, then froze at the faint but familiar rumbling of dual exhaust pipes in the distance.

She slammed the door. "They're coming!"

Molly put the rifle down and turned on the store lights. "We're getting soft in our old age or stupid. We should've buttoned up this place an hour ago."

After they got Lynn settled on the couch, Molly scampered, and CeeCee limped through the store, looking for things to secure it, shouting suggestions back and forth. They pushed the metal drink cooler against the back door, feeling confident it wasn't going anywhere since it took everything they had to slide it that small distance. And thanks to a bucket of nails and a hammer found in a corner, they boarded up the front door using wooden shelves off the walls. Nobody could get in easily. Or out. They turned off the lights and waited.

"You just rest and try to relax," said CeeCee as she sat by Lynn. "We aren't sitting ducks like we were on the porch. Everything will be fine."

Molly plopped down in a chair. "Found some stubby candles that fell to the floor." Thunder and lightning suddenly rocked the building, and Lynn shrieked.

"Dammit," said CeeCee. "Now, all we need is for the—"

<Click.>

"—power to go off."

CeeCee went to the window. "I don't like this at all. The porch light gave us an advantage. We could see them, but they couldn't see us. Now I can't see anything, including my own hand."

Molly felt around for the box of matches and lit one of the candles. "Just in the nick of time."

"Blow it out," Lynn yelled, grabbing Molly's arm. "Blow it out!"

The women sat in the dark silently for a long while, listening for the men's return.

"Remember when we used to pass the candle in sorority meetings?" asked CeeCee.

Announcing the progression of one's love life became a tradition in the Greek community. The sisters would gather in a large circle, sing a sorority song, and with growing anticipation, pass a lit candle from hand to hand. With each lap, the seriousness of the milestone grew. If a girl blew out the candle the first time around, she'd been asked to wear the boy's fraternity lavalier, or they were going steady. Twice around meant pinned, three times engaged, and if it ever went four times around, it meant married, which never happened.

"Who was that chick, Jane somebody, who got pinned to the ex-boyfriend of another sorority sister?" asked CeeCee. "We were in total shock, especially the ex-girlfriend who ran out of the room crying. Nobody knew what to do. Act excited or appalled."

Molly snickered. "They hadn't even been dating that long. That took some balls, all right. They were a temporary item, but the line was drawn in the sand and divided us into two camps for quite a while."

"Yep," said CeeCee." Not exactly a good example of sisterhood, but in a way, I admired her courage. She had to know what would—"

"Shhh!" Molly peered out the barred window. The highway and surrounding woods lit up as headlights approached, then turned into the parking area, high beams aimed at Big Jon's. The engine idled, revved, idled, and revved, but the vehicle itself didn't move, and no one stepped out.

CeeCee joined Molly at the window and craned her neck. "Those rat bastards just don't know when to stop. Anybody get out?"

"No, but they could've, before the truck turned in, maybe hiding in the woods."

"Oh my God, what are we going to do?" asked Lynn, her voice once again a few decibels higher than normal.

"We're going to defend ourselves, that's what," said Molly. "We don't have a choice. I know how you feel about guns, but you'll have to put that aside for now. Think you can do it?"

"I don't understand," Lynn said. "We only have two."

"That's sort of true," said Molly. "The owner keeps a shotgun underneath the counter. Saw it earlier. Kind of surprised he'd leave it here, but I'm glad he did."

"Great," said CeeCee. "I'll go get it. Wouldn't it be fun to blow a hole through the front door and scare the snot out of those assholes?"

Using the miniature flashlight Big Jon donated, she limped away and returned with the weapon. "I have good news and bad."

"What is it?" asked Lynn.

"In summation, we have one shell. No other ammo."

"It's better than nothing," Molly said, still looking out the window. "You think they're taunting us, like a cat with a mouse?"

"This is a calculated move on their part," said CeeCee. "The first encounter? They had no plan, but they've put some thought into it this time. They left with their tails tucked between their legs, and now they're back to teach us a lesson."

The truck's engine revved again.

"Know what this reminds me of?" asked Molly. "One of those frogs that inflates itself with air and raises its hind parts to appear as large as possible to ward off predators."

CeeCee nodded. "Or a gorilla that pounds his chest."

Suddenly, the engine rumbled, and the tires crunched on the gravel as the truck rolled closer to the store.

"Man your stations," Molly said. "Hurry."

The girls got in place, but nothing happened. Instead, the truck made a slow U-turn, and a window rolled down.

"Sleep tight, ladies, if you can. We'll see you soon."

Chapter Twelve

Saturday

An urgent need to empty his bladder woke Adam around two a.m. As he got his bearings, he tried to recall the last thing he did or said, but the cobweb of booze prevented him from finding anything useful. Since he was on the leather couch, one thing he knew. He'd passed out.

He sat up, put his bare feet on the thick Peruvian rug, and wiggled his toes in the dense fibers. It felt good. Bill slept on the opposite couch, facing the back cushions, and snored softly, so Adam quietly stood and tiptoed toward the light coming from a small stained glass lamp across the room.

It projected colorful rays of red, gold, and green onto the ceiling and reminded him of a similar lamp in his grandmother's house decades ago. The memory gave him a brief feeling of warmth when he'd cuddle up with her on the worn-out couch, munching chocolate chip cookies and reading aloud to her. Those good times, however, came *after* his grandfather died and the prolonged abuse of his grandma ended. He started spending more time with her, and the two formed new memories. Better memories. His love of books began there, and the stories helped bury the deep-seated anger his grandfather's behavior created. *Buried but not forgotten.*

Adam managed to find the bathroom located behind the stairwell and avoided knocking anything over on the way, including himself. He still had a buzz from too much scotch and wasn't steady on his feet.

After using the lavatory and washing his hands, he headed for the kitchen. A blooming headache signaled the need to eat something before he got sick. He massaged his temples, then opened the fridge. Blue LED lights lit up the dark kitchen, having the opposite effect of the stained glass lamp, and created a cool bluish glow. Adam grabbed some grub and walked over to the sink to eat it. He took a big swig of diet soda while looking out the window at the two SUVs parked there, taunting him. He felt anger welling up again. *Damn you, Lynn.*

How dare she leave him here. He didn't care what her stupid letter said. She was constantly goading him until he couldn't take it anymore, causing the logical side of his brain to shut down and be replaced by raw emotion and fury.

Adam slowly pulled out kitchen drawers, searching quietly for what he needed to carry out his plan. Not wanting to wake Bill, the process took longer than he could tolerate, and by the time he turned on the outside lights, his fury had taken away all reasoning.

He opened the back door and stepped off the porch onto sharp chunks of gravel. *Shit.* He'd forgotten his shoes, which were in the great room where Bill slept. Retrieving them wasn't an option, so he ventured another step and jammed his big toe into a large rock. Adam grimaced, cursed, and picked up his foot to survey the damage. Blood dripped across the adjoining toes, and the toenail barely remained attached. While he hopped around, the screwdriver from the kitchen drawer fell out of his pocket, taking his anger to the breaking point. He bent to pick it up, then squinted at the offending rock as if it were an enemy in combat. He snarled as he picked it up, then took several quick steps and hurled it at the passenger window of the SUV. Adam smiled as the glass broke into a spider web pattern, but his expression changed quickly when the car alarm shattered the quiet night.

Panic set in as the deafening sound bounced off the house and the lake. He knew how to turn it off with a key fob, but obviously, he didn't have it. With rage building, he picked up the rock and smashed it into the window repeatedly until a small hole appeared, giving him hope. As the alarm blared, a larger hole finally formed, one big enough for Adam to insert his hand into the car. He unlocked the doors using the automatic button, but nothing happened.

"Shit. Shit. Shit." Maybe if he opened and closed a door. Nope. Perhaps it has to be the driver's door. He hobbled around the SUV, cutting his left heel on the way, and opened the door. He climbed in, closed the door, and looked around for an answer, any answer, but the horn continued to honk, and the lights blinked. It was driving him nuts.

A sudden rap, rap, rap on the window shocked Adam, but not as much as when Cory ripped the door open and jerked him out of the car.

"What the hell are you doing?" He shouted into Adam's face, and spit flew. "Are you out of your mind?"

Cory grabbed the front of Adam's shirt and pushed him backward, then lunged and landed an uppercut into his diaphragm, followed by a left hook to the side of his head. Adam fell to the ground, heaving, spitting blood, trying to catch his breath.

"You fucking idiot!" Cory spat as he climbed into the car, opened the glove compartment, and grabbed a wrench and flashlight. He pulled the handle under the dash that popped the hood and ran to the front of the SUV. With the flashlight in his mouth shining on the engine, Cory disconnected the bolts on one of the battery terminals and removed a cable. Silence.

He walked back towards Adam. "Get up, you piece of shit. I'm going to kick your ass across this lake."

"Stop!" Bill shouted, running toward the two men. "What the hell's happening here?" He stepped between them.

"Do you see what this moron did?" asked Cory.

Bill put both his hands up towards Cory. "Hold off for a sec." He helped Adam to his feet. "Can you breathe? Are you okay?"

"If he is, he won't be for long," Cory said. "I hope you throw up your toenails, you son of a bitch, the ones you have left."

Bill asked again. "Adam?"

"Okay. I'm okay." He wiped the blood off his mouth with the back of his hand. Still a little drunk, he lost his balance when he attempted to brush off his clothes, so he leaned against the car, trying to compose himself. It hurt to breathe.

"Somebody better start talking. Now!" Bill shouted.

"Besides getting the crap beat out of me by that Neanderthal?" Adam bent over and tried to take a breath. "Oww... I decided to hotwire the car and get the hell out of here. That's all." He knew how stupid it sounded but continued in his courtroom voice that usually worked in his favor. "I had a client a few years back whose specialty was stealing cars. He said older models that don't have push-button ignitions can be started with a screwdriver."

"So, based on that bit of knowledge, you decided to try it," said Bill.

Adam nodded.

"You know you broke into Cory's car, not *yours.*"

"Course I knew that. You think I'm some sort of nut job?"

"Beginning to wonder, yes," said Bill. "Why didn't you break into your own?"

Adam turned and pointed at his shiny Cadillac Escalade. "That would be pretty stupid to damage a brand new car when this old thing is sitting right here. It doesn't even have a push-button ignition. Don't you get it? And who would've thought it had an alarm? It must be at least ten years old."

Bill shook his head. "I'm going back to bed. Unless somebody dies, don't wake me up." He paused. "And both of you need to think about getting some serious therapy. A thorough check-up from the neck-up."

****

Bill woke up early, as was his routine, but he didn't feel refreshed. After last night's ruckus, he'd found a big, comfy, four-poster bed upstairs and slept fitfully for only three hours. The booze probably contributed to that, and he was feeling the after-effects. He didn't like it and wasn't used to it. When it came to alcohol, Molly's husband was considered a lightweight.

He slid his feet onto the floor, stretched his arms over his head, then touched his toes, which made his head throb. Bill needed Excedrin. *Shit.* His bag was downstairs, not where he wanted to go, but he forced himself to traipse down the hall towards the stairwell. He peeked over the handrail into the great room and saw Adam sprawled on the couch with a red checked blanket draped over half his body. His face had turned different shades of purple and blue from last night's altercation. *He's going to be one sore SOB today.*

Although Adam's snore rivaled the base pipes of an organ, Bill tiptoed down the steps, grabbed his bag, and walked softly towards the bathroom on the main floor. He didn't want to wake the attorney for many reasons.

After freshening up, Bill shuffled to the kitchen, wondering how today might play out. *Do I smell coffee?* He found sweetener and cream sitting on the counter beside the coffee maker, which held a fresh pot. He searched a few cabinets until he found a black bear mug, poured some coffee, and stepped out onto the front porch. He leaned against the railing, taking in the beauty of the tall hardwood trees, and listened to birds tweet and sing. *Ahhh, this is nice.* He breathed in the fresh cool air, then blew on the coffee and took a sip.

"Good morning!"

Bill jerked, choked, and burned his mouth. Cory sat in a rocker with the same bear mug in one hand and a book in the other. "Sorry, man. Didn't mean to startle you."

Bill ignored the apology and looked down at his shirt, checking for brown stains, which miraculously were not there. He managed to tamp down his anger.

"I guess I have you to thank for the coffee. Appreciate it."

"You're welcome. I'm an early riser. Can't stay in bed like prince charming in there."

"Me, either." Bill brought the cup to his nose and took in the aroma. Properly this time, he took a sip without the knee-jerk reaction of being poked with a stick. "This is good stuff, not like we have at home. A special blend?"

"Not really. I kind of doctor it up with some things, like chicory and cinnamon. Depends on the day."

Bill nodded, blew, and sipped. "So you like tinkering with coffee?"

"I like to dabble here and there, and working at a fire station allows me to explore my culinary skills. Those guys will eat anything, although they still like to complain about it."

"Nice. After almost burning the house down, Molly doesn't allow me in the kitchen anymore."

"You kidding?"

"Wish I were," Bill said, half smiling. "You know what would be great with this coffee? A hot Krispy Kreme donut, one still dripping with glaze, right off the conveyor belt." He closed his eyes, picturing it, tasting it. "Man, I'd give my right nut to have one melting in my mouth right now."

Cory chuckled. "Can't tell you the last time I had one. A donut, that is. Or a nut, for that matter." They both laughed. "CeeCee and I try to eat healthy food, but we're not fanatics about it."

Bill nodded. "How's your hand?"

"Sore and swollen, maybe even a fractured bone or two," said Cory. "But it was worth it. Normally I'm not a violent person—angry, yes—violet, no. But last night, that prick challenged me one time too many."

"As they say," Bill added, "you had only one nerve left, and he was standing all over it."

Cory nodded. "Maybe I should go check on him."

"Or maybe you should let sleeping dogs lie."

"I don't know, man. What if Adam has a concussion or something?" Cory rose from his chair and placed his book and coffee on a small table. "Besides, I'm pretty sure there's a part in the EMT manual that says, thou shall not beat the shit out of people. Especially if those people are lawyers."

"Good luck. I'm going for a short walk," said Bill. "Holler, if you need a witness. Or an alibi."

****

Cory walked over to the couch expecting to see Adam asleep, but he was M.I.A. He picked up the blanket to examine the cushions for blood, happy to see none, but a piece of paper partially wedged in one of the creases caught his eye. He picked it up, and as the commode flushed and the bathroom door opened, he automatically stuffed the paper into his pocket.

The attorney entered the great room, bent over at the waist and holding his ribs. The left side of his mouth showed scrapes, and the swelling of his face increased its size by half. A whopper of a black eye would be next. He looked like hell.

"Hey, let me help you," Cory said.

"Don't get near me," said Adam in a weak voice. He held up his hand. "You've done enough."

"I just want to check you for a concussion. Won't take but a second."

"Do not. Touch me. I don't have a concussion. Broken ribs? Probably. But no concussion."

Cory rubbed his forehead. "That's not good."

Adam glared.

"Listen, I know you don't want me around you. The feeling's mutual, but we need to tape up those ribs to keep them as stable as possible. Trust me. It will help, plus a few doses of ibuprofen for the inflammation. And ice."

"You get a medical degree overnight? Thought you were a fireman."

"I am, but I'm also an EMT," Cory replied. "Although…."

"Although what?" asked Adam.

"Well, I have to be honest. The taping is a remedy my dad taught me, used in the old days. Doctors don't wrap ribs anymore. They're more concerned about people being able to breathe deeply, but I believe if your ribs are jiggling around causing pain, you're going to avoid deep breaths at all costs."

Cory went to the pantry to search for supplies and returned to see Adam sitting on the edge of a chair at the breakfast table. *This is good.* Cory poured some coffee and placed it on the table. "You take anything in it?"

Adam shook his head, lifted the cup slowly to his swollen mouth, and successfully took a sip. "Man, that hurts."

"Listen, all I could find is duct tape, but it'll do."

Adam scowled. "Are you messing with me?"

"Tape is tape, man."

"Whatever. Let's get this over with. Where's Bill anyway? I may need a witness."

"That's weird. Bill said something similar before he went for a walk."

Cory reached for the bottom of Adam's t-shirt, gently guided his arms out of the sleeves, and left the shirt resting on his shoulders. "Damn, you're hairy."

"So, you're going to insult me, too? Just forget it." Adam started to get up.

Cory placed his hands on Adam's shoulders. "Sit. Please. I think you need to keep your t-shirt on, and I'll tape over it. Otherwise, when the tape is ripped off, you're going to get a wax job you'll never forget."

"Will that work?"

"Hope so. It's better than having all your hair follicles ripped out of your skin. It's your call. I guess we could always shave you, then tape you up."

"You're not shaving anything!" Adam blurted.

"What's this about shaving?" Bill asked as he walked up behind them. "I don't want to see any razors being bandied about between you two."

"Let's try the t-shirt thing," said Adam.

"We'll take the wrap off in about an hour to reevaluate, and if you don't get any relief, we'll just keep icing the area. How's that?"

"Just do it, man," sighed Adam. "I'm dying here." He looked at Bill. "Don't let him kill me."

Chapter Thirteen

Josh awoke with a pounding headache and a bright light assaulting his eyelids. In the haze of a bad hangover, he worked his way through the possibilities and landed on the only logical conclusion. He must be on an operating table.

Wait.

His eyes flew open, then slammed shut. Pain radiated like a laser, cutting through his corneas. He rubbed his eyes gently, turned away from the light, and tugged the cotton sheet over his head. It smelled like fabric softener, lilac with a hint of vanilla. He also got a whiff of his breath, which reeked of bourbon.

His hand slid across the soft sheet, reaching for her comfort, but only sadness greeted him. For one split second, his brain had been in neutral, not recalling, not grieving, not breaking his heart, but giving him a bit of peace instead. Then, *bam!*

He opened his eyes and stared at the space where Carolyn usually lay. The unchangeable truth jolted his stomach as if he were hearing the news of her death for the first time. He tried to picture her in Heaven, smiling and laughing. Instead, memories of her on Earth clicked through his mind like a slide show while tears trickled down his face. Then unexpectedly, she appeared in an open field, wearing a floral sundress, running gracefully away from him. Her movements were slow, and exaggerated the bounce of her long brown hair. She turned to smile and wave, more than once, until her image disintegrated into the sky's fluffy clouds. Sadness draped over Josh's body like a weighted blanket, causing him to plunge his face into Carolyn's pillow.

An hour later, Josh rolled to the side of the bed and, despite the exhaustion, forced himself to stand. During his wife's diagnosis, illness, hospital stays, chemo, the funeral, and all the plans that went with each step, she'd never seen him cry. Not once. Instead, he stayed hopeful, positive, and strong for her, the kids, and himself. He'd been in fix-it mode and didn't dare let a negative thought penetrate his focus to keep his wife healthy and alive. Some called it denial, but he knew the truth. He just chose to *fight* and *believe* until the apparent end of Carolyn's life was undeniable. With that, the tears fell, and his heart, along with his resolve, broke.

The bathroom mirror reflected red, swollen eyes and the saddest face he'd ever seen belonging to a man wearing a wrinkled lavender shirt, boxers, and one dark blue sock. The shirt color had been a request of Carolyn's, so the family added a touch of it to their funeral attire. Their son, Ben, hated purple and normally would've rebelled, but he'd do anything for his mom. Even that.

Josh turned the faucet handle and shucked his shirt while waiting for warm water. Bending down, he quickly scrubbed his face with Carolyn's fancy face soap, rinsed, then dried with a hand towel that left pink lint stuck to his stubbled face. He dropped the towel onto the floor next to the discarded shirt, briefly wondering if he should throw it away. He didn't need a reminder of yesterday every time he opened the closet.

As he brushed his teeth, the lights above the mirror danced on a bottle of perfume sitting on the vanity. Josh reached for it and pressed the gold nozzle, releasing a spritz of a citrus bouquet. Instantly his memory flew to Paris, where he'd bought the *parfum* in a small shop on the Champs-Elysées. Carolyn had looked lovely that day, wearing a large-brimmed hat, black sunglasses, gold-hooped earrings, and a sundress... *oh my God*... the same floral dress he'd envisioned earlier as she ran in the field.

Tears he didn't think he had rapidly returned. Unable and unwilling to fight the emotion, Josh eased himself onto the edge of the tub, holding the perfume bottle with both hands, and let the grief engulf him. When he finally stood, he gently placed the bottle back on the vanity, knowing it would stay there for a very long time.

A shower and fresh clothes did wonders, but much-needed coffee could no longer wait. Josh put an ear to the bedroom door, listening for human sounds. *Probably still asleep.* He opened the door quietly, peeked down the hall, then padded barefoot to the kitchen, where he fixed a cup of Melozio coffee in the Nespresso machine. Cinnamon, cream, sweetener, and a quick stir finished the concoction, which swiftly found its way to Josh's lips. He leaned against the counter, savoring the taste and the aroma.

In his previous life, Carolyn would be seated at the breakfast table in her blue silk robe, tanned legs crossed, sipping tea, and smiling at him as he entered the room. Never a morning person himself, it was difficult to match his wife's cheerfulness, but somehow she managed to bring him out of his I'm-not-awake-yet funk. She'd hold up the newspaper, point to a specific article, and say, "You have to read this. It's hysterical." Or she'd read a comic strip using different voices and foreign accents for the characters, which always made him smile. Or roll his eyes. She became quite the impersonator and sometimes took that talent to the bedroom for some excellent role-playing.

But the kitchen, eerily quiet now, would remain that way after the kids left to resume their lives. The new normal, as they say. He hated the new normal. Josh looked at the beautiful cabinetry, appliances, and granite countertops meticulously chosen by Carolyn during a major renovation years ago. It was love at first sight when they saw the house, saying many times they couldn't believe they owned a home in the historic district. Translation: it needed updating—and lots of it.

The kitchen project began the long process of tearing down walls, ripping up floors, and replacing old fixtures with trendier ones. Now he lived in a brand new house sitting inside a very old shell, the perfect home in the perfect neighborhood with a bereavement wreath hanging on the front door.

Josh made it back to his bedroom sanctuary uninterrupted. He wasn't ready to get out of his head where Carolyn lived right now. He felt her fragile presence and wanted to cling to it as long as possible. He walked by the bookcase, pushed a button on the CD player, and heard the whirring of the disc as he sank into the cushions of a velvet chair. He'd kidded Carolyn about the feminine decor of their bedroom, which was rose, blush, and pastel green, but he didn't mind. It reflected her soft side; he loved it, even the tasseled floral drapes and gazillion pillows on the bed.

Josh propped his feet on an ottoman and looked out the window at the manicured lawn. Throughout the years, he and Carolyn spent many hours researching plants, building hardscapes, and placing bird baths in just the right spot. And when they raked leaves in the fall, sometimes they played loud music and danced, causing some of their fuddy-duddy neighbors to stare. But yesterday changed all that.

He lifted the old blue coffee mug, a staple in the house, to his lips. The writing said, "My husband ran away with my best friend. I'm gonna miss that girl." Carolyn bought the mug as a joke, but since that day, he rarely drank coffee out of anything else.

Soft instrumental music now filled the room as well as his heart. The CD, a favorite of theirs, featured a group they'd seen in concert many times. Josh closed his eyes, listening, escaping, slow-dancing to the beat. He smiled. With her wrists crossed behind his neck, his wife of many years teased him with her green eyes as his hands slid slowly down her back to caress soft curves below.

"Knock, knock!"

Josh jumped at the sudden intrusion, then cleared his throat. "Yeah?"

"Dad, think you can eat something?" The voice, soft and lilting like her mother's, belonged to his daughter, Kathryn. "I'm heating a French toast casserole somebody brought. It looks delish. Plus, we have fruit if you're counting calories."

Just the thought of food turned his stomach sour. "Not now, Kat. Thanks."

"Dad?"

"Yes?"

"Will the pain ever go away?"

Not anytime soon. "Yes, baby girl. We'll be fine. Enjoy your breakfast. I'll see you in a little while."

Josh stayed sequestered in his room most of the day, reminiscing, crying, and napping in between.

Twice he left to check on the kids, who were hanging out in the den with friends who came and went. Like many funerals, the occasion allowed people to catch up with others they rarely saw. It also allowed Josh to be alone, knowing his children were kept busy.

The abundance of food containers grew throughout the day, scattered on countertops, inside the fridge and freezer, and spilling onto the dining room table. *We'll never be able to eat all that stuff.* He wondered who started the tradition of people bringing food when someone died. As a child, he'd called it death food and wouldn't touch it. Now, he figured it made people feel good, helping in one of the few ways they could, nourishing the grieving family. He admitted some of it looked and smelled delicious, but he only managed to nibble on saltines and peanut butter. Eating seemed selfish. Carolyn wasn't eating, so why should he?

She hadn't been able to eat much in the last week of her life, no matter how much he'd begged her to try. Then he reminded himself of *another* thing she no longer dealt with—pain, sickness, and chemicals dripping into her fragile body. A double-edged sword, death. No more pain meant no more Carolyn. *If I could only talk to her one more time.*

That evening, the kids coerced Josh out of isolation. Even though they weren't children anymore, he felt guilty for abandoning them all day. They were hurting, too. He told himself he'd stay just long enough to see how they were doing, answer questions, then say goodnight. But one thing led to another, and before he knew it, they were huddled under blankets, eating popcorn, slurping sodas, and watching an old Halloween movie. Things seemed almost normal.

"Remember how scared Mom would get?" Ben asked. "And she'd cover her ears and close her eyes during the good parts?"

Josh chuckled. "Our definition of *good* did not match up with hers."

"But she still watched it, even though she didn't want to."

"That's because she loved you and wanted to be near you. Seems like she watched *you* more than the movie."

"Don't forget *you*, Dad. She loved you, too."

He smiled. "I know. The day I met your mom? Best day of my life." *And yesterday, the worst.*

The discussion with Ben and Kathryn felt good and natural, lifting the cloud of gloom and giving Josh a feeling of hope. *I'm supposed to be comforting them, but it's the opposite.* He didn't know how to handle that, but one thing he knew was Carolyn would be happy that he even noticed it. She'd often teased him about not living in the present.

Josh grabbed the remote off the coffee table and muted the TV. "Hey. I want to thank you for letting me veg in my room today. I had to do it and needed to do it. For all of us."

"It's okay, Dad," said Kathryn. "We knew the dam would crack after all you've shouldered."

"When did you become so wise?"

She giggled. "I've always been smart, but in this case, Mom told us it would happen and to let you be until you were ready."

He nodded slowly, then encircled them with a big bear hug. "I love you so much."

"We love you, too."

Josh handed the remote to Ben and got up from the couch. He looked at them both, proud to be their father. "We're going to be fine. It will take time, but we'll get there. Together. And no more solitary confinement for me. You need me? Come running. Okay?"

"Okay. 'Night Dad."

Josh watched the eleven o'clock news and tried to read a few pages of the latest Jack Bowie thriller, but he grew tired quickly. He turned off the television and lamp, then settled in, facing Carolyn's side of the bed. Loneliness tightened its grip on his heart, causing him to grab her pillow and cradle it against his chest. He took a deep breath, detecting a faint scent of moisturizer, and breathed into the pillow again, squeezing it. He heard a slight crackling and curiously massaged the pillow, searching for the cause when it happened again. *Probably that tag you're not supposed to remove or face being prosecuted to the fullest extent of the law.* He felt around for the opening and crammed his hand inside.

Josh sat up, almost knocking the lamp over, clumsily found the switch, and turned it back on. Shock registered when he saw Carolyn's handwriting on the paper he held, with his name on it.

My dearest Josh,

If you're reading this, it means, well, you know what it means. I thought we'd grow old together. I wasn't crazy about the 'old' part, but I loved the 'together' part.

It's hard to write this. I don't want to go, but we both know I have no control. I try not to think about everything I'll miss, but it creeps in every once in a while, like the Kathryn getting married, grandchildren, you, and friendships.

Speaking of friends, I hope you and the kids are uplifted by the service. No doubt the girls will do a fabulous job with their part. If they don't, you tell them to look for signs of my displeasure. I should've asked for a preview, but that would've been super weird, even for me.

I'm writing this note not because I like to have the last word, which I do, but to ask for one more favor. You've done so much already, but... ha ... Would you please go to the cabin and spend time with the girls and hubs before they leave? I'm guessing you're holed up in our bedroom, not talking, not eating. That would be okay, but time is of the essence. They are here for a few short days.

I'm asking you to grieve later. Cry later. You may never see them again, which would break my heart. I know everyone promised to keep in touch, but we both know how time has a way of whittling away good intentions.

Please do this for yourself and me. Have one more conversation with Molly, CeeCee, and Lynn, as if it's your last. Make it meaningful. Say things I can no longer say. Speak to them using your voice and my soul. Comfort them. Please. Share my last month with them if you can. They'll want to know. They'll *need* to know because they're part of me.

I don't want the memories they have of me, you, and our precious family, to stop with the day I die. There is more life to live and more love to give. I'll see you again one day.

Until then, my love, find happiness. Not *too* soon. Ha. But find it.

I Love You,

Carolyn

Chapter Fourteen

Molly volunteered to be on watch while Lynn and CeeCee slept. With flashlight in hand, she prowled around the store like a security guard peering out windows and checking the status of doors. The routine got old quickly, so she slouched on one end of the couch with her head propped on the arm. How anyone could sleep through this storm baffled her. The store's inadequate insulation allowed the wind to whistle through various openings and howl through others, and Mother Nature was putting on quite a show. Molly could think of a million safer places to be, yet her counterparts slept like babies.

A pop of lightning lit up the store briefly and allowed Molly to scan the shadows. Again. Her nerves were raw, and she couldn't wait for sunrise. Being in the dark by choice was one thing, but *this* was torture.

Tonight could not end fast enough. Another bolt of lightning struck, making Molly jump off the couch.

<Crack!>

The unmistakable sound sent her scrambling to the window just as a tree crashed to the ground, and her car alarm confirmed it was a direct hit.

"Shit!"

Under branches and leaves, the SUV lights blinked in unison with the beeping horn as if sending out an SOS. Molly grabbed the key fob out of her purse and pointed it at the car to stop the noise, hoping it would work through the debris. It didn't disappoint, and she smirked at her misplaced relief.

"My car is destroyed, but I'm happy the remote works?" she asked no one in particular. "Heaven forbid I wake anyone, including the dead, when my $60,000 car just got flattened."

"Did I hear a horn?"

Molly screamed and spun around to see Lynn standing so close they could've been inside the same shirt. "You scared the shit out of me. Jesus! And yes, your Uber is here." *What is wrong with people?*

Lynn looked out the window as another flash in the sky showcased the mess outside. She gasped and leaned in to hug her friend. "Oh, no-o-o. I'm so sorry."

Molly remained motionless like a mannequin, staring into space, wanting to cry. "Bill is going to kill me."

CeeCee unfolded herself from the chair, stretched her arms, and yawned, then looked from Molly to Lynn. "What's up?"

Molly agonized over the damage to her car, but they all agreed to wait until the storm passed and daylight arrived before they did anything. After three hours of anguish, they finally unboarded the door and stepped out to fresh air and wreckage.

Lynn and CeeCee put their arms around Molly as they approached. Molly sighed. "I guess it needs more than a brake job now." Her attempt at humor during a terrible situation usually made her feel a little better, but this time it didn't. Twenty-four hours ago, she was in the hotel drinking bad coffee with Bill, and her biggest worry was speaking at the funeral. If she'd only known then what she knew now, she wouldn't be staring at a two-foot diameter tree sprawled across her SUV. She walked closer and discovered the glass in the windshield and back hatch was shattered, and all four doors were jammed.

"This weekend keeps getting better and better," Molly said.

"Ya pissed off yet?" CeeCee asked.

"Getting there," Molly replied. "Only coffee can keep me from snapping."

The girls made their way around the car and walked to the edge of the woods, where the remains of the splintered tree stood. Smoke still rose from the lightning's strike point and stung their nostrils.

"Dang," said CeeCee.

"Exactly," Molly replied. "When I see something like this, it reminds me how unimportant we are and that we have no control over anything."

"I know what you mean," said CeeCee. "One second, the tree stood proudly in the forest. The next, it didn't. But if the Universe deemed the tree to fall..."

"What kind of mumbo jumbo are you saying?" asked Molly. "Are you really getting philosophical at a time like this?"

"No, what I'm getting at is, we should be thankful it fell where it did." CeeCee pointed to her left. "A few more degrees in that direction, and we could've been killed."

"So, I should be happy my car got annihilated?"

"Let's just say it took one for the team."

After the girls finished their inspection, Lynn went to the bathroom to freshen up; CeeCee stayed on the porch, and Molly walked toward the back of the store. "I'm going to get my phone or what's left of it."

"It's *outside?*" asked CeeCee. "That thing's toast."

"That's what I'm afraid of. Like my car, it's new. I dropped the old one into the commode."

"I bet that happens a lot, but people probably lie about it." As Molly rounded the corner, CeeCee shouted, "Will you check our barricade while you're there?"

Molly returned shortly, empty-handed. "I have good news and bad news. The door is secure, but my phone isn't. I looked everywhere. Even searched through the muddy sections that smell like pee."

"Ew," said CeeCee. "How could it not be there? Unless…."

The hairs on the back of Molly's neck stood up. "Oh my God, somebody *did* get out of the truck last night, lurking in the dark like the snakes they are."

CeeCee's eyes widened. "We were in more danger than we thought. But why take the phone? It doesn't even work here."

"To intimidate us, that's why."

"Well, it's working," CeeCee admitted. "Creepy is what it is. Makes my skin crawl and my stomach hurt."

"Mine, too," said Molly. "We've got to get out of here or form a plan, but I can't think straight, especially without coffee."

Lynn stepped out onto the porch. "Did I hear something about coffee? Too bad we don't have a generator or something."

Molly grabbed her up into a big hug. "You're a genius!" She trotted to the back of her car and gently reached through the broken glass. "Bill gave me this converter thing for Christmas, which I did not love, plus it pissed me off he got me an appliance of any kind." She pulled it out and showed it to them. "I guess his present wasn't so dumb after all."

CeeCee laughed. "I'm sure he'll see the compliment in there somewhere."

Molly unzipped the converter cover and briefly scanned the instructions. "Okay, all we have to do is plug it into the cigarette lighter. Who wants to crawl through to the front while I get Big Jon's coffee maker?"

"I'll go," said Lynn, "but I get the first cup."

"You're getting bossier by the day. But it's a deal."

After consuming two pots of coffee and eating chocolate snack cakes filled with white cream, Molly and CeeCee rested in the rockers on the front porch while Lynn napped inside. Last night's events were still taking their toll on her, so no one told Lynn about the backdoor visitor. CeeCee propped her leg on a wooden crate with the makeshift compress, a plastic bag filled with slushy ice from the cooler and two cans of soda, on her swelling knee.

"I need protein," said Molly. "And fiber before my stomach explodes."

CeeCee giggled. "Saw a squirrel earlier. We can cook it up over a fire along with some other vittles."

Molly laughed. "Or we wait for someone to show up and take us to the hotel where there is real food. Why do you think no cars have come by?"

"I've been wondering the same thing," CeeCee replied. "I know the weather is iffy, but people still get out and about, especially on a Saturday. And where is the storekeeper? I would think weekends are big for bait shops."

Molly shook her head, trying to figure it out. "You think the roads are blocked? Maybe our tree isn't the only one that fell."

CeeCee frowned. "I hope not. I'd hate to think we have to stay here another night."

They discussed the pros and cons of walking to the cabin and finally determined CeeCee couldn't handle it. Her knee seemed to be getting bigger by the hour despite the ice. They would wait it out, hope someone would show up, and if not, they'd prepare to overnight inside Big Jon's again. Rolling thunder confirmed their decision to stay put, and hard rain soon followed. They listened to it beat on the tin porch roof until Molly found the rest she needed. And sleep.

Chapter Fifteen

Cory peeled a banana, deposited half of it in his mouth, and studied the cabin's construction.

“I don’t know how they got supplies back here, especially concrete trucks and flatbeds to haul these logs. It has to be three miles from the main road.”

Standing against the railing, Bill nodded, then sauntered over to an exterior corner. “Have you looked at the way these suckers are connected? Dovetails.”

Cory joined him and admired the workmanship. “You’d think a place like this, as expensive as it is, would have a way to communicate with the outside world. Still doesn’t make sense.”

“Probably built before technology exploded, now that I think about it,” said Bill. “No internet, no computers, and it would cost a fortune to run a cable all this way. I’d love to ask Josh about it if I ever see him again. Probably doubtful."

"You may be right, and that's a shame in a way. He's kind of like a distant relative that you know but don't know. Ya know?"

Bill laughed. "I do know what you mean. I think Molly sees him as a brother-in-law because of the girls' closeness. Sisters from another mister, so to speak."

"You got a brother?" asked Cory.

"Two."

"So, if your brother passed away, would you still include his wife in things? Would you stay bonded, or would you let her fade away as if she died, too?"

"Damn, that's harsh," Bill said.

"Probably could have worded it better, but you know what I'm saying."

"I do. I love my sister-in-law and can't imagine not having her in our lives. And their kids."

"So," Cory continued, "Should we expect our wives to write off Josh because Carolyn died?"

"Hadn't thought about it, but the right answer has to be no."

"So, maybe that's where we come in. We can't just kick him to the curb or out of the circle. He's lost enough already."

Bill looked at him as if he'd just grown another head. "Profound, man. Where'd that come from?"

"I have no idea," said Cory, "but if you tell anybody, I'll have to kill you."

"Your secret is safe with me."

"What secret?" asked Adam coming out the front door, balancing a turkey sandwich in one hand and a beer in the other.

"I'm going to walk to the main road and catch a ride to the hotel," Cory said.

Bill frowned. "That's news to me."

"Why is that a secret?" Adam repeated.

Cory shrugged. "That's *not* the secret. And we were just kidding around, but if you keep asking, I'm going to provoke the patient-doctor privacy act."

"That's not what it's called," said Adam.

"Anyway, I'd like to leave soon," Cory said. "Within a half-hour."

"I'm going with you," Adam declared.

"See?" Cory replied. "That's why I wanted it to be a secret. You can barely walk from the kitchen to the porch. How do you think you can walk three miles?" He flicked a beetle off the railing. "How are you feeling, by the way?"

"Nothing wrong with my legs," Adam shot back.

"That may be. But your face, and I'm guessing your ribs, say different. No one in their right mind would let you in a car. You look like a decomposing eggplant. No offense."

"And whose fault is that?" He turned to Bill. "Knowing this Neanderthal, he'd get to the hotel, not tell anybody, and leave us here to rot."

Cory rolled his eyes. "Don't be so dramatic. First of all, you would not rot. Second, you need to learn the definition of Neanderthal. They were very intelligent beings, not like cavemen."

Adam snorted.

"If anyone goes, it should be me," said Bill.

"Yeah, why's that?" asked Cory. "You think I can't make it?"

"Didn't say that. Damn, you guys get your knickers in a wad faster than anyone I've ever met." He paused and took a deep breath. "I'm trying to say that I'm a wilderness hiker and run several miles a week."

"I'm in pretty good shape myself," Cory said. "You know, from carrying people out of burning buildings?"

Bill held up his hands in surrender. "Okay, I give up, but we need a plan."

Fifteen minutes later, Cory gathered bottles of water, trail mix, and apples from the kitchen. He guzzled orange juice straight from the container and stared out the window at the garbage bag covering the window of his SUV. Last night's scene played in his head. *Maybe I am a caveman*. He took another swig and turned to see who had entered the kitchen.

Cory's reflex to swallow and his urge to laugh clashed violently, causing an instant eruption of orange all over the countertop. A coughing fit ensued, and juice trickled out of his nose, burning like hell. He snatched a dishtowel from a hook and covered his face until the sputtering stopped.

There Adam stood, decked out in nicely creased dress shorts, a heavily starched shirt with rolled-up sleeves, and leather loafers. No socks. The only thing out of place was the duct-taped tee shirt.

"I'm confused," he said, barely able to keep a straight face. "Is there a champagne brunch on the front lawn today?"

"This is all I brought."

"You have to be kidding. You can't hike through the woods dressed like that. Maybe you can wear something of Bill's."

"Didn't realize the forest had a dress code." Adam lifted his bag, grimacing as he struggled to put the straps over his shoulder. "I can take care of myself."

Cory eyed the mass of Adam's bag. "We have to come back for our vehicles. Lighten the load."

"I'm not coming back to this place. Ever. Lynn can drive the damn SUV home, or off a cliff with her in it. I'm taking the first flight out. Either way, we're done." He walked outside, slamming the door on his way.

Cory grabbed the water and snacks, scampered outside, and handed some to Adam. "Come on, man, you don't mean that. I know you're upset, but that's pretty drastic. Even by *my* standards. Surely you guys can work through this."

"Upset? Upset is in the rearview mirror, my friend. I'm in warp speed towards divorce court."

Bill joined the two men outside and looked questioningly at Cory.

"Don't waste your breath. He knows *everything*, remember? Let me go get my pack."

The men set a suitable pace and walked three abreast for several minutes. The crunch of gravel and the snap of dead leaves created a cadence similar to a snare drum. When the road narrowed, they separated, choosing individual paths as they dodged tree roots, prickly vines, and standing puddles from the previous night's rain. Bill led. Cory took the rear.

The hike had been uneventful at first, with easy footing, but that began to change, as did the landscape. Deep, rocky ruts caused by years of erosion, loose mud, and exposed roots and stumps slowed their movement, making it more demanding, especially for leather-soled shoes with no grip. As the incline increased, Adam's strides shortened and slowed drastically. It was hot and muggy for a fall day, and he struggled to breathe, not a good thing for someone battered and bruised.

A moss-covered log about fifteen feet into the woods caught Cory's eye. "Hey, how about we stop for a second? I could use something to drink and catch my breath."

No one objected to the stop, so the three men trudged in that direction, circumventing thorny undergrowth that could snag or trip them up. Cory dropped his pack to the ground with a thud and kept walking toward some mountain laurels. "Gotta see a man about a horse."

"Watch for poison ivy," Bill shouted. "That's the last thing you need."

"You got that right," said Cory when he returned. "I had a severe case a few years back. Talk about torture. I thought I would have to die to feel better."

He gave the log a thorough examination before he deemed it appropriate seating, then plopped down and opened his backpack. The beer can hissed as he popped the top, then he took a couple of gulps before tossing trail mix into his mouth. "Took six weeks for the blisters to go away, all caused by a stupid little leaf."

"You brought beer?" Adam asked as he unscrewed the cap to his water.

Cory nodded. "Didn't you?"

"No."

"Too bad. Nothing better when you're hot and sweaty in the middle of nowhere."

"You have more?"

"No, but I'll give you a sip if you won't spit in the can."

"I'll pass. How far do you guys think we've gone?" asked Adam.

Bill looked at his watch and tapped it with his index finger. "I've taken about three thousand steps. Normally that's about a mile for me, but this walk isn't normal."

"Not sure it matters since we don't know how far the road is," Cory said, taking another swig of his beer.

Adam continued to sweat profusely. Large sections of his shirt were ringing wet, and his fashion footwear made his feet and ankles swell. He looked miserable.

Bill took his ball cap off and fanned himself. "Peaceful, isn't it? Just us and Mother Nature." Suddenly thunder shook the ground, and a few seconds later, lightning crossed the sky.

"And Mother Nature bites you in the ass sometimes," said Cory.

"Dammit!" Adam shouted and sprang to his feet, slapping at the back of his leg.

"Look! She just bit one now," Cory said, laughing at his own joke.

Bill chuckled.

"Something stung me, I think. Man, that hurt." He bent to see the source of the pain and found himself staring into the eyes of a snake. "Snake! Get up! Get up!"

Cory and Bill lept off the log, high-stepping like drum majors in front of a college band.

"Are you sure it's a reptile and not an amphibian?" asked Cory. "I want to make sure we use the right terminology.'

"Screw you."

"Did you notice what kind it was?" asked Bill.

"Yeah. I got its phone number, too."

"Any markings?"

"All black, maybe. Jeez, what difference does it make? A snake's a snake."

"Okay. Calm down." Bill and Cory both crouched and saw two small punctures on the back of Adam's calf. A pink circular pattern already surrounded the punctures, which caused the men to exchange worried looks.

The snake had slithered under the log and disappeared, but Bill stepped cautiously towards it to grab his backpack, then walked backward, never taking his eyes off the reptile's hideout. Quickly he unzipped a side pocket. "I can't *believe* this."

"Me either," said Adam. "What else can happen to me in this God-forsaken place?"

"No, not that. I always pack mosquito repellent, band-aids, antibiotic ointment, things like that, including a snake bite kit."

"Seriously?" asked Adam. "Who does that? You still a boy scout?"

"Used to be, but experienced hikers do this, that's who," Bill said. "But since you're being a turd, I don't feel bad telling you it's not in my pack. I know I brought it, though."

"Where is it?" Adam asked, taking a different tone.

"Well, I'm guessing it's in the car, the one Molly took."

"You've got to be shitting me," Adam said, his voice getting higher and louder.

"We can't go any further. We need to go back," said Bill.

"I need to get to a hospital!" screamed Adam. "I'm dying!"

"Yes, probably."

"*What?*"

"I meant, yes, you might need to go to a hospital," Bill said. "But you must also get off that leg to prevent the venom from circulating. Our best hope is that Josh has a kit in the cabin."

"If I don't die first, I'm going to kill that bitch," Adam said. "This is her fault, just like every other thing that goes wrong with my life."

"You are some piece of work, dude," Cory said. "I bet you're fun to live with."

After searching the area for a proper walking stick to give to the snake-bite victim, Cory picked up Adam's bag. "What the hell you got in here? Bricks?"

Adam looked embarrassed. "Just stuff."

"Well, we need to chuck it. I'm not carrying more than I have to," Cory said. He dropped the bag to the ground and tore it open.

"Hey!" Adam shouted. "You can't just rifle through my private things. I'll do it myself."

A lightning bolt flashed across the sky, followed by thunder minutes later and gusty winds.

"Fine, it's your life. But if *my* clock were ticking, I'd make it snappy," said Cory.

Adam pulled out a hairdryer, another pair of leather shoes, binoculars, and a bottle of scotch. "Somebody's going to have an early Christmas when they find this stash," he muttered.

Cory walked over, grabbed the scotch, and took a swig. They passed it around. Twice.

"Hey. I'm wondering if we should douse the bite with alcohol," said Cory. "Or a better idea. Maybe Adam drinks a lot of it and treats it from the inside out."

Bill smiled. "Let's just stick to the plan."

Cory lifted Adam's bag again. "Better. Still feels heavy."

"Oh, put it down." Adam unzipped an inside pocket and pulled out ten rolls of quarters. He shrugged. "Thought we might play poker or something." He felt around more and lifted out a hardback novel.

"Hey, is that Josh Langston's latest Sci-fi?" Cory asked. "Any good?"

"Didn't start it last night for some reason. Oh yeah, I was too busy getting my *head* pounded in."

"Boy, you're not going to let that go, are you?" said Cory as he spied a navy blue necktie in the corner of Adam's bag. "Hand me that tie."

Adam looked suspicious. "Why? You going to strangle me now?"

"Don't give me any ideas, but no. I'm going to mark this location, so we can find your things later. Okay with you?"

After placing the belongings behind some brush, the men slowly retraced their steps. The downhill terrain made walking more manageable, but Adam struggled to keep up. He stopped.

"I feel like I can't get enough oxygen. Don't know if it's the bite or my ribs, but I may pass out."

He put his hands on his knees and hung his head, breathing slowly. "I'm not sure how much further I can go."

Cory handed his and Adam's bag to Bill. "Think you can carry all that?"

"What are you doing?" asked Adam.

Cory squatted. "Climb on."

"No way that's happening."

"It's happening," snapped Cory. "One way or another. Conscious or unconscious. Your choice."

"Oh, for God's sake," Adam grumbled as he reluctantly climbed onto the other man's back.

Bill picked up the walking stick, put it across his shoulders like a yoke, and attached the bags to it. "It may work. It may not."

The winds increased sharply, as did the frequency of thunder and lightning. The men trudged on until large raindrops fell, along with pea-sized hail. They huddled under the canopy of some small trees until the ice pellets stopped falling, then continued, hoping to avoid getting struck by lightning. Finding secure footing got more challenging and demanding for Cory, and 180 pounds of dead weight on his back did not help. He knew each step rattled Adam's ribs, but a man cannot tiptoe in this situation, so he plowed on as quickly as his body would allow. Bill, however, seemed to walk faster with his new method of carrying the bags.

"Time out," Cory shouted as he set Adam down. He mopped sweat and rain from his forehead with his shirt and waited for his respiration rate to return to normal.

"I'll walk from here," said Adam. "I'm wearing you down."

"No. I'm fine, but I need to change to a fireman's carry, which means putting you across my shoulders. That will evenly distribute your weight, and I can walk faster. The bad news is, it will jolt and hurt like hell."

Finally, the graveled road appeared, and Cory's spirits lifted, knowing the cabin would soon come into view. When it did, he placed Adam on the ground and shouted, "Home sweet home!" Even in the heavy rain, they clapped each other's backs, made a few dance moves, and high-fived as if they'd climbed to the summit of Mount Everest.

Cory felt a hand on his shoulder and turned.

"Thank you," said Adam. "I mean it. You saved my life unless I die. Either way, I owe you."

"If you die, that will be reward enough," Cory said, smiling. "I'm kidding. You don't owe me anything. But if I have to do this again, you could stand to lose a few pounds."

****

Bill's concern grew as he opened and slammed cabinet doors, not finding what he needed. He rushed into the pantry and, on the second shelf, spied a first aid kit, all kinds of ointments and bandages, plus a snake bite kit.

What if this doesn't work? He tried not to think of the consequences, but his mind wouldn't let him. *What if Adam dies? And for what? So our wives could feel better forcing friendship on us when we were perfectly happy without it?*

Bill got angry at the carelessness of the girls' lame-brained scheme. They probably never considered the men's safety or need for medical attention should an emergency arise, and now someone's life was in his hands. *Dammit.*

"You're not going to cut me open like I'm some kind of cantaloupe," Adam shouted into his armpit. He lay face down on the kitchen table, waiting for Bill to open the kit and for Cory to cut off the duct-taped tee shirt, so he could get dry.

"You know what irks me?" asked Bill. "I'm dealing with an emergency here, trying to help someone, and the instructions on the package are so small only a flea could read them. Does no one have any common sense these days? I'm sending these people a scolding email when I get home."

"Bill? How about we focus?" asked Cory.

"That's what I've been *trying* to do!" Bill exclaimed. "Okay, it says here, a bunch of don'ts. Don't put ice on the wound, don't use a tourniquet, don't let the victim move around, which causes the venom to circulate, and don't cut anything. So far, we're batting a hundred."

"I think you mean a thousand," Cory said.

Bill gave him a scathing look while Adam released the breath he'd been holding. "Who cares? What else does it say?"

"Oh, and keep the wound below the heart."

"No problem," said Cory. "Doesn't have one."

"Hardy har har," Adam responded. "Can we get this clown out of here, please?"

"Think you could prop up on your elbows without hurting your ribs?" asked Bill.

"Doubt it."

The two men grabbed Adam's feet and slid him to the end of the table until his legs dangled. Bill handed Cory a small plastic cup. "Put this over the bite, attach it to the pump, then push the plunger." He read on. "It should retrieve the venom quickly and is most effective on parts outside the muscle area.

"What did you say about muscle area?" Adam asked.

"Nothing important," Bill lied, exchanging a concerned look with Cory. Silently he kept reading. *In muscle areas such as the calf muscle, venom quickly enters the circulatory system, and the pump is less effective.*

Cory joked, "You don't have any muscle either, so you're good."

"Still not funny," said Adam.

"We don't even know if the snake is poisonous," said Cory. "Probably your garden variety black snake, who we know is our friend."

Bill applied antibiotic ointment to the wound and wrapped it in gauze. "A fun fact. Most snakes in the United States are not venomous. And if it is venomous, 25% of the time, it's a dry bite."

"Meaning?" asked Adam.

"No venom," Bill said. "I like our odds, and we're lucky Josh had this stuff on hand. How are you feeling?"

"Fine, so far, but I'm tired." He headed for the great room. "Think I'll crash for a while."

"Just keep your chest above the leg," said Cory. "We'll check it soon to see if it's fallen off."

Adam nodded and collapsed onto the soft leather couch. "*Still* not funny."

Chapter Sixteen

The storm eventually drove the girls off the porch, and once inside, they repeated the process of securing the front door. With no power or sunshine, the store became dark again, so Molly lit the candles she was so proud of finding, opened a deck of cards, and shuffled. "Who's up for Hearts?"

Lynn pulled her chair closer to the makeshift coffee table. "I haven't played since college. May not remember the rules. But I *do* know that I kicked your asses daily, which made me the *Queen* of Hearts."

Later, with a cigarette hanging out of the corner of her mouth and a sun visor on her head, CeeCee said, "I'm going to have to talk to Big Jon about updating these cushions. I feel like I'm sitting on the floor, and a metal coil is getting too familiar with my rear end."

"Just deal the cards," said Lynn. "You're stalling because you're losing."

Molly laughed. "Speaking of cushions, I've got a story for you."

"Bill and I bought a new sofa a while back, and I asked him to spray it with a protectant while I ran errands. When I got home, the cushions were still in the original position."

Molly deepened her voice, impersonating Bill. "Yep. Got it done in no time. Wasn't a big deal."

"Pointing at the cushions, I said they must've dried pretty fast since they're back down. He said, 'What d'ya mean? I didn't move them in the first place.'

"I asked if he'd sprayed the underside or the backs, and he said no. In my mind, I pictured him spritzing the entire couch as it sat and calling it a day. I guess he read the look on my face and said, 'I have a feeling that's not right.'

"I tried not to look too judgy but finally mentioned that we flip the cushions over from time to time. He looked a little dejected and said, 'Didn't think of that.'"

Lynn laughed. "Of course not. He needed a flow chart and written instructions."

Molly snorted. "Instructions? He doesn't even look at the ones provided when 'some assembly is required.' He thinks it's insulting or some such nonsense."

"Men are funny," Lynn said. "You know how Adam and I love to work in the yard? We buy four hanging baskets each year for the shepherd hooks in the backyard. More than once, Adam proudly announced, 'Hey, I watered the baskets today.' I'd ask if he watered all of them, and he says no, just these, pointing at the two closest to the garden hose. It's not long enough to reach the others, so I asked about them. 'No, they look fine, though.' But they're not fine. Never are. So, I have to get them, water, and hang them back up."

"I don't get it," said Molly. "Why not water them all? Inconvenient?"

Lynn shrugged. "Who knows? In his mind, he's helping, and in mine, he's done it half-assed, and I have to complete the task."

CeeCee finished dealing the cards and stubbed out her cigarette. "Oh, I've got one better than that. Let me tell you what happened a few weeks ago. Get yourselves comfortable."

"I know what *that* means," said Molly.

CeeCee gave her *the* look. "Ya wanna hear it or not?" She grabbed the three piles of cards she'd just dealt, stacked them neatly, and spaced them evenly in a straight line. Each stack represented a different building location. Once the girls got the lay of the land, she began.

"Cory's SUV started acting strange when shifting gears, not constantly but enough to get our attention. The same thing happened with his previous car, which broke down on vacation. What a nightmare. I worried the same thing would happen with this one but in the middle of Atlanta traffic instead. Can you imagine anything more terrifying? Everyone there drives like a maniac."

Molly raised her hand. "Can I ask a question?"

"No. Then, on Friday afternoon, the problem got worse, scaring us both, so he parked it in the garage, and we used my car over the weekend. Sunday night rolled around with no mention of getting his car fixed."

She looked at her friends. "You know that kind of thing makes me crazy, but I kept my mouth shut. Anyway, he thought the transmission was the problem and knew where he'd take the vehicle but couldn't do it on Monday. *So-ooo,* Tuesday morning Cory still hadn't made an appointment or even called. Had all of Monday to set things up, but nope. Didn't. So, I reminded him of *my* appointment at 9 a.m. and that I wouldn't be any help to him until 11-ish. He told me not to worry; it was his problem, and he'd take care of it. So I rolled my eyes, as I do on occasion, and went about my business."

CeeCee took a few sips of water, then pointed to the first pile of cards. "He planned to drop off his car here, the repair shop, then walk up a long hill to a gas station that's right beside the car rental agency." She tapped the second stack of cards to reinforce the location.

"So I asked, are you just going to show up at the transmission place? What if they're closed? He assured me they wouldn't be. After a bit of nagging, Cory called the place, and it didn't open until 8:00, so in the meantime, he lined up a rental car. 'Stick by your phone in case the car dies. I'm leaving now.'

"He made it safely, which made me happy, but his car was one of many in line for repair, and the owner couldn't say when he'd get to it. As he walked up the busy highway in eighty-degree heat, he got a call that the rental car wasn't available yet, so he went into the gas station to cool off, make a few calls, and buy a lottery ticket hoping the rental place would call soon. It didn't. With no place to sit in the gas station, my brilliant husband decided to walk *by* the rental car place across hot asphalt parking lots to Burger King where he could sit down and drink a diet soda." CeeCee pointed at the third card stack and said, "Exhibit C, or BK, as it's called."

Lynn and Molly smiled.

"After my hair appointment, I called him. Mind you, it's past 11:00 by now, and he still had no word about the rental car, but he was back at the gas station, waiting, sitting on a curb outside in the heat. I couldn't stand it, so I told him I'd pick him up."

She looked at her friends. "Okay, this is the good part. So I pulled up beside him, and he climbed into the car and said, 'This whole thing is weird.'

"I asked what he meant. He said, 'Earlier, the rental guy called and told me a car is available, then called back five minutes later and said it would be a while. I guess I shouldn't have reserved it online.'

"I asked if he'd called back or gone inside to talk to them. All I got was, 'Nah.'

"I couldn't believe my ears. The rental agency stood just 50 feet away. Fifty short feet. Right in front of our faces. Then Cory says, 'So, I'm not sure what to do. What do you think?' There I sat staring at the building, wondering if that was a trick question, reviewing all the facts, and trying to remain calm. Finally, I drove the 50 feet, where he got out and two minutes later appeared with keys in his hand."

Molly laughed. "You're making this up."

"You cannot make this stuff up, but wait. I'm not finished."

"There's more?" asked Lynn.

She nodded. "So Cory walks over to my car, pleased as punch he has a rental, and says, 'I guess I'll see ya at home.' I asked if he was going to work and again got, 'Nah. Too late now.'

"So, to wrap it up, it took more than three hours to drop off a car and pick one up, all because he wouldn't make a phone call or, God forbid, go inside and talk to a real person. And the car he got? Some sporty little two-door job. He had to fold himself in half to get inside—for three long days."

Everyone laughed while throwing out editorial comments, which caused the hysteria to grow and happy tears to roll down their cheeks. They finally calmed down, but even later, an occasional giggle escaped when someone replayed a piece of the story.

CeeCee looked at the three stacks of cards, which would be forever known as Repair Shop, Rental Place, and BK. "You want to play this hand or what?"

"I'd like to close my eyes for a bit if you don't mind," Molly said. "All that laughing wore me out."

When she woke up two hours later, she heard the familiar sounds of boards being pried off the front door, which could only mean one thing.

Lynn shouted. "Molly, wake up! They're coming!"

Chapter Seventeen

Bill took his brown leather bag upstairs to the bedroom and dropped it on the unmade bed. The soft flannel sheets and handmade cotton quilt seemed to beckon, and he thought about crawling under them. Cory sat on the porch reading, and Adam slept on the couch downstairs, so he welcomed the opportunity to think and relax. He stared at the bed again and felt his eyelids getting heavy, so he pushed the bag aside, shucked the wet clothes, and lay down.

An hour later, refreshed, Bill unzipped the bag's center section and retrieved navy plaid boxers, a green tee shirt, and a burgundy pullover. He threw them on the bed, put his bag on the dresser, and headed for the shower. He thought he felt something brush against his foot but ignored it.

The adjoining bathroom was rustic like the rest of the cabin but beautifully finished with all the bells and whistles. Thick cotton towels hung on bronze bars, and a woven basket on the back of the commode held every toiletry item imaginable. The vanity top, constructed from one big cedar plank, had a glass-like sheen. Bill ran his hand across it. Nice.

He opened the glass door to the shower, admiring the tile's design of leafless trees against a white background. The floor, made of raised pebbles, massaged his feet as he shoved his face under the showerhead and scrubbed away 24 hours of tension. He liked the soap and wondered if Josh would miss the extra bar in the basket. *Is that considered stealing?*

After Bill shaved and brushed his teeth, he walked into the bedroom to dress. His bare foot touched something on the carpet, reminding him he'd felt something earlier, and he jumped back. Moving the quilt out of the way, he cautiously bent down and peeked under the bed, ready to bolt if necessary, but the mythical monster was simply a piece of paper. Instead of getting on his knees, he deftly picked it up with his toes, a skill that Molly envied. No matter how hard she tried, she never got the hang of it. She was the athlete. Not he. He smiled, just thinking about her. *But I'm still mad.*

The folded paper had Bill's name on it. *Maybe Molly's sharing some insight.* He opened it, and the glaring difference lept off the page. The handwriting did not belong to his wife.

As Bill sat in a chair next to the bedroom windows, a brief opening in the clouds allowed sunlight to spill over his shoulder and onto the shocking note he'd just read. He replayed his last conversation with Molly, where she'd evaded questions about the weekend, but instead of pushing the point, he let it go. And just before going down to the dock, he caught her looking at him. "What? Something on my face?" he'd asked and swiped at his chin.

"Nope. Just love you. That's all. Thanks for coming on this trip."

He'd told her he'd do anything for her. Then she squeezed his arm and turned away. *She was trying to say something but couldn't.*

And that *something* was someone needed his help. Bill sighed. *Why didn't she just tell me?* Bill grew aggravated. Communication is something he and Molly did well, or so he thought, but he couldn't dwell on it now. Time to put on his psychologist's cap and see what he could do, if anything.

****

Adam awoke, feeling like someone had let all the air out of him, so he remained in bed and watched the ceiling fan slowly rotate. He'd been on the couch earlier, but Cory talked him into finding a bed so he could stretch out and get some real rest.

He bent his right knee, placed his left ankle on it, and slid the gauze down to look at his calf. With no signs of increased swelling or reddened skin, he eased himself off the bed and headed for the bathroom, where he encountered an alien in the mirror. Adam saw bruises in various shades of purple and blue and scabs on several minor cuts. His swollen duck mouth reminded him of women with too much filler injected into their lips. He and Lynn often joked about it, saying, "Her lips entered the room two seconds before the rest of her."

"She'd get a laugh out of this," he said to the thing staring back at him. He mashed down several oily sprigs of hair, but they sprang back in defiance. He needed a long hot shower, but his things, the ones allowed, were in the dining room—where the snake venom exorcism had taken place. The rest of his stuff still lay in the jungle out there. Not sure he had the energy to heave the bag and himself back to the second floor, he pondered the situation, but being clean won. He sighed and slowly walked downstairs, feeling deflated, ugly, and dirty. He hated being dirty.

Cory had his foot on the bottom step when Adam came down. "Just on my way up to check on you. How are you feeling? Anything weird going on?"

"The bite hasn't changed, but my face is revolting, ribs hurt like hell, and I smell like a goat. Other than that, I'm great."

"Glad to hear it," Cory said. "You need your bag?"

Adam nodded.

Cory turned towards the dining room.

"Hey, something dropped out of your pocket," said Adam.

As Cory bent to pick it up, Adam recognized his name on the note written in his wife's hand.

"That had better not be what I think it is," he said, pushing Cory aside and snatching the letter off the floor. It hurt like hell to bend, but he had no choice. Spit flew from his mouth as he hissed, "Who the fuck do you think you are? I swear to God, if I had a gun, I'd put a bullet right between your eyes."

Cory stepped back, hands in the air. "I didn't read the damn thing. Jeez, forgot I even had it."

"That's what all the guilty people say. But yet, there's the evidence in your pocket. You're no better than they are. Something to scrape off the bottom of my shoe."

Cory's eyes flashed with anger. "And you might be pulling *my* shoe out of your ass if you say much more. I'll never understand how a sweet lady like Lynn ended up with a piece of shit like you. It must feel like curling up to a copperhead. She knows you're going to bite, just not when."

"Why did you have it?" Adam screamed.

Cory cocked his head, looking at the attorney. "I found it on the couch earlier, and I just jammed it in my pocket to return to you, but I forgot all about it. So, I'm going to tell you one more time. I did *not* read it. Period. You can spit and spew like a rabid skunk, but that won't change the facts."

"I don't believe you."

Cory shrugged. "I don't give a damn what you believe. That's *your* problem." He started to turn away but stopped. "Ya know, I may not be the most educated man here, *counselor*, but your hysteria over a little letter makes me curious. What's in it that's so bad you don't want anyone to know?"

"I'm wondering the same thing," said Bill as he descended the stairs.

"Wonder all you want," Adam shouted. "It's none of your goddamn business."

Bill walked past the two men, calmly dropped onto the leather couch, and patted one of the cushions. "What do you say we sit down and talk about this like adults?"

Adam smirked. "I'm not talking to a shrink about anything, especially one who's not a real doctor. And a fireman? Get real."

"Insults tell me you're putting up a front because we threaten you in some way, but you might change your mind." Bill held something up between two fingers and showed it to Adam. "Anything look familiar?"

Adam walked closer, recognized Lynn's handwriting, and collapsed into the chair next to the couch. His world was crashing.

Cory sat, too. "What is that? I don't get it."

"You want to tell him, Adam?"

"I don't know what it is, but I can speculate," he said. "That's a note from Lynn."

"She wrote to Bill?" asked Cory. "Why?"

"My guess is, she ratted me out." He looked at Bill. "Is that about right?"

"I see it as a cry for help," said Bill. "I hope you'll look at it that way, too."

Adam looked down at his bare feet and said nothing. His stomach churned, and he felt cornered like a wild animal. He wanted to scream, lash out, break things, shout every vulgar word he'd ever heard, and call the two men condescending names, but it wouldn't change anything. He knew what he needed to do and *had* to do, so he slowly unfolded his wife's letter.

The paper quivered in his hand as he stared at it, trying to form the words Lynn wrote, but shame flooded through his entire body, making him want to vomit. He threw the note at Bill and turned to go back upstairs.

"I'm not doing this. I don't want to, and I don't have to. Read it yourself if you're so damn interested."

"Okay," Cory said. "What's happening here?"

Bill opened Lynn's letter and read it aloud.

Dear Adam,

I can imagine how mad you are right now, the anger building with every minute that goes by. Actually, I don't have to imagine it. I've seen it many times, as you know. I do wonder how you're getting along with the guys. Are you playing your little game, keeping up the façade? Thinking you're superior and they're not worthy, even though it's the other way around?

As you like to say, the bottom line is this: I've put up with your abuse for too long. I've hidden the ugliness that lives secretly inside you, and I've changed into someone I don't recognize. You've turned me into a liar, and I hate liars. You've made me weak, a victim, and a statistic of domestic abuse. I despise you for it.

Leaving you this weekend is the hardest decision I've ever made in my life. Not because it's the wrong decision. It isn't. It's fear. Plain and simple. Afraid of my own husband. It's laughable really. Or it would've been twenty years ago. That younger me would never have questioned my ability to stand up for myself. It was a given, and God help anyone who doubted it. But here I am, an empty shell leading a life of shame, thanks to you.

My friends are one thing that keeps me going, and no, they don't know about your behavior. After all these years of living with a monster, I've protected you, your image, your manhood, everything. And for what? So I could be talked down to, bossed around like a child, made into a servant, and threatened if I didn't behave? What does that say about you and your insecurities? What does that say about me?

You have a lot of issues, Adam, and I can't fix them. I've tried like hell, but that ends now.

I often wonder what happened to that college boy I fell in love with.

Lynn

Hidden in the hallway at the top of the stairs, Adam listened to Bill read the letter. Tears rolled down his face as humiliation crept in, putting a death grip on his heart. He walked down the stairs and sat near the fireplace.

"You must be exhausted from this mental charade," said Bill. "The anger, the hurt, feeling less-than. Your life is miserable because you've never dealt with it, fearing what would happen if you did. Who and what you'd lose. Like respect, influence, money, control. And Lynn."

Hearing his wife's name, Adam looked at Bill and nodded. "Especially Lynn."

The men sat silently for several minutes. Then Adam stood, walked to the bathroom, and splashed his face with cold water. He returned but did not sit.

"I don't know what gets into me. I know better. But something snaps. It just snaps. The rage is too much, like a poison pulsing through my blood. I can't control it, so I strike. And afterward, I hate myself."

"What are you so mad about?" asked Bill.

"I don't know, man."

"Does abuse run in the family? Any role models with anger problems?"

"You kidding? Plenty."

"Your dad? Or mom?" Bill probed.

"No, no. I mean, they weren't perfect, and their arguments got loud and nasty, but I figured all parents did that."

"What about your grandparents?"

"My grandfather was cruel to my grandma. Well, sometimes. One moment he'd be okay, then something would happen, and he'd just turn into something else. His whole face distorted, and it happened so fast, you had no warning."

"Like what happens to you," said Bill.

Adam nodded, sniffing and dabbing at his eyes. "I dreaded going to their house, afraid he'd have one of his episodes. That's what grandma called them—*episodes*—like they were innocent tantrums that came and went. I felt helpless because I couldn't do anything about it. Not then anyway."

He sat down on the hearth, put his head in his hands, and cried silently. Cory went to the kitchen, brought back a glass of water and a fist full of paper towels, and handed them to him.

"Thanks." He took a long drink and blew his nose. "My grandma would try to appease him, back down, hang her head and walk around like a whipped puppy until he calmed down. Then she'd try to explain it away to me, but it was very confusing.

"And if he caught her fussing over me, he'd get mad and say, 'You're going to mollycoddle that boy into a pansy if you don't watch it. He's already on the edge.' I didn't know what he meant, but I knew it wasn't good. Grandma would wink at me, lead me into the kitchen as if nothing had happened, and we'd make cookies or biscuits. I'd stand on a little wooden stool while she told me stories, and when she rolled up her sleeves, I'd pretend not to see the bruises. After grandpa died, I stayed with her a lot, which soon became one of the best times of my life. When she died, the guilt ate me alive."

"Because you couldn't protect her?" Bill asked.

Adam nodded again, closed his eyes, and envisioned his grandma's living room where they'd sit for hours, reading. "Seeking information is what reading is all about," she'd say. Then she'd ask him to read a paragraph out loud and tell her what he learned. If he said, "Nothing," she'd say, "Now that can't be right. The author put it in there for a reason. It must mean something." So Adam would read it again and realize he'd missed something, minuscule but still there. This exercise saved his rear more times than he could count when reading briefs in college and later in his career. Often he caught things others missed. Thanks to grandma, it became his superpower.

"Do you hate Lynn?" asked Bill.

"What? Of course not."

"Do you wish her harm?"

"No!"

"Do you like her?"

"What do you mean? I love her."

"That's not the same," Bill said. "If she worked in the same office, for example, would you be friends?"

"If she'd have me," said Adam. "She makes people feel comfortable and is genuinely interested in them. She's smart, funny, and loyal. Anyone would be lucky to have her as a friend. She has a warm heart and a beautiful smile that lights up a room."

Adam thought back to their early years before they dated. He'd purposely position himself near Lynn's group of friends in the student grill, where she acted silly and laughed until she cried. She was the most beautiful girl he'd ever seen, and he loved her before he even knew her. Then one day, they barely avoided a collision, but her soda, already in motion, doused the front of his shirt and pants. She ran to get napkins to blot the stain, apologizing repeatedly and offering to have them cleaned. He declined and finally found the nerve to say, "I'll forgive you if you go out with me this weekend." And that began their journey.

Adam got up and paced in front of the fireplace. "She was a free spirit, tough as nails but as delicate as a butterfly." He sat back down on the hearth, choking back tears. "But when I finally caught her, I pulled her beautiful wings off one at a time until she could no longer fly." Adam broke down and sobbed. "How could I be so damn ignorant?"

Bill put his elbows on his knees and leaned toward Adam. "It's not about intelligence," he said. "It's about rage, a cycle that has to stop. Today. Or you're going to lose everything. Is that what you want?"

Adam shook his head. "I just don't know what to do." Then he plunged his misshapen face back into his hands.

****

Cory sat silently, listening as he witnessed a monster of a man crumble before his very eyes. He wondered if a confession of this magnitude compared to breaking a bucking bronco; Adam being the horse and Bill, the cowhand. He'd heard that people couldn't fix what they don't acknowledge, and Adam just admitted a doozy. *What happens now? Is Adam's demon spirit broken? Or will he continue to buck, snort, and kick?*

"I think we could all use a stiff adult beverage," Cory said.

It was growing dark because of the stormy skies, so he made a sweep through the room, turning on stained glass lamps that gave the house a romantic feel. He smiled at the ridiculous thought as he poured two fingers of scotch into three glasses, dropped an ice cube in each, and handed out the drinks.

"Adam, I've seen men throw themselves into harm's way to save others," said Cory, "but what you just did took a lot of courage. Letting guys you barely know read something so personal? That takes guts. I don't know if I could do it. No, I take that back. I do know, and I couldn't. You've harbored a lot of issues for a long time, and now that I know that, I want to apologize for things I've said."

Adam looked shocked. "I don't deserve an apology. I've been a total prick."

"I agree with both of those statements," said Bill. "Adam, maybe now's the time for *you* to apologize to the fireman, who, according to you, saved your life today, and to a fake doctor who might be able to help save you from yourself."

Adam nodded and looked down at his hands in his lap. "I don't know how I can ever make it up to you, but I hope you'll both let me try. I'm sorry for how I've treated you and for my shitty behavior in general. I mean it. I have no excuse for being so arrogant and treating you with disrespect. I hope someday you can forgive me."

"Thank you for saying that," Bill said.

"You've said some bad things," said Cory, "but so have I. You weren't in a good place and haven't been for some time, so I'm giving you a pass." He waved CeeCee's letter around. "I'm no angel myself, and I'm wondering if the good doc here has room for one more patient."

Dear Cory,

I know you are going to be mad, and hurt, but I hope you'll be able to forgive me. No, I take that back. I'm not going to ask for forgiveness this time. For the first time in my life, I'm not going to apologize.

We both know we need to make some changes in our relationship, or soon we won't have one at all. You know this is true.

You also know how important these women are to me, even though you've made it less than easy to keep them in my life. It always has to be convenient for you and fit into your schedule. You question what we do and what we talk about. I believe you've mocked my friendships because you never had this kind of relationship with other men, especially your father, and you're jealous. It makes me sad to think you'll never know what it's like to have people who uplift you. To validate you. To laugh and cry with you. To truly feel what you are feeling.

So I'm asking you to give me three days to get to know these men, who love the women I love and who love me. Someday, you'll need people to help you cope with some very sad things. Right now, you have no one but me. And I may not be here when that time comes.

I'm going to reemphasize how important this weekend is for me. I want you to share your life with others and offer your friendship. Please give them a chance. Invite them in. You have so much to give.

I'll see you Sunday. I love you.

CeeCee

Chapter Eighteen

In the beams of the headlights, three tall silhouettes, holding weapons, approached the store.

"They're one man short," Lynn announced, watching from the darkness. "Guess we're even now."

A guy spoke, the others laughed, then one peeled off to his right towards the back of Big Jon's. The other two shined flashlights into the shattered hatch of the SUV, then ambled towards the front windows, making another sweep with their lights.

<Rap. Rap. Rap.>

"We know you're in there," said the leader.

Lynn took a deep breath, trying to shake off the fear and keep the anxiety at bay. The only thing keeping her upright was the lorazepam she'd taken earlier, but its effects had limits. She felt pretty safe knowing the thugs couldn't see her. On the other hand, they were lit up like Christmas trees under the porch light, making it quite easy to see their movements and expressions. *Like sitting ducks.* The power, restored just minutes earlier, made it possible to stick to their original plan.

"Noticed your car," he shouted through the door. "Under a big tree. That's too bad, but it makes me wonder why it got hit in the first place. Said you were leaving." He turned to his buddy. "Isn't that what they said?"

"Yep."

He scratched his scraggly beard. "But *I'm* thinking maybe you couldn't leave. I'm thinking maybe something was wrong with your car all along."

"*I'm* thinking," CeeCee whispered, "if these were different times, I'd blow a new asshole into your forehead and let your shit-for-brains seep out."

"I'm thinking you really need help now, so why don't you open up and let's have a little discussion?"

The women stayed silent.

In anticipation, they'd already dragged more shelving racks to the back to reinforce the metal cooler, just in case, and added a booby trap, also just in case. The women felt confident about their preparation.

"Hey, little ladies. You in there?" asked the leader, pounding on the door once again. "We come in peace. The least we can do is give you a lift. That's what we gentlemen do, right Rick?"

The other man chuckled. "Yessir."

"You know what ticks me off, though? A woman giving me the silent treatment. It makes my gentlemanliness kind of go sideways. Ya know? So, let's be civil here, and you unlock that door."

Nothing.

"I said, unlock the door, or we're going to put a bullet in it and unlock it for you."

Lynn volunteered to be the spokesperson since the guys hadn't heard her voice yet. Softly she said, "Please just go away, sir. We're fine. As we said earlier, we don't need rescuing, but thank you for being concerned."

"Oh, who do we have here?" he yelled through the door. "You must be the one with your head screwed on straight, not like your friends, Thelma and Louise."

Lynn giggled intentionally like a little girl. "I know! They got a little carried away, I thought."

"I'd say threatening people with guns is a little more than getting carried away. Last time I checked, it's illegal."

"I agree, and I gave them a good talkin'-to," said Lynn. "Their behavior was ridiculous. Would it help if they apologized?"

He laughed.

Guess not.

The third man reappeared from the back of the building and mumbled something to the leader, who nodded. CeeCee watched them and signaled for Lynn to take her position at the counter area where the shotgun lay. They all hoped she would not have to use it. Lynn especially.

CeeCee stood in the middle of the store on top of the storage trunk coffee table, so she could see over the shelving and racks. She and the Glock were ready if need be. "Hey, asshole! You're getting on my nerves. What do you think is going to happen here?"

"How 'bout I show you instead?" He kicked the door hard, then cussed.

"They say a picture is worth a thousand words," she shouted. "So why don't you draw some stick figures and slide it under the door?"

"Real funny, Thelma. I like a sense of humor in a woman."

"Actually, I'm Louise," CeeCee continued, "but you can call me *Detective* Johnson since we're friends now."

"Yeah, right. And I'm a lie *detector,* so I know bullshit when I hear it."

"I just wanted you to know who you're dealing with before you make another bad decision."

"A cop? That's funny."

"Eighteen years with the NYPD," said CeeCee. "Before that, special military ops."

Lynn's head whipped around, and she looked at CeeCee, wondering how she came up with these things.

More talking outside in low voices. "Bullshit."

"Don't say I didn't warn you." Then she yelled. "Lock and load, ladies."

This command was intended to sound like three women were inside the store, but in reality, Molly hid in a predetermined position in the woods. As soon as they'd heard the truck coming, she hurried outside, and CeeCee and Lynn renailed the boards over the door. Molly's location, behind a large rock in thick undergrowth, gave her a direct line of sight to the front porch. Earlier, she'd changed into darker clothes and covered her red hair with a black bandana to camouflage herself. If the men tried to break into Big Jon's, her job was to fire a warning shot over their heads.

The guy yelled, "You're going to regret this, bitches."

The air suddenly rumbled, shaking the store and everything in it, including CeeCee and Lynn. Windows rattled, objects fell off shelves and crashed to the floor, and the hanging collectibles swayed erratically. Following the explosive thunder came a bolt of lightning, too close, sounding like the crack of a howitzer. Then came another from a rifle. CeeCee and Lynn ducked and froze in position.

Lynn heard the men's footsteps dancing on the creaky boards of the porch. "We're getting the fuck out of here, man," one guy yelled. "This is stupid. I've got a wife and kids, and I'm not risking one more second with these psychopaths. Stay if you want, but me and my truck are outta here."

Lynn and CeeCee both popped up from the floor and saw two of the men leap off the porch and run to the vehicle. The leader stood his ground, glaring at the front door, then spat on the porch.

"Ain't worth my time either."

He stepped off the porch, flipped a bird in the direction of the store, and jogged to the truck. After the loud exhaust pipes faded, CeeCee and Lynn tore the boards off the front door and ran outside.

"Molly, where are you?" Lynn shouted.

"Here," Molly answered.

A flashlight flickered through the trees, and Lynn ran in that direction. Molly, visibly shaken, thrust the rifle at her. "Get this thing away from me."

"What happened?" asked Lynn.

"That lightning strike scared the bejesus out of me. That's what happened. I was so focused on those idiots and staying still that nothing else existed in my sphere. It's a wonder I didn't keel over from the shock. Instead, my finger hit the trigger. What if I'd shot one of those guys? My God! What the hell are we doing? I'm almost a murderer!"

"Well, you aren't that accurate, so they were pretty safe," CeeCee replied. "But I want you to know we'll visit every Sunday if you go to prison."

Lynn shot her eyes at CeeCee and jammed the rifle into her hand. "Not the time. Can't you see she's upset?" Lynn turned back to Molly, hugging her tightly. "My heart sank into my feet when I heard that shot. We were both terrified, even though CeeCee is making jokes. We all know it's her mechanism for disguising emotions. And don't even deny it, Cynthia Corrine. I know you all too well."

As the friends walked back inside, giant raindrops fell, plinking like pebbles thrown against a tin can. Just as the sky opened up, they closed the door and repeated their process of securing their small fort, just in case.

"Is this one of those things we'll laugh about one day?" asked Lynn as they settled back into the worn furniture.

****

"I don't think I'll be able to laugh for a very long time," CeeCee said, slumping into the cushions. "Right now, I'm drained physically and mentally, and my nerves are shot. Can we just take a moment?"

She dangled her legs over the chair arm, eyes closed, listening to the pounding rain on the roof. The sound brought back memories of summer camp, racing to the nearest shelter to escape a sudden thunderstorm. She could smell the scent of wet pine needles and the sulfur of a match lighting a cigarette, the first one she'd ever smoked, although she took only one puff. For several minutes CeeCee coughed so hard, she thought her lungs would pop out. Her camp buddies, who dared her, laughed, but she didn't mind.

She had wondered about it. Now she knew. No matter what the cool kids did, smoking was not for her.

CeeCee took a big draw off the Virginia Slim. *Boy, was I wrong*. She swigged the beer she snagged from Big Jon's cooler and looked at her friends and sisters in crime.

Molly sipped wine out of a red plastic cup and tossed a chip into her mouth. "What are you grinning at?"

"You and Lynn."

Lynn heard her name and opened her eyes to exchange looks of unstated love, trust, and respect.

"Tell me again," said CeeCee. "Who had the bright idea to leave the guys at the lake, in a beautiful, well-furnished cabin, with real beds and bathrooms and all the food and drink you'd ever need? And who said we'd go to the spa for some much-needed pampering?"

Molly and Lynn answered in unison. "Me?"

"At no time did you say, 'Hey, you know what would be fun? Let's confront some macho nutcases and threaten them, not once but twice, with guns. And just to spice things up, let's do it in the middle of nowhere, with no phone service, a disabled car, and no way to escape.' I do *not* remember discussing that at all."

"It's hard to believe, that's for damn sure," Molly said. "You know how they say truth is stranger than fiction? No one will ever believe this story."

"It's not over yet, and I'm not sure we should even tell it, given the legal repercussions," said Lynn.

CeeCee shivered, grabbed her jacket, and wrapped it around her. "I keep replaying everything in my mind. The outcome could've been so different."

"Kind of like those people on TV who punch on their phone when they're in danger instead of defending themselves?" asked Molly.

"Okay, maybe your little lecture at the bakery helped. I don't know. But, what if we'd played along like many women would, thinking those guys were just trying to scare us? What if they were sociopaths who kidnapped, raped or tortured people? Something about those guys was crazy scary. They were way too calm."

"No, those guys were just drunk and acting tough," said Lynn. "*You* were the scary one, but in a good way. Wish I had half that amount of courage." She looked away. "Things might be a lot different."

"What things? How different?" asked Molly. "You're not talking about tonight, are you?

Lynn looked down at her hands. "My life is a mess, and I don't know what to do."

"Well, the first thing you can do is refuse to jump out of a fucking airplane," said CeeCee. "If you're terrified, just don't do it. Why your husband, of all people, would demand something like that is beyond me."

Lynn didn't respond, but CeeCee saw the fear on her face. "Please tell us what's going on."

Lynn took a deep breath and stared straight ahead. "Adam is...."

"Having an affair. I knew it!" CeeCee pounded the seat cushion so loud it made Lynn jump.

"That's not it," Lynn stammered. "Sometimes, I wish he were. That's something we could work on and talk about, but it's worse."

"He's abusing you, isn't he?" Molly whispered.

Lynn hesitated, nodded, then put both hands over her face. "How did you know?"

"For years, I've thought something seemed... off," said Molly.

CeeCee wanted to hit something. Adam mainly. *I'm going to kick that bastard in the nads the next time I see him.*

"I've never told anyone. For years and years, but I can't hold it in any longer." She wiped her nose with the back of her hand and continued in a monotone. "Adam is not what he seems. He's not the persona he perpetuates. He can be very charming and engaging, but it's an act. He's mean. Controlling. And emotionally abusive."

CeeCee closed her eyes. "How long?"

"Years. Eight or nine, maybe."

"Oh, God, Lynn. Does he hit you?" asked CeeCee.

"Not yet, but his physical actions are escalating. He gets within inches of my face and practically snarls while telling me how lucky I am he's with me or wants me. He demands sex even when I don't feel well, like before the funeral."

"What happened?"

"He got furious because I got out of bed. No, skulked is more like it because that's what I've been reduced to. I didn't want to wake him, so I tiptoed to the bathroom to take a shower."

"Why would—"

Lynn held her hand up to quiet CeeCee. "I heard him call my name but ignored it. I knew I'd pay for it, but I didn't care. I needed time to myself to cry for my friend and to think, but all he cared about was sex. So, of course, he stomped in and went into a rage."

CeeCee couldn't believe what she was hearing. "Couldn't you lock him out?"

"Oh, I'm never to lock the door. Ever." Lynn dabbed at her eyes.

"I *hate* that son of a bitch," growled CeeCee.

"Cee, let her finish," Molly said.

"He ripped open the shower curtain, jerked me out of the tub by my wrist, and grabbed my face, forcing me to look at myself in the mirror. He told me how ugly I looked and some other things. It's a blur because I've heard it so many times. But you know what? It still shocks me to see him transform into this other being, even after all this time."

"Like Jekyll and Hyde," said Molly. "His anger is always your fault, right?"

Lynn nodded. "How do you know all this stuff?"

"You learn a lot being married to a psychologist."

"Goddammit!" CeeCee got up, put her hands on her hips, and limped around in a circle.

"CeeCee! You never say GD," Lynn said.

"Well, I'm pissed. Aren't you?"

"My days of getting mad are far behind me. I'm such a fool, a weakling, whatever you want to call me. I've been too embarrassed to tell anyone, especially you, Molly."

"Why especially me?" Molly asked.

"I admire you so much," Lynn said in sobs. "The things you've accomplished, the kind of woman you've become. You'd never let this happen to you. Never. I didn't want you to hate me or lose respect for me. I don't want to be a failure in your eyes."

Molly, oddly quiet, put her hands on Lynn's shoulders. "Look at me, please, and listen. You're not a fool, and you're definitely not weak. You're one of the strongest women I know, and you could never be a failure in my eyes or anybody else's."

Lynn grabbed her purse, found a tissue, and blew her nose loudly.

"Then why have I put up with this? I *know* better."

"Because you love the bastard," Molly said, "at least the one you fell in love with, and when he's nice, you think, maybe this time he's changed."

"Ridiculous, isn't it? I kept thinking if I did everything right, he'd appreciate me again. And we'd be those happy-go-lucky kids who couldn't bear to be apart." The cadence of Lynn's voice got faster. "I can't even remember when it started. Subtle at first, I'd brush it off, thinking he had a bad day at work. But then it got to be more frequent, and the anger intensified.

"And you know the worst part? I've seen a million TV shows about this. I'd shake my head at those poor women and scream at the screen. 'Why do you keep going back? Don't you know how stupid you're being? Over some man who doesn't deserve you?'"

"Did you ever talk to him about it?" Molly asked.

"Lots of times. He blew it off, of course, turning it around on me, blaming hormones or an overreaction. Then he'd get lovey-dovey, apologize, and do something nice like flowers or a gift. Until the next time. With each incident, my self-esteem cracked a little more until I lost my will, my purpose in life, thinking maybe he's right."

"I'm surprised you're able to come to the beach with us," said CeeCee.

"It's not easy. And it's held over my head because he knows how important it is. He says things like, 'I'd hate to see you miss your beach trip this year.' Always in a menacing tone, and conditions are always part of the deal."

"All those calls you make aren't because you miss him. You *have* to call, don't you?" Molly asked.

Lynn nodded. "Pathetic isn't it?"

"I noticed the calls, too," said CeeCee, "but figured it wasn't my business."

"Since when did that stop you?" asked Molly, smiling.

CeeCee ignored her. "Have you thought about leaving him?"

"Every second of every day, and I've come close several times. Once in an argument, I threatened to leave, and he laughed like some mad scientist. He said, 'Go ahead. I'd like to see the lawyer who could beat me in court or the judge who would rule against me. You'd get nothing and be out on the street living in your car.'"

CeeCee wanted to scream. "Jesus Christ! We cannot allow this piece of shit to violate you for one minute longer."

"No, CeeCee!" Lynn yelled. "There is no *we*. You can't say anything. Ever! This is *my* fight." She grabbed another tissue. "I thought about counseling, just for me, because he'd never go. But if he found out, it would make things worse. I even called one of those hotlines but hung up when they answered."

"Does he look at your phone, the calls you make?" asked Molly.

Lynn nodded. "Plus, he uses it to spy on me. One of those locator apps."

CeeCee laughed. "Bet he can't find you now, and I hope it's driving him fucking crazy."

Lynn grinned.

"No wonder you have stomach problems," said Molly. "And you've lost weight. It kills me that you've gone through this alone. Did you think about telling Bill so he could help?"

Lynn started crying again. "Yes. But I didn't want him to have to keep a secret like that from you. It wouldn't be right. But I guess that cat's out of the bag now. Oh God, what am I going to do? I can't go home with him after sneaking off and leaving him with Bill and Cory. He'll be homicidal."

"You'll come home with one of us, that's what," Molly said. "Wonder if Mr. Hyde will show up at the cabin."

Lynn shrugged. "His rage is always directed at me, so I don't know. He may not be able to control himself if the right buttons are pushed."

"Cory's specialty is pushing buttons," said CeeCee. "He can be a hothead, but he's not in Adam's category."

"Well, let's hope those two hotheads clash like rams banging horns during mating season," said Molly. "That would certainly get Bill's attention."

"Or maybe he'll learn about it another way," said Lynn. She looked at Molly. "I wrote a note to Bill, too."

Chapter Nineteen

The scrumptious aroma of sizzling steak filled Bill's nostrils and made his mouth water. It seemed like years since he'd bitten into a medium-rare juicy slab of beef, and he couldn't wait. His job was to stand by the stainless-steel grill and make sure the grease didn't cause a fire. The firefighter's instructions were very clear. "Don't touch anything, doc. Just come get me."

Bill knew next to nothing about cooking, but he figured he could handle this assignment while the chef prepared side dishes he refused to reveal. The psychologist analyzed this secrecy for about two seconds, then shrugged. He swirled the red wine in his glass and inhaled its bouquet as he'd seen other people do. *Did he smell pears and tobacco?* He took a sip. *Delicious.* He walked over to the small outdoor table where the bottle sat and looked at the label for future reference. The graphics were fancier than most labels, and the words were in French. "Looks *and* tastes expensive."

"It is," said Cory as he reappeared to check the steaks. He gave them a turn. "Any fire activity?"

"Nary a spark."

He nodded, took the blue checkered kitchen towel off his shoulder, and wiped his hands. "That wine you're gulping down costs about $500 a bottle, so you might want to go easy."

"Are you kidding?" asked Bill. "My whole wardrobe didn't cost that much." They both chuckled. "It's yummy."

"I'm sure that's just the description the winery wanted," Cory said. "You should write a review."

"Any more of it?"

"A whole case."

Bill smiled. "In that *case*, pun intended, get your own bottle and leave me alone."

"I'm not the one you have to deal with," said Cory. "It's Josh. You know, the guy who bought it?"

"Ah, yes." He lifted his glass. "To Josh and his good taste, and you, the chef."

Cory nodded, plated the steaks, and turned off the grill. Bill followed him into the cabin and sat across from Adam. The dining room table, meticulously set with casual white china plates, linen napkins, and crystal glasses, looked magnificent and could compete with any fine dining restaurant. They glanced at each other inquisitively as Cory served them, pouring wine and water, then placing steaks, twice-baked potatoes, asparagus, and garlic rolls in front of them.

"Where did all this come from?" asked Bill.

"Well, the meal CeeCee and I brought. Tableware came from the kitchen cabinets. Figured this deserved more than paper plates and plastic forks."

"It looks amazing," said Adam. "How did you learn to cook like this?"

Cory sat down and placed a napkin on his lap. "I'm self-taught really, but I watch a lot of cooking shows, read recipes online, and practice on my buddies at the station. Their critiques can be brutal."

The men spent the next few minutes sampling the different foods and nodding their heads in approval.

"I can't imagine what they'd have to complain about," said Bill before shoveling in another fork full.

"Ever consider opening a restaurant?" asked Adam.

"Every day. That's always been a dream, but my father crammed my head with so much bullshit I started doubting myself. 'That's woman's work, son. People will think you're not a real man.' That kind of thing."

Adam nodded. "Sounds like my gramps."

"Yeah, I guess we have a not-so-great thing in common. So, I played sports I didn't want to play, joined the Marines, and now I fight fires when all I want to be is a chef."

"So, it sounds like you're all crusty and tough on the outside but have a gooey inside," said Bill.

"Is that an official diagnosis, doc?"

They all laughed.

"Well, if this dish is on your menu, I'll be your first customer," said Adam. As he reached for the bottle of wine, the lights flickered, and a rumble of thunder rolled through the lake basin, so intense it rattled the windows. Lightning flashed, igniting the sky like fireworks on the fourth of July. Then everything went dark.

"Dammit," said Cory as he pushed his chair back and pulled out his phone for light. He returned to the table with a couple of candles, set them down, and struck a match. "Saw these earlier in the pantry."

"Romantic," said Bill. "Just so you know, I don't put out on the first date."

Cory raised his glass, and the others followed. "To second dates then." They clinked glasses and dug into their meals, making appreciative guttural sounds until their plates were clean.

"Hope you have some room left," said Cory as he walked over to the fridge. He reached into the dark cavity, grabbed three ramekins, and carried them to the table. He lit a small butane torch and caramelized the sugar on top of the creme brulee, making the room fill quickly with the scent of freshly made waffle cones.

"If you weren't married," said Adam, "I'd be on bended knee proposing." They all laughed, then thumped the top of the brulee to crack the sugar.

"This may be the best creme brulee I've ever had," Bill said. "Unbelievable. This whole meal was outstanding. Thank you, Cory."

As Adam and Bill cleaned up the kitchen, the wind gained strength, whipping tree branches around like paper streamers and slamming twigs and leaves against the cabin windows. When they heard the grill scraping across the deck, they left their post to look outside.

"We'd better close the lid on the grill," said Adam, "before it takes flight."

Everyone scrambled around the house's porch, grabbing things that could become airborne, and brought them inside. They found flashlights and more candles in the supply room and scattered them about the first floor. In the glow of the candles, they finally noticed they looked like three very large, drowned ferrets, and for some reason, this caused a laughing frenzy. They were getting punchy. And drunk.

"Whew! The last time I laughed this hard, I was smoking a doobie," said Adam trying to catch his breath. "My ribs hurt like hell."

"*You* smoke pot?" asked Bill. "An officer of the court?"

"Not anymore."

"Too bad." Bill pulled a plastic bag out of his shirt pocket, opened it, and showed them a joint. He gave it a quick sniff, then bobbed his eyebrows up and down.

"Now we're talking," Cory said, slapping Bill on the back. "Light her up."

An hour later, the storm was gone, and so was the joint, but the haze of marijuana smoke lingered near the ceiling. Cory lay on one of the leather couches with the flashlight propped on his stomach, pointing upward. "Ever noticed the colors in the smoke? They're all in there, just hanging around like a rainbow. I bet we could go to the top of the stairs and breathe it in all over again, colors and all. What d'ya think?"

"I think that's groovy, dude," said Adam, "which reminds me of a story." Soon an avalanche of exaggerated tales shot across the room like rapid fire. They spoke of childhood dreams, disappointments, puberty, and losing their virginity, things they'd never shared with other men.

"Bill abruptly leaped from his chair. "I'm starving. Think we have any M&Ms?"

The three men went to the kitchen and sifted through cabinets, drawers, and grocery sacks. Anything that looked remotely odd cracked them up.

"Look what I found!" said Cory. "Jiffy Pop! When is the last time you saw this?"

"Hey, we could build a fire outside and cook our corn there," said Adam proudly. He was referring to the beautiful stone fire pit near the lake.

"Everything's soaked," Bill said. "Be hard to get a fire going with wet wood, but I yield to the gentleman from North Carolina who is an expert on the subject."

Cory took a bow and peered outside. "Looks like the rain stopped, and the skies are clearing. And if I remember right, the pit has ceramic logs and uses propane gas. Probably safer than building fires in the woods, in case somebody gets sloppy."

"You talking about me?" asked Adam.

"Probably."

Armed with flashlights, towels, Jiffy Pop, and beer, the guys made their way toward the lake and the fire pit. Cory pushed the igniter button sending flames into action and lighting up the area around them. Glass stones around the rim of the firepit turned blue as they got hotter.

"There's our sign, boys," said Cory as he removed the round cardboard cover and placed the popcorn container over the coals. They all leaned in, watching and waiting for the aluminum to swell and the corn to pop.

"I'd forgotten how long this takes," said Bill. "Kind of like watching paint dry. No wonder it's extinct. We could've thrown back two big bags of chips and a pack of hotdogs by now."

"Yeah, where's the Jiffy part of this?" asked Adam, cackling at his joke.

"I don't think I can feel my toes," Bill said.

"They're overrated anyway," Adam replied, standing up and raising his beer. "Okay, I have a toast! Ya ready?

"Friends may come, and friends may go.

Friends may peter out, you know.

But friends we'll be until the end,

Peter out, or peter in."

Another burst of their laughter echoed across the lake.

"Good one, counselor," said Cory. "You should use that as a closing argument someday."

Adam tipped an imaginary hat towards Cory. "I say we go swimming. We're already wet."

"Not a good idea," Cory said. "You don't want that bite to get infected by some kind of weird bacteria, but there's no reason Bill and I can't go."

"Fine, buzz-kill," said Adam. "I'll just hang out and watch you dorks sink to the bottom."

The guys managed to make their way onto the dock without falling into the water or on top of each other. Bill and Cory grabbed oversized innertubes and jumped in, floating, singing, and listening to their voices bounce back at them. Someone in the distance yelled, "Shut up!" which made them snicker like little kids.

"Something just nibbled my toe," Bill said.

"Thought you couldn't feel your toes," Cory reminded him.

"Well, I can now, and I don't like what I'm feeling." He stiffened his body on top of the innertube to lift it out of the water. As he studied the sky and a few scattered stars, an upside-down image of the diving board floated into view. *Cannonball.* He paddled over to the dock and scrambled up the ladder to the second tier.

"What the hell are you doing?" asked Adam. "You're going to kill yourself."

"You're not my mother." Bill approached the end of the board to do his famous cannonball jump and shouted, "Bombs away!"

As he planted his feet at the end of the board, he lost his balance, and his right foot slipped off the side. A domino effect of injuries began with the inside of his ankle, then his calf and thigh, and ended with his genitals, all scraping the sharp edge of the board. Bill screamed in agony, then belly-flopped onto the water's surface with a loud splat. The impact knocked the breath out of him, making him panic and thrash around like a hooked fish.

Cory jumped off his innertube and pushed it across the water. "Grab on! I'm coming."

Bill got choked from coughing and trying to scream at the same time. "I think I smashed my right nut," he whimpered. "I'm not kidding." He tried to hold back tears, but the searing pain radiating from his genitals, down his legs, and throughout his abdomen was more than he could handle. He thought he might die. Cory pulled him to the ladder and tried to coax him out of the water. Instead, Bill hung on the tube like a limp noodle, his lips pressed against it, moaning and sounding like a humpback whale.

When he finally mustered the courage, Bill tried to place his right foot on the wrung of the ladder, which made the intense pain shoot through his body again. "Oh, Jesus, Mary, and Joseph!"

"Didn't see you as a name-dropper," Adam joked, squatting on the dock with his arm extended. "Gimme your hand."

"Don't touch me!" Bill yelped. Suddenly, he was lifted onto Cory's shoulder like a sack of flour and carried to the dock, where he screamed again.

"Man, I'm getting tired of carrying your two asses around," said Cory, breathing hard. "Something's gotta give."

"I said not to fucking touch me!" Bill shouted.

"I didn't think you were making good decisions," said Cory. "And you're welcome."

Bill hunched over, cradled his genitals, clenched his teeth, then fell to his knees, where he promptly threw up his entire dinner, including the Jiffy Pop popcorn.

****

Cory worried that Bill had torn the flesh of his scrotum and wanted him out of the lake water as fast as possible. He'd seen this kind of injury a few times and knew the situation could go wrong quickly, especially if an infection developed, but he didn't want to panic anyone, so he said nothing. With lots of urging and help, Bill finally stood and slowly made his way off the dock and up the pathway to the cabin. His friends stayed protectively close until he was safely inside and seated on the couch.

Using a flashlight to ensure his footing, the fireman ran upstairs, taking two steps at a time, and quickly returned with ibuprofen, dry clothes, towels, and a mirror.

"You want me to do what?" asked Bill.

"Since you're being a jackass and won't let me look at the—uhm—battered appendage," Cory said, "you'll have to do it yourself with the mirror. We need to see if it's injured."

"I can tell you with great confidence it's injured," said Bill, "if not obliterated. And what difference does it make? We can't get to a hospital anyway. Dammit, Molly!"

"There it is," Adam announced. "Finally! Some emotion about our circumstances."

"Not the time, asshole," said Bill, wincing.

"Adam, make yourself useful," Cory said. "Get ice while we still have some and wrap it in a dishtowel. Bill, it might relieve the pain if you lie down and pull your knees to your chest. When you give us the go, we'll turn our backs and point the flashlights so you can see. Candles aren't going to do the job. This is important, Bill."

"Okay, I'm ready."

Cory and Adam placed their flashlights behind their necks and shone them downward as Bill gave instructions. "Okay, hold'em right there," he finally said.

"What do you see?" asked Cory.

"Looks weird."

"Describe weird."

"Kind of like Adam's face."

"Oh, for God's sake," Adam said. "Just let Cory examine you. It's not like we don't have the same parts, but he might need a magnifying glass in your case."

"Fuck you."

When Bill described the injury, Cory sighed with relief, happy there was no open wound and that everything remained in its proper place. Discolored and painful, but no contortion, meaning treatment could be administered here and not in a hospital, which wasn't an option.

"Didn't you say yesterday that you'd give your right nut for a Krispy Kreme donut?" asked Cory. "How do you feel about that now?"

Bill managed a weak laugh. "I take it back."

"Here's the plan," said Cory. "No moving around unless necessary, apply ice with light pressure, take ibuprofen, and last but not least, and my personal favorite, put a rolled-up towel in your underwear to lift the scrotum to your body. This particular step also makes you very popular with the ladies at the beach. You're supposed to wear a jockstrap, but who even has one these days? And if you say you brought one, that's another conversation. Can we turn around now?"

"Yeah, freak show's over."

Adam plopped down in a chair, exhaling. "Man, you had me scared. I mean it. Every time you screamed, my stomach flopped."

"I guess Cory is the last man standing," Bill replied. "The only one unscathed."

"Well, in my case, he was doing the scathing," Adam joked.

Cory heard the comment but didn't answer. Instead, he headed out the back door, sat on the steps, and stared into the woods, reliving the day's events. He was used to being physically tired and knew he'd recover quickly, but the mental and emotional stress weighed heavily on him.

Between Adam's snakebite and Bill's injury, he felt overwhelmed with responsibility. Too many what-ifs passed through his mind, and he couldn't seem to shake them. He needed CeeCee. Although tiny in stature, she was the rock in the family, and he didn't know what he'd do without her. Cory didn't show his appreciation nearly enough, but that would change tomorrow.

He wondered what the girls were doing and pictured his wife curled up in a hotel terry cloth robe, her hair wrapped in a towel while admiring her new nail polish. Of course, she'd be holding a glass of wine and laughing with Molly and Lynn. He smiled at the thought. Sunday could not come soon enough.

Chapter Twenty

Sunday

At 3:00 a.m., Josh made an impulsive decision to go to the lake house. He couldn't sleep, so he got dressed and tiptoed out of his bedroom. He stopped in his office, made a copy of Carolyn's letter, and placed it on the kitchen counter for the kids to read when they got up.

When she wrote the note, his wife didn't know her friends planned to leave their husbands at the cabin. She'd assumed everyone would be there, so Josh debated where to go, the hotel or the lake. Knowing the girls were returning later today, he called the hotel to leave a message that he'd see them at the lake. Instead, he discovered they never arrived. *Did they change their minds?* Molly seemed adamant about their mission, but they were nervous about it, too. Maybe they couldn't go through with it.

He poured some coffee into a thermos, then grabbed a bag of trail mix and a pastry, which he swiftly stuffed into his mouth. As he groaned out loud at the sweet, buttery taste, he turned with a wide grin on his face and took the whole box.

Traffic was light this time of night, so Josh made good time. After driving to the lake so often, the truck practically knew the way on its own. He looked over at the empty passenger seat. "Are you happy now?"

As he made his way northwest, the skies got nastier, and the roads got curvier. He knew he wouldn't have cell service soon, so he guided the vehicle to the side and pulled his phone out of the cupholder. The screen lit up, and he punched the weather app, which showed a lot of green, red, and yellow blobs on the map. Bad storms were all over the area, and he'd be driving right into them. Josh grimaced and shook his head back and forth. *I should've left earlier*. After chastising himself, he thought about the situation for a moment, tossed some trail mix into his mouth, washed it down with coffee, and eased back onto the roadway.

Lightning flashed frequently, and thunder reverberated through the mountains while the wipers swished and thumped against the windshield. The surge of rain soon overtook the wipers, and Josh's vision decreased by half. As he slowed the truck to round a sharp curve, a huge oak tree lying on the road caught him off guard. He stomped on the brakes, causing the truck to fishtail, but it stopped just a few short yards from the outstretched branches. He pounded the steering wheel.

"Dammit!"

He wrestled with his windbreaker inside the vehicle's cabin, threw the hood over his head, and climbed out. The wind whipped small limbs off the trees, and debris soon covered the hood of his truck. The headlights allowed Josh to survey the possibility of getting around the tree, but his luck ran out. The journey ended there. He grabbed a road-hazard triangle from the truck and put it on the road, hoping to warn anyone as foolish as he.

Josh felt an unexplained urgency to get to the cabin, and turning back made him anxious. Carolyn always said, "listen to your gut," but he rarely did. This time, however, felt different, but what could it be? *I mean, what could possibly happen at the cabin?*

Chapter Twenty-One

Sunday morning Lynn walked around the store with a cup of coffee, searching for something useful, but she didn't know what until she stepped behind the cash register counter. And there it was. A map. Previous folding and unfolding had caused its dirty creases to split, so she handled it like a fifteenth-century museum document and tenderly placed it on the cracked acrylic countertop. She accidentally knocked over a tin can holding pens and pencils, causing them to splatter all over the floor. *Crap.* She crouched to pick them up and found herself eye level with a telephone handset, a spiral cord attached to one end. Thinking it fit the category of Big Jon's weird collectibles, she shrugged, picked up the pens, and spread out the map.

"Holy shit! Hey you guys, come over here."

"What is it?" asked CeeCee as she hobbled to the counter. Molly was right behind her.

Lynn stabbed her index finger at the map. "Look. Here we are, and there's the lake. If you follow the shoreline, the cabin is somewhere over here." Her finger traced a path. "I think we can walk there."

Molly looked closer. "And I'm pretty sure this line is the road that leads to the house. It's a lot farther by car."

"So we've been stuck in this hell hole when we could've escaped to safety?" asked CeeCee.

"I might question the *safety* part of that statement," said Molly. "We don't know what we'll face when we see the guys."

"At least they won't be aiming guns at us," said Lynn.

CeeCee grinned. "That's because we have them all."

Excited about having a plan, the women readied for the hike by dumping the contents of their purses and filling them with essentials like water, power bars, billfolds, phones, and ammo. They had no backpacks, so expensive designer pouches would have to do.

"I don't know why we're even taking our phones," said Molly. "They're useless and heavy, especially if the case is rhinestoned." She rolled her eyes at Lynn. "Just sayin'."

"That reminds me," said Lynn. "I saw an old telephone handset under the counter. Cord and all. Weird, huh?"

CeeCee limped back across the store with her friends in tow, looked under the counter, and pulled the handset off the shelf. She handled it like evidence from a crime scene. "Yes, this is weird."

"Unless it's not," said Molly.

"You think there's a phone somewhere?" CeeCee asked.

"Maybe. Seems like someone could look."

"You mean me."

"Nevermind, Hop-along." Molly pushed by CeeCee, then eyeballed the area for clues. She finally noticed a wooden box on the wall tucked between two shelves holding styrofoam cups of live bait. It was painted the same putrid color as the wall and well camouflaged.

"What might this be?" She reached to open it, using the tiny brass knob, but it didn't budge. "Are you kidding me?"

"What's the problem?" asked Lynn.

"I think the phone is in there. It's the right size anyway. Why in God's name would you lock up a phone?"

"Let me get this straight," said CeeCee. "Not only could we have escaped from those morons by simply walking around the lake, but we could have also called for help. Unbelievable."

"Thanks for the recap, Sherlock," Molly replied. "This Big Jon is a strange dude. He leaves a shotgun out on the shelf for anyone to see and locks up the phone. Kind of backward, don't ya think?"

"It's called supply and demand," said Lynn. "Phone service is in high demand with low supply, and guns are everywhere. Economics 101."

"And let me guess, professor," said Molly. "You made an A."

"Yep. Who would you call? Can't reach the guys."

"9-1-1, I imagine," said Molly. "Or AAA?"

"Too late for AAA," Lynn said. "I'm afraid that car of yours needs the jaws of life."

CeeCee disappeared for a few seconds and returned with a screwdriver and the hammer they'd used to board up the store. "Rip it open. Let's find out for sure."

Molly put the screwdriver tip into the seam between the door and the box and thumped it with the hammer. Nothing. She put more force into the next blow, and the whole box detached from the wall while also jarring the shelf above. A styrofoam cup fell, and a wad of worms wriggled and writhed at Molly's feet.

"Oh my God!" She shook a worm off her shoe. "Get these things away from me."

"You can freak out later," CeeCee said. "Look."

And there it was, a yellow phone base with a rotary dial. Molly inserted the matching spiral cord into the bottom of the receiver, pressed the hook, released it, and listened.

No dial tone. She repeated the steps and shook her head. "Maybe it never worked the storm knocked down a line. Either way, we're walking."

The women's temporary feeling of hope dissipated, forcing them to go back to their original plan. So, they quickly swapped their capris for long pants, sandals for socks and athletic shoes, and layered long-sleeved shirts over tee-shirts for added protection against briars, poison ivy, or bugs. While gathering things for the hike, Lynn found a corkscrew-willow, walking staff in a pile of old fishing rods, and handed it to CeeCee.

"Here. Let's trade." She took the Glock from CeeCee and shoved it between her waistband and spine. "Damn, that's cold."

"What did you expect?" CeeCee asked as she tapped and stepped, tapped and stepped, trying out her new assistant. "This works pretty well."

Lynn looked at CeeCee's swollen knee and nodded. "Good. You can thank Big Jon for that later."

"Truthfully, I hope there isn't a *later*," CeeCee replied. "At least in person. But his décor tells me he would rather receive a proper handwritten thank you note."

Lynn snorted.

As Molly approached the front door, she slung the rifle strap over her shoulder and looked at her friends. "Are you weirdos going to stand around all day?"

****

Bill sat on the dock in one of the Adirondack chairs, enjoying the silence, sun, and a beer. He took a deep breath of the fresh air cleansed by the previous night's rain and slowly released it. The scent reminded him of camping trips with his boy scout troop and leader, Mr. McGuire. That's when his love for the outdoors was soundly confirmed and continues to this day. Still friends with some of the boys, men now, he heard from them occasionally as well as McGuire. They'd spoken about a reunion that never happened, but a place like this would be perfect. They wouldn't even have to pitch a tent, but that would defeat the purpose. Someone would still insist on digging a latrine and bragging about its perfection or on blazing a trail of some kind. Hell, he would, too. The former boy scout made a mental note to contact the guys when he got home.

He adjusted the plastic bag of ice tucked between his thighs and, as ordered by Cory, had placed a small towel inside his boxers for support. He felt ridiculous, but the treatment seemed to lessen his discomfort, so he didn't dwell on his appearance. Bill's muscles started to relax, so he closed his eyes and thought about the last three days. Nobody back home would believe it, but his experience as a psychologist taught him many years ago that truth is stranger than fiction. He smiled as he recollected Molly's statement about observing the different personalities and jotting them down. She certainly knew what she was talking about, and he might do it. Bill's thoughts were interrupted by the dock bobbing up and down and the sound of footsteps getting closer.

Adam slid into the chair beside him. "Feeling any better?"

"I'm okay if I don't move or breathe. This has to be the worst thing a man can go through."

"You mean worse than getting your face bashed in, ribs cracked, and bitten by a snake?"

Bill felt like a chump. "Shit. How are you? Seriously."

"Okay, as long as I don't move or breathe."

Both men laughed, then said, "Oww," and laughed again.

They heard the low hum of an electric motor, turned their heads to the right, and saw a small boat off in the distance following the shoreline of the lake.

"Wonder if they're catching anything," said Bill automatically, even though he didn't wonder or care. He pulled his cap over his eyes, breathed in the morning air again, and went back to thinking about Molly.

"Morning!" someone shouted, causing Bill's body to jerk. *Dammit.* He raised his cap and saw a tan Jon Boat approaching the dock. Two men sat on the built-in bench seats, and a big black innertube rested in the hull between them.

"Morning," Adam replied. "Hooking anything?"

"Not unless you count this innertube," said the fisherman in the boat's bow. "We found it up the lake hung on a branch. Is it yours?"

"Yes," said Bill. "Thanks. We forgot all about it. Could you throw it on the dock? I'd rather not get up if you don't mind."

The fisherman looked at the bag of ice on Bill's crotch. "Damn. Does that have anything to do with the innertube?"

"Indirectly. I decided to do a cannonball off the diving board last night and missed."

"Great balls afire!"

"That about covers it," Bill said, laughing. "You live around here?"

"Yeah, born and raised. Our little slice of Heaven and a great place to raise a family. You all visiting?"

Bill nodded. "Belongs to a friend of ours."

"Josh and Carolyn. We know them. Nice couple."

"Yes, they were," said Bill.

"What d'ya mean?"

"Carolyn died. We came for the funeral."

"Ah, no." The fisherman bowed his head reverently for a moment and closed his eyes. He looked at his buddy. "Did you know?"

His friend shook his head.

"Damn, that's going to tear my wife up. Carolyn was a wonderful lady."

"I know what you mean. Our wives were very close to her." Adam grabbed a beer out of the small cooler. "Want one?"

"Sure."

He tossed one to each fisherman. The cans popped, then hissed, and some foam spewed into the lake, making tiny ripples.

After three large gulps from the can, the guy said, "Ahh, that hits the spot. I swore I wouldn't get within ten yards of a beer today, but this European stuff goes down pretty smooth." He took another swig. "Me and my buddies tied one on both nights this weekend, stayed up way too late doing stupid stuff. The wives were not amused."

Adam laughed. "As long as you don't get into trouble, they'll get used to it. Might even encourage it."

The guys drained their beers, so Adam tossed them another one.

"You probably live where there are things to do," the fisherman continued, taking another sip. "That's the tradeoff for living in such a beautiful place. It gets a little boring sometimes, so you have to make your own fun, but I admit we got a little carried away."

"How so?" asked Bill. "If it's okay to ask."

"Probably shouldn't talk about it. What do ya think, Hank?"

The fisherman sitting in the back of the boat stood and stretched. A cell phone fell out of his pocket and thumped on the boat hull. He quickly grabbed it and shrugged. "Your call."

"Ah, what the hell? You don't know us from Adam, and we don't know you."

Adam smiled.

"Well, the bottom line is, we got two guns pointed at us, if you can believe it."

"You're kidding!" said Adam. "Is this normal?"

"Heck, no. Locals are as nice as can be. These were tourists or something, sitting around drinking. We thought they were stranded and offered to help, but they took offense for some reason. Got all snarky; you know how they are."

"They?" asked Bill.

"Women," the fisherman said. "I still think something was wrong with their car, but they wouldn't admit it. I mean, why would somebody stop in the middle of nowhere, at night, and have a party?" He winked at his buddy. "So we thought we'd play with them a little, you know, scare them. But the next thing we know, we're looking down the barrels of a rifle and a damn Glock."

Molly. Bill's stomach sank as he realized why the fisherman's dropped phone looked familiar. It had a yellow smiley face on the back, as did his wife's. Hoping to sound interested instead of panicked, Bill asked, "Where did this happen? Hope you called the police."

"Nah. It'd take too long to get to Big Jon's. You probably passed it on your way up."

Adam nodded. "We got a few things there."

The fisherman laughed. "Did you get sick?"

"Nah. The owner warned us about the expiration dates," Adam replied. "In fact, we tried to hike there yesterday, but I got bitten by a snake, and we came back."

"No shit! You okay?"

" I think so."

"Is that what happened to your face, too? You fall or something?"

Adam frowned. "No. That's a whole other story."

"Well, you could've swum there faster," said Hank.

"Where?" asked Adam.

"Big Jon's."

Bill boosted himself to the edge of his chair, and the bag of ice fell to the dock. "What do you mean?"

The fisherman pointed behind him. "If you follow the lefthand bank for a bit, you'll see a bridge that crosses over the lake. You wouldn't know that since this is your first time here. Anyway, you go under that and keep going until you see a deep cove. There's a little opening in the rocky shoreline where people anchor their boats and hike up to the road to buy supplies and bait. It's a steep hike, but there are plenty of things to hold on to for the climb."

"Had no idea it was that close by water," Bill said. His heart raced, but he tried to remain calm. He didn't want to spook the guys until he got more answers, so he got up slowly from his chair and faked a stretch.

"I'm going to the cabin to get some more beer for our new friends and some of those homemade biscuits Cory whipped up this morning." He turned and looked at them. "You like ham biscuits?"

"Oh, don't bother. We'll just motor on and leave you to it."

"No, I insist. Josh would be all over us if we weren't hospitable. You won't believe how good these things are, and they're huge. Like cat-head huge. Plus, we can drink a toast to Carolyn."

"I'll go," said Adam. "You need to rest your boys."

"No. I'll go," said Bill. "I need to walk a little and get rid of some of this beer. Be right back."

"You might as well listen to him," said Adam, shrugging. "He pitches a hellova hissy fit."

****

Ten minutes later, Cory appeared with a small cooler, and Bill carried a plastic sack.

"Hey, I'm Cory."

"Hi there. Heard you're a good cook."

"Working on it." He headed for the screened part of the dock. "Let's go over to the table. I need to get out of the sun. I brought some homemade apple butter, too."

The two men tied their boat to a cleat on the dock and climbed out. "Now, this is what I call service. Hope you guys are staying awhile."

"Just the weekend," Bill said, "Unless something happens."

"What *else* could happen?" asked Adam as he took a seat. "I mean—"

"They don't want to hear about our boring lives," said Cory as he pulled out biscuits for the two visitors, tossed one to each of them, then napkins, and opened the jar. "Bon appetit."

The two fishermen spread the gooey brown butter on their biscuits and took giant bites. "Man, you weren't kidding about the size, and they're as good as any I've ever had."

Cory nodded. "Appreciate that. More in the kitchen if you're still hungry."

"Nah, this is more than plenty."

"Bill tells me you boys got schooled this weekend," said Cory, smiling. "By a bunch of girls. That's pretty sad, man."

"They weren't girls," one said defensively. "They were women around your age, I'm guessing."

"That's even worse," Cory chuckled, goading them on.

"Says you. You weren't there, but we couldn't let those bitches have the last word, so we went back last night."

"Didn't learn your lesson, huh," said Cory locking eyes with Bill.

"They were still there?" asked Adam. "Wonder why?"

As the stranger described the scene at Big Jon's, the women's husbands listened intently, interrupting periodically to ask questions. Adam still had no idea who the men were talking about, which made his curiosity and questions seem more authentic. "Sounds like they were ready for you," he said.

"I guess so," said the fisherman. They'd barricaded themselves inside the store, had the front and back doors secured."

"Someone fired a rifle at you?" Cory asked.

"Yeah, had somebody in the woods, probably the redhead."

"She had you in the crosshairs," said Bill.

Cory laughed. "I think you meant to say she had him by the *short* hairs."

"Real funny. They probably couldn't hit the broad side of a barn."

Cory knew that wasn't true, but he went along with the jab and nodded.

"But the storm opened wide up, so we said, 'fuck it,' and left."

"Wow, that's a *whale* of a story," said Cory as he stood and held his hands out, three feet apart.

"I know what you're implying," said the fisherman, "but I'm not exaggerating." He pushed his chair back. "Thanks for the grub and beer. Tasty." As he started to rise, Cory put his hands on the guy's shoulders, pushed him down, then grabbed the fisherman's wrists and pulled them behind the chair back.

"What the hell, man?" During the struggle, his chair fell over, and he hit the deck, squirming. "Get off of me!" His strength wasn't a match for Cory's, and he soon found himself restrained but still cussed and screamed for help.

The fisherman's pal, Hank, pushed his chair back forcefully, and it, too, crashed onto the decking, blocking his way out. Before he could step over it, Bill grabbed his arms from behind.

"Don't move, asshole!"

The fisherman ignored the command, twisted out of Bill's grasp, and then lunged at Adam, elbowing him in the ribs. Adam hunched over in pain, unable to help, but Bill regained his ground and jerked the guy's right arm back and up into a rear wrist lock.

"Just cool it," he shouted. "We're not going to hurt you."

"Somebody want to clue me in?" grunted Adam, holding his ribs.

Once the fisherman stopped squirming, Bill reached into his pocket, took out some binders twine, and quickly wound the guy's wrists together. He looked at Adam, still bent from the blow, resting his hands on the table. "Think you can tie some knots, then do his buddy?"

"*Do* his buddy?" asked Adam. "You with the mob now? What the *hell* is going on?"

"Yeah, what the fuck, man?" shouted the fisherman.

"You chose the wrong people to mess with, that's what," said Bill. "Those women? Are our wives."

Adam's face turned red. "Are you saying these bastards tried to hurt my Lynn?"

"You and your big, fat mouth," said Hank, glaring at his friend. "This is the last time, Gus."

Gus suddenly found Bill in his face, eyeball to eyeball. "The big guy here is going to stay with you and your buddy while we take your boat for a ride. You'd better pray we find our wives unharmed. Comprende, amigo? And Cory? Don't hesitate to do what's necessary if these fuckers make a move."

Bill walked over to Hank and grabbed Molly's phone out of his pocket. "And you? You're buying my wife a new phone." He stormed out of the screened area towards the boat, and Adam followed, grabbing the bag of ice off the dock before getting in.

****

Bill pushed off from the dock, and Adam shivered as he placed the ice under his shirt and onto his ribs. "Man, if I don't die this weekend, I never will."

"And if I don't kill somebody this weekend," Bill said. "I never will."

The electric motor purred along at one mile an hour, which made the trip excruciatingly long. They'd passed under the bridge and finally saw the cove the fishermen mentioned. Adam slowed their speed and settled the boat onto the sandy area between rocks. A few boats were tied to trees or logs, and some young men sat in the shade eating sandwiches. Bill eased himself out and held the boat in place. He'd ditched the rolled-up towel at the dock, so with no support to keep things stable, his movements were slow. He managed to tie the boat rope to a nearby stump and waved at the picnickers. "This the way to Big Jon's?"

"Yeah, but it's probably closed today. The storm blew down a lot of trees and blocked the road."

The two men started their climb at a break in the rocks and slowly made their way over and around boulders, using limbs and tree roots to get to the top. They had to stop several times to relieve the strain on their injured bodies. The ascent would be a minor challenge for a healthy man, but Bill and Adam were not those men right now. Only the situation's urgency gave them the strength to endure the pain of torn and bruised tissue and cracked ribs. Once they reached the top of the cliff, the terrain changed from rocks to hardwood trees, but it still sloped upwards instead of leveling off as they'd hoped.

"I need a break in the shade," said Bill. "Plus, a strong pain killer."

After several minutes, Adam wiped his sweaty face with his shirt. "Ready?"

"No, but let's go."

They followed a well-trodden path in the woods that eventually leveled off and led them to the highway and Big Jon's. When the store came into view, Adam picked up his pace slightly, leaving Bill to get there when he could. He half-jogged across the graveled lot, but after two or three strides, he slowed to a walk again.

Bill saw his wife's SUV buried under a large tree and panicked. He tried to shout Molly's name but didn't have the wind, so only a whisper surfaced. He coughed, and with legs that felt like lead, he staggered towards the front porch and watched as Adam pushed on the door. It opened freely to reveal an empty store.

****

Climbing down over the rocks took twice as long as the trip up, and both men were winded and sweating heavily, their tee shirts drenched. In a hurry to get to the girls, neither man thought to bring water, and the beer they drank earlier didn't help. Both felt like hell. When they finally reached the bottom, a couple of men stood in front of their boat with their arms crossed. The bigger of the two wore a black tee shirt and a fluorescent yellow vest, much like public service workers wear.

"Jesus Christ. What now?" Bill said to Adam's back as they reached the water's edge.

"Can we help you?" asked Adam.

"Looks like Gus's boat," one man said, stating the obvious.

"It is," Adam answered. "Is there a problem with it? Is it in violation of something?"

"How would I know?"

"Thought you might be with the fish and game commission or something."

"Why would you think that?"

Adam looked at Bill and shrugged. "The vest? I don't know."

The fisherman's buddy chuckled.

"What are you doing with Gus' boat?"

"We borrowed it," said Bill.

"Don't sound like Gus. He's pretty picky about his toys. Who'd you say you were?"

"We didn't," said Adam as he walked by and got in the boat. Bill untied the rope, joined his friend, and mumbled, "Must be something in the water up here."

"What d'you say?" asked the guy on the shore.

"I said, have a good day, gentlemen. We'll let Gus know you're looking out for him."

"You do that and tell that rat bastard he still owes me twenty bucks."

****

Adam felt like he'd been punched in the gut when he and Bill discovered the girls were not at Big Jon's. Now they moved along the water in silence, giving him time to think. *Was Lynn afraid?* He grimaced. *Probably more fearful of me. What if she's hurt? What if it's worse than that and I never see her again?* He wanted to scream her name across the lake to let out some angst. Instead, he stared at the back of Bill, who sat on the boat's bow turning his head from side to side like the beacon of a lighthouse.

"Bill?"

"Yeah?"

"What if I never see her again? What if I don't get to tell her what a jerk I've been?"

"I think she already knows that."

"You know what I mean. I want her to know I'm going to change—this time for real. I want to tell her how much she means to me. She can't be dead."

Bill whipped his head around, his body following, to face Adam. "Nobody said anything about anybody being dead. Jeez. They left a note, remember?"

Adam stopped the trolling motor leaving the boat to coast on its own. "But anything could happen. Look at *us*. We can hardly walk or breathe. I have to talk to her. I have to." He sniffed and wiped his nose with the back of his hand. "And I want you to be there when I do if you don't mind."

Bill's eyebrows rose. "You do?"

"Yes. I think it will give me the courage to say the things I need to, and Lynn may be more likely to believe me if there is a witness. Especially if that witness is a shrink." Both hands shot out, palms toward Bill. "Sorry. Psychologist. I didn't mean to be disrespectful."

"I'm happy to stand with you if that's what you want, but you'd better be serious. Uncontrolled anger and abuse is no game, and there is no quick fix. You have to continue to work on your issues with another psychologist."

"I know. And I will. Thank you. I mean it."

"You're welcome. When I get home, I'll find someone in your town for you."

Adam nodded, scooped some water from the lake, and splashed it on his face and neck. Then he started the electric motor and aimed the boat toward the cabin.

****

Bill let out a sigh of relief when he saw the fishermen and Cory still on the dock and no dead bodies. He waved Cory over.

"What happened?" he asked as he secured the rope around the cleat. "Where are the girls?"

Adam whispered. "Not there."

Cory's eyes grew wide. "What do you mean?"

"They emptied their purses and are heading here," said Bill. "They left a note."

"And they have their weapons," said Adam, "which they shouldn't need since the perps are here."

"Perps?" asked Cory.

"Police lingo."

"I know what it is. I watch TV, too."

"We checked out that antiquated wall phone, too," Bill said, "the one the owner was on when we stopped? The line's dead, so the girls had no help that way. And one more tiny thing, a tree totaled Molly's SUV."

Cory closed his eyes for a second and then shook his head. "This just makes me sick."

"I'm sure Molly felt the same way."

"No, not that, but yeah, I am sorry to hear about the car," said Cory. "Thank God they weren't in it. But I'm talking about their situation in general, out there alone, being under attack."

"I know," Bill replied. "I feel horrible, too, but it sounds like they got the best of those shitheads."

"Those shitheads have names," said Adam. "We need to find out what they are."

"Already done." Cory smiled. "I got pictures of them and their driver's licenses."

"Good. We need to let them go."

"But—"

"No buts," Adam continued. "We can't hold hostages. That's kidnapping and makes us just as bad as they are. Cut 'em loose."

"I want to talk to them first," Bill said as he strode to the screened area. The fishermen looked at him suspiciously as he glared at them. "The women weren't there, so you'd better start talking. Now."

Both men looked surprised. "Listen, man," Gus said. "We don't know anything about that. I swear it's the truth. When we left, they were barricaded inside the store."

"Why should I believe you?" Bill growled.

"Look, a rifle shot came from the woods, and the one with the Glock stayed inside with the nice lady."

"Did you have guns?"

Both men looked surprised at the question. "Us? Do you think we're that stupid?"

Bill held eye contact. "I think you're answering a question with a question to avoid answering the original question. So yes, I think you're that stupid. We have your identity, addresses, a picture of you at this table, and your confession."

Gus spat on the dock. "Yeah? It's your word against ours."

"Not really," Cory said as he walked into the screened area, holding up his phone. He jabbed at the screen, and the men's voices sounded loud and clear as they described the incident in detail. He stopped the recording as Adam joined them.

"Remember when you said you don't know us from Adam?" asked Cory. "May I present to you our friend, Adam Ferguson, Assistant District Attorney for the City of Frankfort, in the great state of Kentucky. And if you think *you're* tough, you ain't seen nothing."

Adam smiled. "Thanks for the introduction. Gentlemen, anything you say may be used against you in a court of law. So, here's what you're going to do next."

****

"Look, your wives won't let us get within 50 yards of them," said Gus. "And there's a lot of territory to cover out there. Wouldn't even know where to start."

"We know the answer to that," Adam replied. "They're headed here. Just don't know the route. They may stay hidden in the woods if they're still worried about you two assholes showing up."

"Actually, there were four of us," said Hank. Gus immediately jabbed him in the ribs. "Ow! Why'd ya do that?"

Adam glared at them while he thought about this new piece of information. "Well, that's even better. You can get your buddies to help with the search."

"That might be hard," said Gus. "They'll be at church this morning teaching Sunday School."

"That's rich. I don't care if they flew to the fucking moon. You get them. One more question: if someone fired a weapon between here and Big Jon's, do you think we could hear it?"

"Possible. Sound carries on water farther than folks think."

Adam scratched his chin. "Do you have a gun of some kind?"

Hank snorted, then coughed. "Is that a trick question? 'Course we got guns. We had 'em last—"

"Shut up, you moron," Gus yelled, whose jaw suddenly collided with Adam's fist. Saliva flew out of his mouth, and blood dripped from his split lip. Adam wanted to strangle him.

Cory ran to the screened area and saw the fisherman holding his jaw and checking for loose teeth.

"What happened?" he asked.

"These lying bastards took weapons with them last night," said Adam. "So their crime just changed to a felony.

"No wonder you said they wouldn't let you within 50 yards of them. I ought to pound your head in, but I don't think your buddy could find his ass with two hands and a flashlight, so you're the lead tracker. When, *not if*, you find them, ask Molly to fire her rifle three times, so we'll know they're okay."

"And if one of those bullets happens to go through your head," added Cory, "then, as a wise friend once said, 'it is what it is.'"

Chapter Twenty-Two

Lynn had led the threesome across Highway 41 and into the woods, where they followed a path of fallen leaves until they got to an opening in the trees. They peered onto an outcrop of large rocks rising from the water. No people were in sight.

"I didn't expect this," she said. "The map doesn't show elevations, but we know the property slopes to the lake at the cabin. The terrain has to level out eventually." She peered over the edge again. "Cee, you think you could handle the descent?"

"I don't know," CeeCee replied, shaking her head. "Looks tricky, and as helpful as this stick is, stepping over and down to other rocks might be a problem. I almost face-planted twice on that path behind us." She looked at Molly. "Thank you, by the way, for keeping me upright."

The day's temperature was climbing, so the women shed their shirts and tied them around their waists. They took a few sips of water while looking over the lake and discussed their limited options.

"I think we should avoid the rocks for now," said Lynn. "Follow the shoreline the best we can but stay in the woods, just in case. And we need to be vigilant for hazards. No more injuries, ladies."

"Or, you and Molly can hike down to the shore and leave me," CeeCee said. "I'll get there eventually."

Lynn frowned. "Don't be ridiculous. We're not splitting up. That's the Girl Scout code."

"You weren't a Girl Scout," CeeCee replied.

Lynn shrugged her shoulders. "It has to be in the handbook somewhere."

Molly bent over and stretched her thighs and calves. "Let's get this party started, shall we?"

The rolling hills and rocky woods around the lake made the pilgrimage tedious, but the friends plowed on, zig-zagging around briars or vines that looked suspiciously like poison ivy. Lynn led the way and frequently swiped a stick through the air to keep spider webs out of her face. *Maybe I* was *a Girl Scout.* Sometimes she'd call out a cadence like an army drill Sargeant, the rhymes often so ridiculous, she had to stop marching to avoid wetting her pants.

Lynn had no idea where they were or how far they'd gone, but distant voices across the water gave her the courage to continue. She was just one hiccup away from losing it but remained convincing for her friends, who'd done all the heavy lifting so far. At least they weren't trapped in a bait shop box now. If something happened, their screams might draw help—unlike the ones she'd stifled for years when her husband flew into a rage.

The closer they got to the cabin, the more Lynn's anxiety intensified. Different scenarios raced through her mind, none good, all with Adam's face contorted and his mouth churning out words of hate and intimidation. The image alone upset her stomach, and she prayed it wouldn't cause another eruption of diarrhea.

After an hour, the women saw some large flat rocks stacked on a slant and decided to take a short break. While Molly and CeeCee situated themselves, Lynn bent at the waist and finger-combed her hair over her head. She took an ever-present, green elastic band off her wrist and used it to form a disheveled topknot.

"That feels better," she said, fanning the back of her neck. "Can't do this at home. Adam..." Lynn paused when she noticed the expressions on her friends' faces. "Don't look at me like that. Thanks to you, big changes are coming. I'm not that weakling anymore, and as they say, the truth shall set you free. And that includes my hair."

She smiled at them, secretly hoping they'd bought her act, when CeeCee yelled, "Don't move!"

Lynn twirled and shrieked. "What is it?"

"You've got a bug or tick on your neck. Stand still, and let me see."

CeeCee frowned when she got a closer look. "You got a tattoo? Of a ladybug?"

Lynn covered it with her hand, then giggled. "I'd forgotten about it. That's why I don't put my hair up when Adam's around. It's my dirty little secret."

"Well, aren't you full of surprises," said CeeCee, slapping her friend on the butt, then returning to her seat on the rock.

Lynn smiled and plopped down, a little too hard, onto the cool limestone. The Glock popped out of her waistband, skidded across the rock, and disappeared into a crevice. "Dammit!" She scampered over to the edge, tearing the knees of her jeans, and peered into the large crack.

"Do you see it?" asked CeeCee.

"Yes, but I can't reach it. I'm such an idiot!" She stood up, stomped to the edge of the rock, and hopped off. "At least it didn't discharge and kill somebody. I'll be back. I need to tinkle anyway."

Lynn made her way around the large rock, ducking under tree branches and using them to keep her balance. After she relieved her bladder, she grabbed at the fork of a small tree to help herself up, and something orange dropped out of it. She zipped and buttoned her pants and saw a plastic prescription bottle beside her shoe. She almost ignored it, but curiosity forced her to pick it up and shake it. Nothing rattled, so she unscrewed the top and found several one-hundred-dollar bills rolled up inside.

"Hey, girls! You won't believe what I—"

"I'll take that."

Lynn spun around and saw a large man wearing a fluorescent yellow vest over a black tee-shirt stride towards her and snatch the bottle out of her hand.

"Get up there with your buddies."

Instead, Lynn backed up, terrified, screaming, unable to stop the meltdown in motion. She fell to her knees and locked eyes with the stranger when suddenly Molly's body launched at the man as she shoulder-tackled him into a thicket of thorny underbrush. He grunted as the air gushed from his lungs and looked momentarily disoriented, but when Molly attempted to push herself off the guy, he caught her ankle. She struggled, hopping on one leg and stretching to grab something, anything, to get away. The man tried to get up, cursing the briars tearing at his clothes and arms, but he didn't release his grip. Finally, she stopped pulling away and kicked him in the face instead, forcing him to let go. He shrieked, then scowled at Molly and lunged.

<Thwack!>

CeeCee stood over him, holding her cane like a baseball bat, cocked and ready should he try to get up. She nudged him with her toe, then looked at Molly. "I hope he's not dead."

Both women squatted beside Lynn.

"Everything's going to be all right," said CeeCee. "We're here."

She looked at Molly. "Will you go get her medicine?" Lynn remained still and silent, eyes fixed on the unconscious man.

****

While retrieving Lynn's purse off the slab of rock, Molly heard moaning from the attacker's direction. She tiptoed toward him and saw a different guy hovering over him. Slimly built, with a long blond ponytail, he wore black and white snakeskin cowboy boots and a black hat. As he helped his groggy friend to his feet, he asked, "Did you get it?"

He pointed at Lynn, then rubbed his neck. "S*he* found it for me, but yeah."

Molly's rifle was too far away to grab, so she glared at the two men to buy some time. "Found what?"

"Who's she?" asked the newcomer.

"Don't matter."

"It doesn't matter?" asked Molly. "Do you see my friend crumpled on the ground? I don't know what your deal is, but she needs her medicine, and I will give it to her. You got a problem with that?"

"No ma'am."

The mannerly response didn't go unnoticed, but Molly approached the two men cautiously. She didn't trust anyone today and was right to do so as the injured guy grabbed the purse, pulling it and Molly to his chest.

"I'll take it to her," he said. "You stay put."

"No. *You* stay put, asshole." She jerked the bag away from him and scowled. "What the fuck is wrong with you people up here? Everywhere we go, we find degenerates who want to knock us around. I've had it with you and your other dirtbag buddies, so if you don't want the label of involuntary manslaughter added to my rap sheet, get out of my fucking way."

Molly took a step backward and glared at the guy. "What did my friend find that's so important you had to scare someone half to death?"

"Money," CeeCee answered as she walked to where Molly stood and took Lynn's medicine out of the purse. "In a prescription bottle, no less." She rolled her eyes at the two men. "Not very creative for a drug deal."

"Shut up," said Ponytail.

The guy in the vest fidgeted and rocked from one foot to the other, but his evident agitation didn't prevent Molly from speaking her mind. "You got what you wanted, so why don't you crawl back under your rock."

"You've got a real mouth on you," he said.

"You have no idea," said CeeCee, returning to Molly's side. "Inside the state prison, her nickname was The Maw. Maw-Maw if you were her friend. I see you've had a run-in with the law yourself. Is this your day to pick up trash?"

Ponytail snickered. "Told you not to wear that damn vest." He cocked his head at his friend, indicating he wanted to talk privately.

Molly looked questioningly at CeeCee, who shook her head and whispered, "It's still in the crevice."

When the guys' conference ended, CeeCee snarled, "So what's your plan, genius?"

The guy in the vest glared at her. "I don't like your atti—"

Suddenly the limbs of an evergreen tree sprang forward with a snap, revealing two familiar faces. Molly automatically darted towards her weapon, leaning on a scraggly pine tree, but Yellow Vest grabbed her arm and stopped her. The newcomer grabbed the rifle and locked eyes with Molly, his expression telling her to back off. He spat tobacco juice on the ground. "I don't feel like getting shot today, if you don't mind."

He looked different, less sinister in the light, but the scroungy beard still hung from his chin. Molly noticed he didn't raise the rifle but kept it horizontal to the ground, casually against his thighs and his hand was nowhere near the trigger.

He looked over at the guy in the yellow vest. "What the hell are you doing here, Howard?"

Molly and CeeCee watched, fascinated, as predator number one addressed predator number two.

"We're on an Easter egg hunt, Gus. What the hell do you think we're doing? I'll ask you the same."

"We've been tracking them all weekend," Gus said. "It's personal. And none of your business."

"It's my business now," Howard said, showing concern. "They saw us."

"They don't know jack, and they don't live around here, so take your stash and go."

Howard squinted, checking out both Gus and his sidekick. "What have you gotten yourself into?"

"Never you mind." Gus reached into his pocket, pulled out a twenty-dollar bill, and threw it in the guy's direction. "Now we're even."

Howard picked up the money. "'Bout time you paid up." He turned to leave. "Don't blame me if you end up dead."

"Thanks for the tip," Gus replied. He looked over at Molly and CeeCee and pointed his thumb at Howard. "He's not all that bad."

Still holding her walking staff like a baseball bat, CeeCee looked at him with disbelief. "Says someone with no credibility whatsoever."

"Seriously," he continued. "A lot of folks up here don't have insurance to pay for their medications, so Howard has a little side job that helps them out. This rock is his drop point. Everybody knows about it."

"That's still illegal."

"Maybe. But it keeps people well, so we look the other way, which is what you need to do."

CeeCee smiled. "Yeah. Yeah. Blah blah blah. What the fuck do you morons want now? It's no coincidence that you're here, in the middle of the woods where we happen to be, the same jerks who got their asses handed to them last night."

"No, it's not a coincidence," Gus admitted.

"But it's not what you think," said Hank quickly.

Lynn stepped from behind the slab of rocks, Glock aimed but held with a trembling hand. "How would a peabrain like you know what we're thinking?"

"Jesus, Gus. Just tell them before you get us killed," Hank said, holding his hands up in surrender, but his pal remained silent.

"Then I will." Hank looked at the women. "Your husbands sent us to find you."

The girls laughed.

"That's the best you masterminds could come up with?" asked CeeCee. "Do you think we're stupid? And what? We're supposed to just march through the woods with you like little lambs?"

Gus finally spoke. "No. We don't expect that. And I'd like to put this rifle down so you know we came in peace."

Molly glared. "How about you put it over there where I can reach it?"

He did as she asked and retreated to his original location with his hands up.

"Lynn? Cover me," she said as she retrieved her weapon.

"I have something to show you," Gus said, looking over at Lynn, who still held her stance, "So, for God's sake, don't shoot me."

The women watched his left hand extract a piece of paper from his right front pocket, using only two fingers. He held it up.

"This is for CeeCee, Molly, and Lynn."

Hank bobbed his head up and down. "From your husbands. Like I said, they sent us."

****

Lynn stood in shock, never moving, while the man showed Molly a note of some kind. She hadn't relaxed her arms or grip on the Glock, and her ears rang so loud that she could barely hear what anyone said. She knew her breathing was too shallow and could trigger another panic attack. She'd taken the medication, but it didn't help immediately and only worked if the person remained calm with no continued stimulation. CeeCee looked in her direction, lips moving and hands gesturing, but the fog kept Lynn from comprehending. Her hands felt funny, stinging and burning, and her knees buckled.

Just as CeeCee got to her, the Glock discharged.

****

The sound of the weapon, followed by screams, shot through the woods and across the lake. Molly's screaming turned into a moan as CeeCee fell to the ground in a heap beside Lynn, neither of them moving. She felt like she'd been kicked in the chest by a mule.

"Noooo!"

As tears flowed down her face, Molly dropped to her knees and touched CeeCee's shoulder, afraid to roll her over and acknowledge the possibilities.

"Cee? Tell me you're okay. Please."

CeeCee's hand moved slightly from her bleeding face to her left ear, giving Molly hope. She grabbed her friend in a hug and rocked back and forth while more tears gushed in thankfulness. CeeCee pushed away, touched her cheek, and looked at the blood on her hand.

"Am I shot?"

"I don't know. Let me look."

Molly finally shook her head and told CeeCee the ejected shell cut her cheek, and probably burned her, too.

"What?" shouted CeeCee. "I can't hear a word you're saying! I think the shot blew out my eardrum."

Molly nodded, took her shirt from around her waist, and dabbed at CeeCee's face. Then she indicated time out with her hands and scooted over to Lynn, whose eyes were slightly open. She glanced at Molly, then curled back into a ball.

Gus and Hank squatted beside the women and offered help. Molly didn't have the strength to battle them anymore, and if that note from the guys was authentic, she didn't have to. She told them to help CeeCee to the rock while she attended to Lynn, but she had no idea what to do.

She looked at Gus. "Do you have any experience with people who are traumatized?"

"Me?" he asked. "I have a buddy with PTSD. That's post-traumatic—"

"I know what it is. Can you help or not?"

"Here's my advice. Your friend needs to rest for however long it takes until she's calm. Even then, she may be too exhausted from the adrenaline overload to function at a high level. Does she have some kind of medication?"

"She took something right before you and your buddy showed up."

He looked at his watch. "Okay. I say we leave her be for 45 minutes, then see how she feels." He took off his flannel shirt. "Here. Put this under her head."

As Molly got up, Gus offered his hand, which she ignored. There was only so much help she'd allow from this man. She dusted off her pants and went back to CeeCee, who looked less gruesome after cleaning her face with some water. "Wish I had something to put over that cut, but we'll fix it when we get to the cabin."

"What? I can't hear you!"

Molly motioned for Gus, then pointed at Lynn. "I don't want you anywhere near her. You idiots are the reason she's in this condition in the first place. And now I want to see the note."

After she read it, she gave it to CeeCee, then spoke into her undamaged ear. "I guess they're telling the truth. Seems like their lives are in jeopardy if they don't show up with us."

"Good!" CeeCee shouted.

Hank whispered something to Gus, who said, "Oh yeah, about your rifle."

During the next hour, CeeCee and Molly ate their apples and power bars and waited for Lynn to wake up. After 30 more minutes, Lynn opened her eyes, so they joined her on the ground.

"Hey, sleepy head," said Molly. "How do you feel?"

Lynn ignored the question and scanned her surroundings instead. She looked at CeeCee. "What happened to your face?"

"This little scrape?" she said, her voice overly loud. "It's nothing. How are you feeling?"

"Groggy. Maybe tired? Or out of gas. I don't know." She frowned and looked at Molly. "Why is she shouting?"

Molly shrugged, not wanting Lynn to recall the incident yet. "Who knows? Think you can stand or go sit on the rock?"

Lynn nodded but stared blankly into the woods.

"I need to tell you something," said Molly, "but first, you should know we are in no danger whatsoever."

Lynn looked skeptical but nodded anyway.

"Turns out our husbands sent someone to find us and escort us back to the cabin."

"But how did they—"

"Long story. I'll tell you later, but we'd like to get going if you're up to it."

Lynn nodded again, got to her feet, and brushed some leaves off her clothes. "Ready as I'll ever be."

"There's a couple more things. Our husbands want us to signal them, so I'm to fire my rifle three times. It will be loud, so plug your ears."

"What's the other thing?" asked Lynn.

"The guys from last night are the ones taking us back."

Lynn stared at the ground for a moment. "Where are they?" she asked in a whisper but didn't wait for an answer. Instead, she ran to the place where she'd collapsed, frantically searching the ground. "Where is it? Where is it?"

"CeeCee has it," said Molly, hugging her friend tightly. "You're safe. We're safe." She took a step back.

"Lynn, look at me. I know you want to go into fight-or-flight mode, but please take one second to be present and recognize the facts. First, we have the weapons. Nod if you hear me." Lynn did. "Second, our husbands have threatened these men with their lives to return us safely, and third..." Molly handed her the note. "They sent this."

Chapter Twenty-Three

When the fishermen disappeared into the woods, the three husbands returned to the cabin and busied themselves with nothing in particular. One by one, they gravitated to the breakfast table and parked themselves.

"This is driving me insane," said Adam looking at his index fingernail. He tore off a chunk with his teeth and spat it onto the floor. "Lynn must be scared to death. She's fragile, ya know? And all I've done is feel sorry for myself, act like a moron, get pissed and drunk."

"Aren't those last two the same thing?" asked Bill.

Adam grinned.

"But I know what you mean," Bill replied. "I feel like a complete idiot. Here we are in this beautiful place, handed to us on a silver platter, and I couldn't rise above my disappointment to appreciate it."

"At least you didn't behave like a caveman," said Cory. "I've never assaulted so many people in my entire life. This weekend brought out the worst in me, and it's not who I want to be."

"You're an altar boy compared to me," Adam admitted. "I'd love to be more like you."

"I don't know about that," said Cory. "But instead of being more like me, just be *less* like you." He laughed. "Thanks to Bill, you're on the right path, and when I open my first restaurant, I'm counting on you, your legal knowledge, *and* your wallet."

"It's a deal," said Adam as he rose from his chair. "I'm going to the dock. I can't just sit here twiddling my thumbs."

"Or eating them," Cory said. "I'll go with you."

Bill went to the freezer. "I'll be on the couch icing myself. Holler if you hear anything."

Cory stayed in the screened area while Adam paced the dock and checked his watch every ten seconds. He couldn't wait to see Lynn and tell her everything that had happened, how he'd changed, and his plan to make himself a better person. He was excited about their future but nervous, too. His behavior the morning of the funeral sickened him as his aggression often did after the fact. Since then, they hadn't talked much, but who'd blame her? During the drive to the cabin, Lynn withdrew, curled under a blanket, and slept. Or pretended to. Adam had no idea where he stood.

It had been hours since the fishermen left, and his patience had worn thin. He stomped over to Cory's end of the dock. "What the hell do you think is happening? They should've found them by now, don't you think?"

"I'm going nuts, too," said Cory. "I know it's a lot of ground to cover, but they seemed confident they—"

"Listen!"

Cory jumped up. "A rifle shot?"

They heard two more, not very loud, but they got the message. Their girls were coming home. Cory threw open the screened door, picked up Adam, and cheered. Although his ribs hurt like hell, Adam joined in the celebration instead of complaining, then finally pleaded to be put down.

Cory ran towards the cabin, and Adam followed, holding his side. When they reached the porch, Bill walked out the front door. "Thought I heard celebrating. Do we have news?"

"Yes, they found them," said Cory.

"Or, Molly used three shots to kill the bastards," Adam added.

"A win-win either way," joked Bill.

More hugs and high-fives led to laughing and slapping each other on the back as if they were old

Army buddies at a long-awaited reunion. They made their way to the firepit, where they'd wait for the group to arrive.

Adam jumped up from the stone bench several times, walked a few yards into the woods, and yelled for the women. "Lynn, CeeCee, Molly, we're over here!" With no response, he found another fingernail to chew. "I'm as jumpy as a cat on a hot tin roof." He spat out the nail he'd just bitten off.

The torture finally ended when the fishermen appeared and stepped aside to let the women pass. Molly dropped the rifle and ran to Bill's open arms. Just as quickly, she backed away and looked at his shorts and the bulge created by the rolled-up towel. He smiled.

"It's a long story, but yes, I'm excited to see you." They both laughed and hugged again.

CeeCee and Lynn lagged behind and smiled at Molly and Bill. Adam stepped forward, but CeeCee's glaring eyes and outstretched hand told him to stop. Slowly she hobbled in his direction, touching Cory's hand briefly as she continued, her expression never changing.

She knows.

A primal scream escaped CeeCee's throat as she lunged, delivering a full-strength kick to Adam's crotch. He grunted and doubled over as Cory grabbed his wife and pulled her into his chest. No one spoke. No one had to.

Adam straightened, and with tears running down his face, he looked at his wife, still standing several feet away.

"Lynn?"

She approached him and studied his misshapen, purple face, but she addressed Cory. "What happened to him?"

"Another long story, but I'm responsible."

Lynn nodded, then turned and walked toward the cabin by herself.

The humiliation paralyzed him, but Adam finally urged his feet to move and slowly walked down to the dock. He'd never felt so alone in his life. The heavy guilt for not protecting his grandma and mistreating his wife was more than he could handle, and Adam fell to his knees in shame. He wished he could disappear from the face of the earth, but for better or worse, the time had come for him to pay for his sins.

Gus and his buddy stood awkwardly next to the boat, waiting. Adam looked at them with a blank expression on his face.

"We good?" asked Gus.

Adam nodded. "For now. But if I get a *hint* of misconduct, I'm coming after you. Legally. I'll let CeeCee take care of anything physical."

Chapter Twenty-Four

After a few calls to local know-it-alls, Josh got the information he needed. Overnight, crews worked to make roads passable and repaired the power lines, so the coast was clear. The kids were still asleep, so he repeated the process of coffee and pastries and scribbled a note at the bottom of Carolyns's letter that still sat on the counter.

That odd feeling of urgency had never left him, so Josh navigated the winding road towards the cabin like an elite NASCAR driver at the Bristol Motor Speedway. His driving skills came from decades of restoring classic V8 muscle cars and testing their power before handing the keys to the owner.

As the red Ford F-150 rounded the bend and breezed by Big Jon's store, he saw the owner's faded truck parked in its usual spot. A burgundy vehicle, or what was left of it, was *not* usual.

Is that Molly's? Josh pressed hard on the brake pedal, squealing the tires until the vehicle came to an abrupt stop. He jammed the gearshift into reverse, gunned it until he reached the parking area, and slid in beside Jon's old heap. Impressed, Josh took a moment to congratulate himself on his maneuver or, more likely, his good luck, then jumped out and hurried inside.

He found the owner struggling to move a big metal Coke cooler from the back of the store.

"Whoa, Jon, let me help." Together they slid it back into its original location. "What's going on?"

The store owner wiped his brow with a flannel shirt sleeve. "Beats me. Came in this morning and found the place in disarray, not that most folks would notice. The back door was blocked with this cooler and some racks; things moved all around; my phone box on the floor along with dead worms, and there's some old boards leaning against the wall, nails still in 'em."

"Anything missing?"

"Not that I can tell. I don't think they were here to steal, though, they most likely needed a place to stay. They left some things behind. A pot of coffee, which I appreciated, and girl stuff. I thought it smelled too good in here."

"What kind of things were left?"

"Go see for yourself. It's over there on the trunk table."

Small piles of receipts, nail polish, pens, an emery board or two, gum, breath mints, cough drops, mini-perfume sprays, business cards secured with a rubber band, two small containers of hand lotion, and a rhinestone-covered phone case. In the middle of the cache lay an envelope with a note.

Hiking to J & C's place along the lake. Send help if we don't show up.

Molly, Lynn & CeeCee

"Jon, did you see this note?"

The older man with two bad hips duck-walked over to Josh. "No. What's it say?"

"That crushed SUV belongs to my friends. Something's happened."

Jon scratched his head. "Meant to tell you something else. I found four pairs of work boots in the parking lot. Would they belong to your friends?"

"No! I'm headed for the cabin. Call me on the bat phone if you learn anything."

"Can't. Line's down."

****

When Josh arrived at the cabin, his body felt physically and mentally depleted, but it was a different type of exhaustion, not the kind wrapped around grief. Focusing on someone other than his wife had given him a few hours of what, relief? A bit of time to breathe in *life* instead of death? He suddenly felt guilty about the reprieve, and salty tears stung his eyes. Josh flipped up the console storage lid, grabbed a wad of fast-food napkins, and dabbed at his face, something Carolyn had done a million times to blot freshly applied lipstick.

His boots crunched on the gravel as he approached the two black SUVs parked near the back door. One had a white garbage bag duct-taped over the passenger side window.

What the hell? Josh hastened his steps into the cabin, shouting names as he quickly covered the first floor, but only echoes of his voice bounced back at him. He raced up the stairs and tore through every room and bath where towels, clothes, and luggage lay in disarray.

No people.

He practically jumped to the bottom of the stairs and searched the porch and the immediate area around the house for clues. His heart rate escalated rapidly, and he thought he might have to sit down before he fell down, but the sound of voices kept his feet moving.

Was this coming from the dock or across the lake? Josh scurried down the flagstone path with dread, wanting to see, and *hoping* to see his friends but fearing the worst.

Relief flooded his body when he reached the dock, where all three couples were alive and well. He looked up at the sky and said a silent thank you. Molly and Cory floated in the lake on innertubes, beers in hand, while Bill and CeeCee sat on the dock's edge, dangling their feet in the water. Adam and Lynn sat knee to knee in the screened area, talking quietly.

When Josh approached the end of the dock, everyone was shocked but happy to see him. He put his hands on his hips and smiled. "So, how was your weekend?"

****

A little after six o'clock, Lynn, having scoured three days of dirt and grime off of her, meandered into the kitchen to find Cory performing magic with the remaining food. He pulled hot rolls from the oven. "Grab a plate and dig in."

"I didn't know if I'd ever see real food again. Smells delicious." She sat but didn't get anything to eat.

"You look a little pale," said Cory. "You okay?"

"A lot to process, ya know? I don't bounce back from trauma like I used to, and my digestive system is the first to complain about it."

He nodded and stirred something simmering in a pot. "Considering what you went through this weekend, I think you're made of steel. I'm in awe of how you handled yourselves, and don't tell CeeCee, but I may be a little afraid of her now."

"Afraid of who?" asked Molly as she entered the kitchen and surveyed the cuisine. "You guys have been dining like kings while we ate old raisins and expired Twinkies?"

"You should know," said the grinning chef. "You girls planned the menu for us royal highnesses."

Molly flipped him off. "Highnesses, my ass." She then grabbed the glass of wine sitting in front of him and took a swig.

"You're welcome," said Cory as he poured another and handed it to Lynn.

Eventually, everyone found a seat at the table. Among the seven, a few looked like a band of broken toys. CeeCee's swollen cheek forced her left eye closed, and her knee was the size of a softball. Bill still donned the rolled-up towel in his shorts and ice on his crotch, and Adam's pummeled face looked like an eggplant, not to mention his broken ribs and kick to the balls. Lynn's injuries were invisible, but she was damaged just the same. She knew they felt sorry for her by the awkward glances in her direction and Adam's. It made her want to scream. Instead, she broke the silence with a calm voice. "What looks good here? I'm starving."

As if waiting on her cue, dishes were passed around, and the hum of people commenting on Cory's culinary skills gave the dinner some normalcy. Lynn chose a few items but as good as they looked, she didn't have an appetite. She mostly pushed the food around her plate and concentrated on refilling her wine glass.

"Okay, who wants to start?" asked Bill. "We want to hear every detail."

CeeCee and Molly took turns sharing the weekend events, stopping for the men to ask questions or get clarification. Lynn contributed little, insisting her friends could tell the story better than she.

At first, the speakers' tones were somber, but soon the tales morphed into exaggerations and impersonations of each other, and even Lynn couldn't hold back laughter. There wasn't a dry eye in the house, including hers. By the time it came for the men to speak, the women had thoroughly tickled the group's funny bone, so they were primed to laugh at anything. And did.

Josh stood to snag the last slice of lemon cake when the muted sound of an old-fashioned ringtone stopped his pursuit. Everyone but him looked flabbergasted. "Ah, the bat phone is restored." He casually walked over to the staircase wall, pushed on a rectangular section of the wood paneling, and a small door sprang open. He grabbed the device out of its hiding place.

"Hello? Oh, hey, Jon. I see the lines are back up. Yeah, everything's fine. I'll tell you all about it when I see ya tomorrow."

Josh returned to the kitchen, grabbed the cake, and sat down. "What's everybody staring at?"

With the table cleared and the kitchen tidied, the group gathered more wine and assembled at the fire pit. Josh sprinkled something on the ceramic logs and said, "This'll add a little color," then lit the gas.

Cinders, multicolored flames, and sparks quickly lit up every face as the gang continued to talk, share, and tell jokes. The laughter provided much-needed relief from the trauma, sadness, and anger experienced over the last few days, and no one deserved it more. Their jubilance echoed around the lake basin, and soon they heard distant neighbors laughing, chatting, and even singing. It was a glorious night to be outside under a sky filled with twinkling stars.

Adam stood to replenish everyone's wine, then raised his glass. "I'd like to make a toast if I may."

Lynn watched everyone focus on Adam and his performance. Once again, he inserted himself into the middle of a situation that had nothing to do with him, but his ego always took over. Everything was all about him.

"First, to our gracious host, Josh. Thank you for inviting us to stay in your beautiful home. I assumed the worst about this trip, thinking it would be a real snooze, but instead, it turned into a test of survival. If I'd known, I would've brought different shoes."

Everyone laughed except Lynn, who sat in Adam's shadow, literally and figuratively.

"Second, thank you, CeeCee and Molly, for your love and friendship that makes my wife so happy. You are fortunate to have each other, and I will never again question the importance you play in Lynn's life."

Molly smiled. CeeCee's expression remained indifferent.

"Third, to my brothers from another mother. Cory, thank you for pounding my head in and readjusting my ribs, therefore changing me on the outside."

Cory grinned. "My pleasure."

"And Bill? Thank you for jumpstarting the changes *inside* my head and heart.

"And the last but most important toast is to this beautiful woman." Adam reached for her hand, and Lynn stood. "I've never been happier to see you than today when you walked out of the woods. When I learned you were in danger, it scared the hell out of me. I should've been there to protect you. I love you so much."

The crowd chanted, "To Lynn!"

Lynn grinned slightly at her friends, said thank you, then raised her glass and flung the wine into Adam's face. As she watched it drip down his chin and onto his clean white shirt, she clenched her left hand into a fist, swung her arm around from her side, and punched him squarely in the mouth. Adam stumbled backward, stunned, while Lynn glared.

"No! You will *not* put on one of your shows for my friends," she growled. "Not this time. They know all about you now and the shit I've gone through, and I will not prop you up, make excuses for you, or defend you for one more second. You've mutilated my confidence and taken away my joy in life, but the old me has risen out of the ashes. So, you can stuff your pretty vocabulary, giant ego, and monster rage right up your hairy ass."

The years of anticipating this moment and the actual follow-through instantly drained Lynn of the energy she had left, so she wilted onto the stone bench before her legs collapsed.

The group sat silently as the startling event unfolded and watched as Adam bowed his head and physically slumped from the public rejection. It seemed like hours before he spoke, but this time the confident courtroom voice shook with emotion. He stepped toward Lynn and got down on one knee.

"Lynn?"

She remained motionless, but her eyes locked onto his, almost daring him to speak.

"To picture you afraid and threatened by those men destroyed me. Then I remembered the fear on your face at the hotel a few days ago, the fear I created. It made me sick to my stomach. I'm no better than they are. Actually, I'm worse for treating you like I have for years, but I can promise it stops now."

Lynn leaned away. She'd heard all this bullshit before, but never in front of an audience. *What is his end game?*

"Please listen, even if it's the last time. You've always been the strong one, not me. I'm threatened by that strength and jealous of your bond with your friends. Even if you're falling apart, you somehow find the will to do what's needed, no matter the situation. And over the years, I've done my best to eradicate your power, crush your spirit, and turn you into a shell of the woman you used to be. I'm so ashamed of myself and the person I've become, and I'm sorry. I'll never forgive myself."

Lynn looked at the sadness in his eyes—the genuine sadness of a broken man. She wished Molly and CeeCee were sitting beside her.

"But I'm asking you tonight—no, begging you—in front of the people you love to please give me a chance to prove I still have the heart of the guy you met long ago."

He wiped tears from his face and spoke in a whisper. "The monster you've been living with will never show his ugly face again. This I promise, and thanks to Bill, I will get the help I need to become the man you deserve."

Lynn looked at Bill, who nodded, and tears rolled down her cheeks. She gazed at the flames dancing in the fire pit, then scanned the faces of her trusted, longtime friends, the people who knew her better than she knew herself. They seemed touched by Adam's words and the courage it took to say them. She looked at her husband's pleading eyes and thought she saw the boy in the student grill. She loved that boy but wasn't sure about the man before her. *Had too much happened? Could he change? And if so, could she trust that change?* She hesitated and looked at Bill again. He seemed to be reading her mind and grinned, then nodded his head again with conviction.

Lynn stood. "Who thinks I should give Adam another chance?"

One by one, Cory, Bill, and Josh raised a hand, but the votes that mattered were Molly's and CeeCee's, and their hands remained in their laps. They looked lovingly at Lynn, then at each other, and stood up. They clasped hands and slowly raised them high into the air.

"Looks like we have five votes," said Josh softly. "But it's up to you."

Lynn nodded, closed her eyes, took a deep breath, and then exhaled. She thought she felt a hand on her shoulder and heard the slightest tinkling of bracelets. *Carolyn.*

"Make that six votes."

Epilogue

Present Day

CeeCee looked around at her friends, who seemed lost in their thoughts and the significance of the story they had just heard. It had undoubtedly shaped the last ten years of their lives, and she wondered where they'd be if that long weekend had never occurred.

Kathryn leaned over and hugged her. "Thank you. I can't express how much this means to me. I don't think I'll ever get tired of hearing you tell this story."

CeeCee smiled. "That's sweet, but I think *I'll* get tired of telling it one day, so you'd better start taking notes. Some of the details are already getting fuzzy, but thankfully most of the culprits, I mean, main characters, are here to keep me straight." She smiled at Cory and squeezed his hand.

She looked over at the empty Adirondack chair and sighed. They'd loved and lost, but the escapades just recited led to the lives they now shared. The experience of that weekend so long ago brought out strengths they didn't know they had and revealed secrets of unhealed suffering. The result was an unbreakable bond of genuine respect and love.

Bill cleared his throat and pulled out a folded note from his pocket. "It's funny how things happen sometimes. I was packing for this trip and decided to use the old leather duffle bag I brought here ten years ago. I'm not sure why. I had to blow the dust off the darn thing."

Everyone chuckled.

"Anyway, I found Molly's note and Lynn's. Forgot I still had them." He passed the note to Lynn. "You may want this as a souvenir. Or not."

She laughed and handed it to Adam.

"You two will be just fine," said Bill as he adjusted his glasses.

"During the storytelling over the years, we've mentioned the letters the girls wrote to us guys, but we never read them word for word. So I thought you might want to hear Molly's."

Dearest Bill.

Before I say anything else, I love you. Because of that, you are at the cabin, and I'm not.

Bill looked up. "As you know, Molly likes to get to the point." Everyone smiled.

You've always told me not to try to read minds, so I won't say how I think you feel. Well, maybe a little. Seriously pissed, curious, shocked, hurt.

All these years, you've told me how much you admire my relationship with my sister-friends. The fact that we've stayed in touch for 20 years and traveled together yearly shows our love for each other. When we married, CeeCee told you they were part of the package. Remember?

Carolyn's death reminded us how special our relationship is and how quickly it can change.

When she told us about her illness, she said some things I'll never forget. She was so sick and frail and could barely sit up on her own, but when she spoke, her voice was as solid as it had ever been. She said, "I know Josh will miss me and grieve for quite a while. That's natural. But one thing he won't be is alone, like a lot of guys would be. He has friends that are like brothers to him, closer even. And I know they will surround him with love and support.

"So, when my time comes, I don't have to worry about leaving him alone, which would break my heart. I've spoken to his friends, and they are ready. They will do whatever it takes to help him heal."

CeeCee, Lynn, and I believe the three of you can become great friends. You just don't know it yet. You may have to work out some kinks, but you'll get there.

Bill paused and said, "Boy, did she have that part right." Everyone laughed, and he went back to the letter.

So, we are giving you guys a weekend to get to know each other. We'll be back Sunday. That's it.

He stopped again. "But we all know *that's it* doesn't mean Molly is finished."

These friends are important to me. YOU are important to me. And because Cory and Adam love the women I love, they automatically fit into the same category. We are all bonded in this life, so why not find out who these guys are?

If something should happen to me, which could be sooner than we think, I need and want the same peace Carolyn had. I want to know the man I cherish will have a safe place to land and friends who make you laugh when things seem hopeless, help you heal when you suffer, and guide you as you renew your life.

I beg you to keep your heart and mind open and take this time out of your life to do this for me—three short days and nights.

I hope you'll forgive me for such an abrupt departure and even more for the one yet to come.

Love, Molly

Bill sat down and put the note back in his pocket. CeeCee dabbed at some tears and looked at the empty chair across from them.

"Ten years ago, that chair symbolized Carolyn's absence, and we'll always honor her memory, but tonight it recognizes another loss, another soul that left our circle too soon."

Heads nodded, and she continued. "She wouldn't want us to dwell on it, so there is only one last thing to say, and I can't think of anything more appropriate for this occasion."

CeeCee stood with her husband's help, hobbled to the edge of the dock, and yelled. "Last one in is a rotten egg!"

Lynn rolled her eyes and looked at the stars. "Even from up there, Commander Molly, you're calling the shots." She ran to join her friends, taking off her sandals before jumping. "Bombs away!"

One by one, fully clothed bodies plunged into the water, and shrieks of laughter echoed across the lake.

But the loudest splash was yet to come, right after one final shout from the diving board. And Bill.

"Cannonball!"

The End

About the Author

Lou Knight has always been a creator. A treehouse in her Tennessee front yard was not allowed, so she turned her not-so-secret hiding place into a crude fort with a river rock floor. To protect it, Lou shaped woody weeds into arrows for her bow.

To her parents' dismay, she mowed a wicket-to-wicket pattern on the lawn for a neighborhood croquet tournament. When her allowance wouldn't afford her a real dollhouse, she remodeled an old trunk into a bedroom suite with a built-in closet. In college, she built a scale model of a house she designed, trimming pine cone needles to represent cedar shakes for the mansard roof. Ten years later, she drew the plans and helped construct a real house, her dream home.

After graduating from East Tennessee State University with a B.S. in Industrial Technology, Lou joined the chemical industry as a mechanical draftsman. Later she created a new safety program for 1,000 mechanics, then moved into corporate communications and community relations, where she continued to hone her writing skills. After concluding a 30-year career, she continued to apply her design expertise and creativity in various fields.

A chance visit to a writer's group in her community rekindled Lou's love of telling stories, especially those that highlight relationships—good and bad. She tells them with passion and a sense of humor. ***The Fallout of Deception*** is her debut novel.

Lou now lives in Canton, Georgia, with her husband, Mickey, and two annoying but loveable Goldendoodles.

Lou Knight's next novel will launch in 2023.

Made in the USA
Columbia, SC
28 December 2022

75121219R00176